The Rendezvous

and Other Stories

By Patrick O'Brian

The Rendezvous

and Other Stories

Patrick O'Brian

W·W·NORTON & COMPANY
New York   London

Printed in the United States of America

Manufacturing by The Haddon Craftsmen, Inc.

ISBN 0-393-31380-8

W. W. Norton & Company, Inc.
500 Fifth Avenue, New York, N.Y. 10110
W. W. Norton & Company Ltd.
10 Coptic Street, London WC1A 1PU

1 2 3 4 5 6 7 8 9 0

CONTENTS

The Rendezvous

and Other Stories

The Return

ALL DAY the fly had been hatching, and where the stream broadened into a deep pool between two falls the surface was continually broken by the rising of fish, broken with rings spreading perpetually, crossing and counter-crossing. It was a perfect day for the hatch, mild, gentle and full of life. Under the willows on the far side of the pool ephemerids drifted in their thousands, and the trout jostled one another in the shade of the willows, drunk with excitement and greed. Great heavy-headed cannibals with harsh, jutting under-jaws came from their stony fastnesses beneath the fall to rise at the fly; tender young trout rose beside them and took no harm.

All down the length of the stream the trout made holiday: they added a fresh, water-borne note to the incessant, imperceptible noise of the country, a note quite distinct from the purl of the water over the big pebbles above the fall, and from the sharp punctuation of the splash of the diving kingfisher, who flashed up and down his beat, darting ever and again on some minnow or tittlebat, some half-transparent fishlet that strayed up into danger from the green, waving forests in the stream's bed.

The best part of the stream lay between the ruined mill and the bridge: a path, some little way from the water, but roughly parallel with it, ran through the grass from the mill to the bridge. On the other side the woods came down to the water's edge, where huge pollard willows stood knee-deep in the stream, making deep quiet bays for chub and quiet-loving fish. Formerly the underbrush had been cut back for the comfort of fishermen, but now it was overgrown, and the riot of young fresh green was brave in the sun.

Immediately below the pool the stream ran with a deeper note,

7

flowing faster through a more narrow course, being constricted by worn rocks, which it could surmount only when the winter rains came down. Here the bridge spanned it in one leap: an ancient stone bridge it was, exquisitely lichened and its lines all rounded with age. There was an appearance of vast solidity about the bridge; it was massive and immovably firm, but it had a wonderful grace. A few self-sown wallflowers, tawny yellow, grew in its sides, and the sun was upon it now. The road that the bridge carried on its back ran clean a little way into the wood, but after the first bend it was lost and overgrown, for it was quite neglected.

The kingfisher perched on a stump close by the bridge to preen itself in the sunlight. It took no heed of the trout, nor of any of the innumerable sounds that came from hidden places all around it, but all at once it froze motionless on the stump, with its head raised questioningly. Then it sped down the stream in a blur of blue-green light, low over the water.

A little while after a man came down the lost road through the wood. At the bridge-head he paused, blinking in the sudden light. The trout stopped rising; a dabchick dived silently and swam fast away under the water. The pool held still to listen. Treading softly over the encroaching moss, the man came on to the bridge: he leaned over the coping and stared upstream. He was a tall, thick man, with a red face and black hair, quite gross to look at, and urbanized now: on his shoulders he carried a knapsack and a rod. After some minutes he looked down at the stones on which he leaned: initials and dates were scratched and cut into them. He knew almost to an inch where his own should be. They were there, J.S.B. in bold, swaggering letters, deeply carved, with a date of many years ago and a girl's initials in the same hand coming after them. Mary Adams: how very clearly he remembered her. A glaze of sentiment came over his eyes. A pace along the bridge there was J.S.B. and E.R.L., more discreetly this time, and, lower down, J.S.B. and T.M. There was a little cushion of moss spreading over the T.M.: he flicked it off and stood up. She had always called him Jeremy in full.

At the far end of the pool a trout rose, with a clear, round plop. The kingfisher flashed under the bridge and vanished upstream. The man walked on over the bridge to the path that led to the mill. From the path in the meadow he could see the stream, but from far enough away that he would not put the fish down.

He sat down in the sweet, dry grass and threw off his knapsack. He put the joints of his rod together, and it quivered pleasantly in his hand: from the pockets of his knapsack he drew old tobacco tins, a reel with an agate ring, his fly box; his fingers seemed too coarse for the tiny, delicate knots in the translucent cast, but the knots formed and the fly was on – a grannom. At last he stood up and whipped the rod in the air: he worked the line out loop by loop; it whistled and sang. He cast his fly at a dandelion clock, and after a few casts the fly floated down and broke the white ball. Satisfied, he walked gently towards the stream: for some time there had been a recurrent heavy swirl under the alders on the far side. Kneeling down – for the day was bright and the water scarcely ruffled – he worked his line out across the stream and cast a little above the rise. His fly landed clumsily in a coil of the cast; the trout ignored it, but did not take fright. When it had floated down, Jeremy twitched it from the surface and cast again. This time it landed handsomely, well cocked on the surface, and as it came down his hand was tense with anticipation; but the trout took another fly immediately in front of it. The third cast was too short, and the next began to drag, and the fly was half-drowned. He switched tiny specks of water from the grannom and cast again: still the trout let the fly go by, and a snag bore it over to a sunken branch. Delicately he tweaked and manœuvred with his outstretched rod, but the barb sank into the wood and held firm.

Will it give? he said, or will I go round and free it? Come now, handsomely does it. He lowered the top of his rod and pulled through the rings. The line stretched and the branch stirred: all around the trout were rising. He gave it a sudden, brutal jerk and the fly shot back across the stream, carrying a white sliver of wood on its point.

9

I did not deserve that, he said, taking the little piece off; I did not, indeed. He walked some way up the pool, waving his rod as he went. At haphazard, he cast to a small rise by the near bank, hardly pausing in his stride. At once the trout took the fly and went fast away with it in the corner of his mouth. The little fish was game enough, but he was finished in two mad rushes: he played himself, and came rolling in on his side, still defying the hook, but with no more power to fight it. The fisherman took another like the first a little higher up, beyond the pool. They were both about half a pound – small for that stream – cleanly run and game, but stupid.

After he had put the second fish into his bag, he rested; there was a crick between his shoulders from the unaccustomed exercise. He squatted on his heels, and almost without knowing it he filled his pipe as he gazed over the water: the kingfisher passed again, and in the woods a garrulous jay betrayed a fox.

It was just at this place that he had taken his first trout, tickling under the rill for them with Ralph, who was simple, but who could poach like an otter. The march of the years between those times and now effaced the unhappy days of his boyhood and adolescence, and now that he knew the value of the happiness of the days that remained to him that his former, smaller self had lived in a golden world. He had so little to show for all that he had lost; and sudden, intense regret for it took him by the throat for a moment.

He took off his shoes and socks, laid down his coat, and rolled up his trousers. The water was surprisingly cold as he waded into the stream; he could feel its distinct movement between each toe and the edged stones hurt his feet. He walked on the beds of water plants, sinking his feet to the ankles in the brilliant green: at each step he could feel innumerable tiny hoppings against his soles. The last time he had walked that way the water had been well up his thighs, he remembered, and in the middle the current had sometimes plucked him off his feet. Above him there was a small pool, with a stone rill above and below it. A crayfish exploded before his white toes, shooting through a cloud of silver minnows. Three or four small trout flitted from the weed-beds

as he walked, speeding up the open, clean lanes between the
orderly weeds; there seemed to be no other fish, but he knew the
ways of these trout, and he waded quietly to the bar of stones,
where the water came through fast from the pool. The force of
the current had washed out a deep hollow here, and the water
was too deep to stand in.

The sun had passed well over noon-height, and a deep shadow
lay slantwise down the wall of stones beneath the water. Nothing
could be seen there, but middle-aged Jeremy, standing thigh-
deep at the edge of the scoop, leaned over and passed his hand
along the stones, feeling gently into the interstices. Almost at
once his fingers touched the firm, living body of a trout: the fish,
working in the strong current, moved a little to one side. It was
not frightened. He touched it again, drawing one finger up its
side, feeling the strong, urgent thrust as the trout pushed continually upstream to hold its position. As his eyes grew used to the
deep shadow, he could see the trout's tail, moving steadily to
and fro. Carefully he continued to stroke its unresisting body,
working the fish into the grip of his fingers: as soon as he could
gauge the full length of the fish he knew that it would be too big
for one hand, so he brought the other down, changing his foothold
as he did so. The trout started and moved restlessly, but the
quiet stroking of its belly on each side calmed it. Up and up the
fingers stole, now touching the gills for a moment, then lingering.
He drew in his breath, made his whole body tense and ready,
and then with an instant grasp behind and under the trout's gills
he flung it over his back on to the bank, where it sprang and
curved in the sun. Grinning like a boy, he waded in a slow hurry
back to the edge, killed his fish – a good fish, a very nice fish
indeed – and sat down to dry his feet on a handkerchief.

He was hungry now, quite suddenly and unpleasantly hungry.
He collected dried grass and twigs: the thin blue smoke of his
fire rose straight up high into the air. He fanned it until it had
a red heart, and he gutted two fish. He washed them in the
stream and cut a green withy: coming back to the fire's black
circle, he spitted them and lapped them with a piece of string to
keep their bellies in. He twirled the ends and cooked his trout

until their skins were wrinkled and golden and their pink flesh showed through the cracks in it. He had a broad leaf for a plate and bread and butter and a screw of salt from his bag. Being rather greedy by nature, he buttered and salted the fish with great care and ate them and the crusty bread in alternate bites, so that the taste came fresh and fresh: and at the end he slit out the little oval pieces from the cheeks of the trout and toasted them on the last piece of crust, so that the morsels spattered for a moment in the heat. After he had wiped his fingers and his mouth, he lay on his back in the soft, cushioning grass with his head under the shade of a bush, and all around him there was a murmur and a drowsy hum, and he slept.

When he woke up the sun had gone down three parts of the way to the horizon. Long shadows stood across the stream, and in the broad motes that came through the trees the spinners still danced in their hosts.

The fisherman raised his head and ran his fingers through his hair: he had not meant to lose his time in sleep, but here he did not mind the loss so much as he might have done on another stream; for he was here on a pilgrimage.

He walked back along the stream so as to fish up the same stretch again, and at the end of the pool by the bridge he saw a big rise – no splash, but the big, swirling ring that it is such a pleasure to see. The trout was on the farther side, well out in the open water, so it was necessary to creep up to an alder and, kneeling precariously on the edge, to cast left-handed from a long way off. Tentatively he worked a long line out, feeling his way across. A capricious little breeze, with no fixed direction, had arisen while he slept: the bushes behind him were a continual anxiety, and his knee kept slipping on the rounded edge of the bank. With his mouth closed tightly, he breathed heavily through his nose and concentrated on the flying line: his fly weaved back and yon, like a detached speck over which he had some occult control. The fly sped out and out, and still further; it was a very long cast. He shot the line, checked its run and bowed his rod; its forward motion stopped and as naturally as a dropping ephemerid the fly touched the surface, precisely where he had wanted it. The trout came straight at it, took it hard and vanished in a series of rings that spread out well across the pool before the fisherman raised his rod in a gentle tightening of the straight line. At once there was a great jar on the line as the trout jerked against the pull and sent the hook right home. The reel screamed, the rod curved, the line raced out. The trout leapt, not once but six times, showing clear a foot above the water at each leap. The man scrambled away from the insecure bank and stood in the water: his rod was thrilling with life under his hands. Three-pounder at least, he said it was, perhaps four, and Aah, would you? he said as the trout turned and dashed for the willow roots. His rod curved almost to a half-circle, checking sideways. The trout leapt again, slapping the water; it changed direction and shot up past him to the other end of the pool, into the deep stones beneath the rill. He could not reel in fast enough, and the line was still slack when the trout reached the stones.

Deep down in the calm water at the side of the rill the fish lay, beneath weeds and a tangle of drifted wood. Anxiously he twitched on the line; it was as dead as if it were tied to a rock. He was almost sure that it must be round the wood if not round the deep weed as well, but with his rod far out on the one side and then on the other he tried to stir the trout. There was no result, no feeling of life. With his rod pointing at the fish, he thrummed on the line, pulled and eased, did everything he knew, but it was entirely of its own foolish will that the trout moved in the end. Moved by some fancy, it turned round from its hole in the rocks and headed downstream with fresh strength. The cast strained shockingly: a green streamer carried away from the weed-bed, the line snaked free through the floating debris, and he was still on to his fish. For a dangerous minute the weed dashed through the water after the trout, but its stems parted before the cast.

Again the reel sang and the line fleeted away in spite of his checking finger and the straining rod: it was a heavy fish and a strong one. When the line was gone to the first knot in the backing, the trout was the whole length of the pool away; he dared not let it run any further, so he stopped the line dead for a second;

it stretched and he let it go slack. The trout stopped, leapt twice, but went on under the bridge, down through the dark tunnel of swift water, and the fisherman's heart sank. But he ran down the bank, now in the water, now out of it, stumbling and panting and sweating. The line was fraying against the stone foot of the bridge both this side and that; the strain was unwarrantable, and still the trout was running. He reached the bridge, with a couple of yards of backing on his reel, and the fish curved across to lie under the shade of the far bank, with its gills opening wide and fast.

Jeremy had been under the bridge; he knew its dark-green slipperiness and the almost certainty of a ducking. The rod might break too. However, there was nothing for it: he pushed his rod through, tip foremost, and bowed his head under the arch. The pent-in water took him behind the knees and nearly had him down at once: its note changed as soon as he was under the bridge. Then the trout began to rush across the stream again, and in his flurry of spirit he was through the bridge and on the shingle the other side before he had had time to think about it.

The heavy strain of the angled line had tired the trout, and its rushes were now much shorter, and they lacked the irresistible fire of the first. He made line on it fast, and fought it hard, never giving it a moment to recover. He thought he had it once, and pulled it in towards the bank as it lay inert upon the water, but before he had got it more than halfway it revived with a desperate rush and very nearly broke him against a stone on the bottom.

The trout lay on the bottom and would not move: the fisherman had been so near success and failure that he grew over-cautious now. He knew that his cast must be in a bad way, and he dared not pull until a sudden feeling of desperation nerved him to it. The fish had recovered, and it had learnt cunning. It meant to go through the bridge again, and he only stopped it with a strain that came within an ace of snapping the cast at the worst fray. Then he saw the line coming back and he scrabbled his way fast up the bank to keep the strain, reeling in as he went. I know I shall trip, he said, and that will be an end to it: but his good fortune was with him, and he kept his feet among the bushes and lumps. He kept the fish on the top now and bore masterfully on it, because there was no other way. Its strength ebbed in short rushes and a few angry leaps; the continual pressure was breaking its heart, and at the end it lost its head, used up the last of its strength in an unavailing burst and rolled sideways in the water.

He reeled in it very cautiously over the shingle where he stood ankle-deep. He was between the fish and the water as it grounded; there was a wild flurry and he had it out jerking and gasping on the grass in the last golden sunlight of the day.

He took the draggled fly from the corner of its jaw – it had nearly worn free in the fight – and he stood above the fish, gazing at it with satisfied admiration. It was a perfect fish: he looked down on its small, well-formed head, the gleaming pools of its eyes, and the golden yellow under the delicate white of its throat, and it lay there quiet with labouring gills. He must weigh a good four pounds, he said, drawing his finger down the fine, pink-flecked line that divided its belly from its gorgeous spotted sides. The fish bounded at his touch, and lay still again. He saw its strong shoulders, the saffron of its fins and the splendid play of colours over its whole glowing body, and he could not find it in his heart to kill the fish. It was the day and an undefined symbolism that worked upon him too.

Bending to the water, he held the trout upright with its head upstream: it was certainly four pounds. Its gills opened and closed and the cool water laved through them: for minutes he held it so, until fresh life and a little strength flowed into it and it lashed free. The trout almost turned belly-up a little way out, but more strength came to it. It turned into the stronger current and sank down to the waving green. He could see it there plainly, working gently under the soft shelter.

He wound his reel and packed his rod. The first owl cried and he went over the bridge: he went away, through the woods by the lost road, in the dying light.

The Happy Despatch

SLIEVE DONAGH on the east and Ardearg on the west hold a valley between them as lovely as any valley in the world. The nearest road is a great way off, however, and the valley is beautiful without praise.

A man standing halfway up the side of Ardearg would see the whole of the valley at once, from the high curtain of precipitous rock that closes the upper end to the curious, bar-like round of hill at its mouth. This bar is pierced by a single cleft that lets the river through, but the cleft is wooded, not to be seen, and the bar hides the valley from the lower world. On each side of the valley's head stand the tall mountains, rising nobly, each in a smooth, steep slope to shale, naked rock and savagery; their ridges, equal in height and unbroken, form the valley's sides. From his vantage point, the observer would see the soaring sweep of the top of the valley, the steep flanks whose slope ends suddenly in the flat green of the bottom: there would be half a mile of swimming air between him and the other side, and this would give him a feeling of immense height. He would see with the utmost clarity the meandering course of the Uisge, whose source is here at the foot of Slieve Donagh.

The Uisge, the bright stream, was high and running fast between its banks; two and three days before it had been over them, flooding the bright green bed of the valley and scouring the rock pools clear. The fishing in this highest stretch of the river was not at all good by most standards. There was no possibility of sea-trout above the falls in the cleft and the brown trout were tiny, elusive fish, never above four or five ounces in weight and mostly half that size.

It was this that made it possible for Woollen to be fishing

there. The lower water had some value and was let to an angling association. On account of his extreme poverty, Woollen belonged neither to this association nor to any other: indeed, there were times when it seemed to him that he hardly belonged to the human race at all, the more the pity, for he was a sociable creature by nature. He was an incongruous figure, with his mild, sheep-like face and bowed, apologetic shoulders, here in this fierce valley – a valley that must have looked the same before ever the Firbolgs came into it – primitive and harsh, a place for cruel and bloody slaughter.

Woollen was as unsuited to the neighbourhood as he might well be. He was an Englishman, and it was widely known that he was, or had been, a Freemason. This was an unusually devout parish, and Fr. Tobin a bitter Anglophobe.

Woollen had a wife, a deathless shrew. There was something wrong with her that caused her to lie the day long on a sordid stuffed couch, from which she screamed abuse in an untiring, metallic voice, rendered piercingly sharp by long wear. Her face was a disagreeable purple and flour lay thick upon it; her body, of ponderous bulk, was covered with a deep layer of pale grey fat. She did not wash: she had many disgusting personal habits. Woollen had married her in haste a great many years since; she had been employed in an inferior boarding-house at the time. As for Woollen, he had been gently bred, of no particular family, but a gentleman. An elderly, ailing parson had brought him up, had disliked him nearly all the time, and had seen him into the Army with querulous relief. With neither connections nor abilities, he had found his way into one of the nastiest of infantry regiments, and he had passed several unenviable years in association with a number of third-rate subalterns who, sensing his timidity, had from the first used him ill. He had been their butt, and they had shown an ape-like ingenuity in making him wretched. Some of them had traded on the kindness of his stupid heart.

When he had thrown up his commission to join an acquaintance in a commercial undertaking, they had said that he would be rooked, and they were right. The businessman from

Manchester, who had promoted a company with a registered office and documents bright with seals, and who had allowed Woollen to come in on the ground floor with the title of Director in Charge of Army Contracts, had taken his small patrimony and his gratuity within six months. All that was left to him was the income of seventy-two pounds a year that an aunt, his last known relation, had left him in trust.

He was, as he very soon discovered, wholly unemployable – these were the bad days, the very bad days – so he had taken the advice of a sort of friend, the senior captain of his regiment, and had come to Ireland with the intention of living in rural ease, keeping hens and so on, in a cottage on the estate of the captain's cousin, Harler.

It had taken nearly all Woollen's loose cash to transport himself, his vile wife and their few possessions to this far, hidden corner of County Mayo. He had been deceived again: the cabin was barely habitable, the possibilities of making money from tomatoes, mushrooms or eggs were non-existent, and the reputation that he brought with him of being a friend of the Harlers damned him. This was a district that had suffered terribly in the troubles, and at least one Harler had been proved an informer. Two sons of the family had been in the Black and Tans. The paltry estate was now managed at a distance by a Harler who was some kind of a broker or attorney, a heavy, unshaven, loud-mouthed fellow who met all complaints, all requests for repairs, with blank indifference.

Woollen, of his own act, had effectually closed the door of silence upon himself. He had thought it best to maintain his status by a certain stiffness – after he had asserted his gentility, he could unbend to the two or three half-gentlemen of the neighbourhood. He never had the opportunity. His poverty was quickly discovered and they felt themselves outraged. Even the poorest of his neighbours considered himself affronted. Woollen had picked up a glaze of military stupidity in the Army and a kind of superficial arrogance – a protective colouring of which he was wholly unconscious – and this unconciliating manner, added to his horrible wife, his native stupidity and to his other overwhelming disadvantages, rendered him perhaps the loneliest man in the county.

Years of slow misery had passed since he first came. All his ill-informed ideas and schemes for making a little extra money had come to nothing: worse, many of them had cost invaluable pounds. Those which had not been downright foolish had wrecked on the indifference or open hostility of his neighbours. They would not teach him anything, and, being town-bred, he knew almost nothing of any value. His pig had died; his attempt at goat-keeping had been disastrous, for the animals had strayed incessantly, and after they had accomplished a great havoc he found them mutilated in the Irish fashion. His hens had gone, victims of a family of stoats: long after the event the memory could bring a choking disappointment. Seventeen pullets, so carefully bred up, fed at such cost, cosseted by him from chicks to the point of lay, housed with such pains, all slaughtered for fun within a few minutes. His beehives had been tipped over so often by unknown hands in the night that he was hardly sorry when the survivors died of Isle of Wight disease. So the list would run on; every enthusiasm, each fresh plan frustrated by lack of knowledge, want of a few pounds, evil fortune; perpetual failure, unending poverty.

It would not have been a gay life alone: in the company of his wife it was hell. That unlovely woman lay, wrapped in a mauve thing, on her creaking stuffed couch, with a malevolent blur in place of a mind. Directly she was legally married she had resolved never to do a hand's turn again her whole life long. She had deceived herself as to her husband's resources, but with incredible persistence she maintained her resolution. She was a teetotaller. She lived almost entirely upon tea and bread and margarine. She was unbelievably ignorant, and her tiny mind had narrowed with the passing years to the point of insanity.

Through countless nights of dumb, aching misery Woollen had revolved plans for removal, for going away to some happier place where children would not shriek after him with stones, to some English backwater, somewhere where he could do something; but every fresh day had shown him their impossibility. Poverty had brought him there, and poverty chained him there. Long ago he had made an arrangement for his tiny income to be sent to him in weekly sums; it was the only way, he had found, of keeping out of debt – it should be stated, with great emphasis, that he had a single-hearted regard for what he conceived to be his duty, and a simple honesty that would put nine men out of ten to shame at the judgment seat. From this weekly sum it had never yet been possible for him to save twopence.

Mrs. Woollen hated fishing. It had been the subject of countless disgusting rows, bellowing, smashing quarrels that had left him shattered in spirit and her exhilarated. Once she had broken his rod, and he, moved out of himself, had beaten her almost to insensibility with the butt-end. This had earned him one undisputed day's fishing a week, for a deep voice had warned him, against his convictions, never to apologize for this outburst, nor, indeed, to refer to it.

The day was Thursday, and this Thursday had dawned fair. He had risen before the alarm clock rang, as excited as a boy, and he had walked the four miles up the river with an eager impatience. The locals were sure that he fished the preserved water, and they would willingly have sworn to it; the water-bailiff often hid up for him. But Woollen had never in his days of life put a fly upon forbidden water. As he walked he averted his eyes from the pools with their widening circles of invitation, and pressed on to the ravine at the bottom of the high valley.

At the top of it, hot and panting, he was in his own place. The lower river, with its chequer-work of farms and small-holdings, was out of sight; his own prison and incubus too. Above there were the impassive mountains, which had always seemed friendly to Woollen, and there was hardly a sign of man. The high valley was notorious for the bog-evil and the poverty of its grazing; no walls divided it – in this it was singular – and the only sign that men had ever been in the valley was a mound with a circle of stones on the top of it. The mound was regular, thirty or forty paces round and five feet high. By some it was called the Torr an Aonar, because it was supposed that an anchorite had lived there, though indeed the stones had been piled by hands that knew nothing of the Cross. Formerly the mound had been at a considerable distance from the water, but the stream changed its course in very rainy winters and now it ran fast round half the mound, following the curve of it.

Immediately below the mound was a large pool, the best in the upper stream; several times Woollen had seen a trout in it that must have weighed over a quarter of a pound, and twice it had risen to his fly. At present he was still a long way from the mound, fishing the quiet middle stretches. The fish were coming up well – rising a little short, some of them, but already he had caught five. One had been too small even for this stream, but two were gratifyingly heavy. He had missed a dozen or more, but that was nothing to a man so habituated to misfortune.

He stalked along now, casting well forward with each step. He was throwing a longer line than was necessary, mostly for the pleasure of seeing it go out straight before him; he was casting easily and well, with a slight, constant breeze at his shoulder to lay the cast out flat. His mild, foolish face had an unwonted happiness on it. He talked gently as he went, in a voice a little above a whisper.

'Behind the rock, in the calm place . . . no, nobody there . . . try each side.' His fly was going down just where he wanted it, on the spot he was looking at each time. To the right of the rock the fly danced down the edge of the main current; there was a silver flash under it and Woollen struck, whipping the fish into the air, well out on to the bank. He had found this to be the only way of taking these mercurial little trout, but it still came hard to him to strike with such force and speed. The fish sprang and sprang in the grass until he reached it; it was of due size and he killed it, not without a qualm for its beauty. Thousands of trout he must have caught by now, and still, each time, he had to justify himself for the final killing.

He smoothed his fly, a red quill in the last stages of decrepitude, and looked over the length of his cast. It had a great many knots in it, most of them clumsy, for he was not a man of his hands, and it was uncommonly short. Both cast and fly would have to last a great while yet, as Woollen knew with a deep certainty. Few things would have given him greater pleasure than a five-pound note to be spent without remorse of conscience in a good tackle shop.

He went on, along the right bank, fishing steadily. The sun came out hot on the back of his neck. For a long stretch no fish came up, and he saw that it must be about noon. Lunch was cold new potatoes and a white pudding – good for a hungry man. He ate it with his back against the deep bank, where the Uisge came down through a series of rocky pools. The warmth beat down upon him; new-sprung ferns shaded his head with a green, sweet, shade, and he dozed for a while.

When he woke up the sun had gone in again and the day was overcast, though still warm. His first cast brought out a better fish than he had caught all the morning, and the omen held true. The three rock pools, generally good for a rise apiece, yielded seven fish, not one of them under two ounces. It was odd, Woollen observed aloud as he arranged the fish according to size on the grass, gazing at them with a childish complacence, it was odd how one's standards changed: he had fished some of the English chalk streams where a half-pound fish was as a minnow; now he was delighted with two-ounce fish. Anything much smaller than that was rather disappointing, but these did in truth look like real trout; small ones, indeed very small ones, but the real fish for all that.

He went up the river slowly now, for the fish were coming up in a most gallant and determined rise. The Uisge had little trout, but there were many of them on a good day. By the time he reached the pool under the mound his cloth bag was heavy in his pocket, and he had lost certain count of his fish, a thing that had not happened to him since he came into Ireland. He was on the opposite side to the mound, and as he stood at the foot of the pool he saw that the flood had bitten deeper into the round of the Torr an Aonar; there was a deep scar of bare earth, and the low scrub that had lined the far bank at the top was now in the water, most of it lying sideways with branches tearing the water, still anchored by the roots.

He wanted to cast diagonally up the pool, straight for the

mound, for the deepest water was just under it, and there he had raised his good trout before. Formerly he had cast up from where he stood now, dropping his fly into the little smooth place on the far side of the incoming current – a natural weir brought it in with some force – so that it poised momentarily before dragging across and down. Now, with this change, the piece of slack water was very much enlarged, and might hold nothing; also, the half-submerged tangle of dwarf willow and bramble, with all the rushes and grass that it had gathered, made the cast a dangerous one. He was undecided still when he saw a rise in the eddy; he could not see whether it was his fish or not, but he made a couple of air casts, feeling his way across the pool, and then dropped his fly neatly into the middle of the slack water. But he had too long a line out, and when he struck with the rising of the fish he could not whip it cleanly from the water. It darted instantly into the tangle, and before he could reel in, the line was fast knit.

Woollen crossed the pool at the bottom and came round to the tangle. It was awkward to get at it, because of the slope of the mound, which ran straight into the water here, but with a good deal of trouble he pulled the whole weedy mess up on to the side. The trout was only a very little fish, not the big one at all. Woollen took it carefully in his wet hand and worked the hook out. He went up to the bank overhanging the slack water so that he could put the fish into a quiet place out of the run of the current. Much more of the bank had caved in than he had supposed, looking from the other side. He knelt and held the little fish in the hollow of his hand under the water; it stayed there for a moment before shooting away into the waving green bed, out of sight.

When he had disentangled his cast and line he began to examine the altered bank, so that he should know the new lie of the pool another day. Huge slices of spongy black earth had been undercut and lay at the bottom with their long grass streaming. One slice had not quite parted; it hung with a deep wide crack between it and the still solid land. Woollen pushed it with his foot and it went over, quite slowly, with a watery sough. The water was shallow under it, and the black earth lay half awash.

Woollen was still looking vacantly at it when there was a slight rumble – tremor rather than sound – under his feet and a great stone slab fell flatlings into the thin water and mud, scattering them far out across the pool. Immediately after there was an indescribable rushing noise as a hundred thousand gold coins gushed on to the slab piling up like wheat, cascading, flowing, flowing. All at once the gush stopped: one last coin rolled down, slid down the side of the pile and rang on the stone.

Woollen had not moved. His breath suspended, his hand to his mouth; his throat was stiff, could not swallow, and his heart was doing strange things even before his reason had grasped the reality of what was before him.

Two things stabbed into his mind: one the word 'escape' and a thousand implications behind it, the other the dreadfulness of the coins on the far side dribbling down to irrecoverable loss in the deep water. With a violent, epileptic jerk he leapt to rescue them. There was no need: they lay in a few inches of water on the side of a turf that had gone in before. The surprising chill of the water checked him, and he stood there gasping, with his sense coming back. Bending, he peered under the dark bank: the earth had fallen away from a stone chest buried deep in the mound; three sides of it and its lid still stood there, canted outwards by long subsidence to such a degree that no single coin remained. The fourth side and a long sliver of flawed stone from the bottom of the chest had fallen under the immense weight of the gold. His mind digested this while he drew breath, and at once he was back with one foot on the bank and the other on the stone slab, saying, 'Easy now, old Woollen. Steady does it,' and picking up gold with both hands. He worked with immense speed at first, but as his natural phlegm began to reassert itself even in the smallest degree he arranged them in neat piles, counting as he did so.

His first wild flurry of spirits, painful in its intensity, calmed, to be succeeded by an all-embracing happiness. This vast hoard was his. He had not the first glimmering of a doubt there. Plans formed and reformed with lightning rapidity in his head; he lost count of the hundreds. He came up on to the bank among the piles to count again, and he suddenly found himself trembling with weariness.

The sun came out, and the gold sent back its light, not a coin but what was brilliant; no tarnish, no obscuring dust. Woollen sat among the heaps, passing the gold through his hands. It was not Armada gold, as he had expected; there were a few Roman aurei, some Greek staters, among them coins of a beauty that struck him even then, and a mass of thick, unintelligible rounds that he supposed to be Oriental. There was no silver, no bronze. Gold; all gold.

He knew that he could not possibly carry a tenth part of it, and while he was weighing in his mind the ways of dealing with it he was possessed with the idea that he might already have been seen – some lurker in an illicit still, some chance wandering youth in the mountainside. He did not ever suppose that there might be other things in the valley watching him, measuring his breath, weighing his shadows: silent things like a round bank of fern or a crag at a vantage point, incessantly recording, communicating with each other, collating, storing up.

There were stills in the neighbourhood, he knew very well. The gleam of the hoard – how it flashed and shone; it would catch a man's eye five miles away. With a chill on his soul he covered some with his coat, strewed the broken tangle over more, tore up bushes to cover the rest. He stared searchingly at the mountains, down the two ridges; there was no movement, only a kestrel hanging in the wind. The valley behind him was empty.

'I must not dig. They would see the marks . . .' His mind's voice trailed off in an anguish of frustration. Illumination came: he sprang down into the water again and tore lumps from the fallen earth. Then leaning under the still overhanging bank to the great chest he levelled its floor with clods, piled it high with gold, built up a wall of stones and turf to serve for the fallen sides, and crammed the chest again. The slab, lest it should draw notice, he moved with a strength that he had never known before, and plunged it into the deep swirling middle water.

Some gold remained, enough to buy half the County Mayo. He dug among the bushes, in spite of his fear; he dug with his

hands and slashed the roots with his knife. There was little trace
when he had done. By now his mind was running fast and clear.
'I will go over to Ballyatha,' he said, 'and I will sell four or five
at Power's there. Then I will buy some decent clothes and have
dinner at the Connaught. To-morrow I will send some to the big
London dealers, and when I have the money . . .' There were so
many possible variations that his mind stumbled in a happy
indecision.

He was ready. A dozen very thick coins weighed down the
pockets of his coat. The sun was well down the sky but if he
hurried he could reach Ballyatha in time. It was clearly essential
that he should not be cheated of one day's happiness; it was less
clear how getting to Ballyatha affected the safety of everything,
but he was entirely certain that it did. The way was over the
pass between Slieve Donagh and Ardearg, right up the valley
and over the curtain of rock that closed its upper end. A chasm,
not six feet wide – a man could touch each side with outstretched
arms – and twenty yards long formed the pass, and below it on
the far side was the town.

There was no path: he toiled upwards with his eyes fixed on
the skyline. When he had gone a quarter of a mile he spun round,
ran in long bounds downhill to the water, to the chest, grasped
handfuls of gold, stuffed his pockets, his trout-bag, hurled the
fish away. Then, breathing in great uneven gasps, he turned his
face to the pass again and forced his labouring body up and up,
on for ever, always uphill and the short grass slippery like glass.

He must get there in time, everything depended on it. The
weight was more than he could bear and the pass was infinitely
high above. The sun hurried down. Woollen, the unfortunate
man in all his days, pressed on and on, and still the everlasting
hill stretched above and beyond him. A despairing glance over
his shoulder at the sun as it dipped made him stumble and fall.
The wind chilled his soaking body. On and on: not to look up:
on, on, on. He did look up, and the pass in the dusk was before
him.

But in the pass he met the keeper of the hoard.

The Dawn Flighting

THE NIGHT WAS OLD, black, and full of driving cold rain; the moon and the stars had already passed over the sky. But anyhow they had been hidden since midnight by the low, racing, torn cloud and the flying wetness of small rain and sea-foam and the whipped-off top of standing water. Dawn was still far away: from the dark east the mounting wind blew in gusts; it bore more rain flatlings from the sea.

Bent double, with the breath caught from his mouth, a man struggled against the force of the living wind. He walked on the top of a sea-wall that guarded the reclamation of a great marsh. At this point the wall ran straight into the teeth of the wind for a long way; there was no shelter. He had to walk carefully, for the mud had not frozen yet, and it was treacherous going. Behind him his dog, an old black Labrador, picked its way, whining in a little undertone to itself when the way was very dirty.

A great blast came, halting him in mid-stride; he staggered and stepped back to keep his balance. The dog's paw came under his heel and there was a yelp, but he heard nothing of it for the roaring of the wind. He leaned against it, and it bore him up with a living resilience, suddenly slackening, so that he stumbled again. The false step jerked a grunt out of him.

Thrusting his chin down into the scarf under his high-buttoned collar and shifting the weight of his gun, the man pushed on. All his mind was taken up with his fight; every long, firm step was a victory in little. The hardness of his way and the unceasing clamour at his ears had taken away every other thought. He was hardly aware of the places where the driven wet had pierced through, above his knees, down one side of his neck, and on his shoulder where the strap of his cartridge-bag crossed over. Earlier on he had been irked by the weight of the bag and by the drag of the gun in the crook of his arm, but now he did not heed them at all; the wind was the single, embracing enemy.

At last the sea-wall turned right-handed, running along the south face of the saltings. At the corner he stooped and slid on all fours down the steep side into the lee. At once it seemed to him that some enormous machine had stopped; in the quiet air he breathed freely, and sighed as he squatted in the mud. The Labrador shook itself and thrust its muzzle into his relaxed hand. Absently the man felt for its ears, but the dog was insistent; the custom must be fulfilled. When he had changed the hang of the strap on his aching shoulder the man searched under his macintosh among the scarves and pullovers for an inner pocket; he found half a biscuit and his pipe. The flare of the match in his cupped hands showed his face momentarily, in flashes, as he sucked the flame down; it showed disembodied in the darkness, high cheekbones and jutting nose thrown into distorted prominence. The foul pipe bubbled, but the acrid tobacco was instantly satisfying; he drew and inhaled deeply for a few moments.

'Well, that's the first leg,' he said to the dog as he got up. He went on under the lee of the sea-wall, walking heavily in the deep, uneven mud. Further on there was a place where he had to leave the wall to strike across the marsh for a stretch of open fresh water: there was only one path that led to the mere. At this time of the year the marsh was impassable except by this track, for the land-water had deepened the mud so that a man could sink out of sight in it almost before he knew he was in danger.

Anxiously he counted the time that he had taken walking along the southern wall; if he missed the path he would not get across the marsh for the dawn flighting. He crossed an old, broken sea-wall that joined the other, and he knew that he was near the path. When he climbed to the top of the wall to look for the three posts that would give him his bearings he felt an abatement in the wind: it blew less furiously, but it was colder now – certainly freezing. A flurry of sleet stung his cheek. The wind was veering to the north-north-east. He found the posts and the track; he was glad, for it was easy to miss in the dark, when all that could be seen looked strange, even monstrous.

The dog went before him now, finding out the tortuous way: sometimes a single bending plank led through the deep reed-beds, loud in the wind: treading on the planks stirred the marsh smell. Once there was a rush of wings, and desolate voices fled away piping in the darkness. They were redshanks or some kind of tukes – inedible, and his half-raised gun sank.

Now the wind was at his back; it was blowing itself out in great gusts. A thin film of ice was skimming the top of the puddles, and a more querulous note sang through the reeds. He looked over his shoulder, scanning the eastern sky for the first cold light: there seemed to be a lessening in the darkness, nothing more. He pushed on faster: the way was a little easier now.

Presently large dim shapes came up out of the blind murk before him; they were the trees surrounding the mere. He stopped to take his bearings again, and then he went on cautiously. The ground rose a little; there were brambles and patches of alder, laced through and through with rabbit tracks. Ahead a buck-rabbit thrummed the earth, and three white scuts bobbed away. Very carefully the man came through the undergrowth among the trees: a flick of his thumb and finger brought his dog in to heel. There might well be duck down on the water. Choosing his steps and crouching low in the bushes and then in the reeds, the man slipped down the bank, down the sheltered way, and crept secretly into the butt of cut reeds at the pond's edge.

After a little listening pause he stood slowly up, holding his breath and staring with wide-opened eyes through the shoulder-high reeds. Still a little bent, he peered intently over the water. There were no duck; only a little grebe swam and dived unwitting on the mere. He slowly relaxed, and sat down on the rough, unsteady plank stool in the butt.

He stretched and shook himself, for he was still desperately tired from getting up at two o'clock in the morning, and his eyes prickled. He looked to his gun, wiped a clot of mud from its barrels, and propped it carefully in the corner of the butt by his cartridge bag; he was warm now in the shelter of the reeds, and he settled himself comfortably to wait for the dawn flight of the wild duck.

Now that he was in the butt, time seemed to begin again: for the whole of the way out across the marsh it had stopped. He had been trying to race the dawn – quite another thing. By and by he pulled out a packet of bread and cheese, with an apple against thirst, for the marsh water was sulphurous and brackish. He ate bite for bite with the dog, but absently, with his senses on the stretch.

By imperceptible degrees the sky lightened, so that when he looked again he could see halfway across the water. The lake had formerly been a decoy: the hoops for the duck-pipes still showed in the overgrown channels, and a cottage, half-sunk and unroofed, marked where the wild-fowlers had kept their gear.

He was unready, for all his vigilance, when the first duck passed over: one hand was scrabbling in his pouch, the other holding his pipe. With his unlighted pipe in his mouth and his gun in his hands, he listened again: the sound was high above, a sound hard to convey. There was a creaking in it, and a whistling. His ears followed the sound, and the dog stared up into the dim quarter-light. The noise circled round the mere twice, coming lower. Mallard they were, by the sound, and they were coming down. The butt stood on a spit of land with the length of the pond lying out on each side, so that the duck would come in across. He stood with his back to the wind, jiggling his forehand nervously and biting hard on the stem of his pipe. Down, and up again: he caught a glimpse of them, five mallard. They came round lower, the flight-note changed and they braced hard against the wind to land. Up went the gun and his fingers poised delicately round the triggers. The sound of wings rushed closer: he saw the duck, picked the right-hand bird, steadied, and fired, swinging his second barrel into them as they crossed so quickly that the two tongues of flame stabbed the darkness almost at the same moment. There was a splash in front of him, then a threshing in the water. His hands, working of themselves, broke the gun and thrust new cartridges into the smoking breech. He stared up, waiting for the duck to circle overhead, but they swung wide out of range, and he heard them go. The Labrador stood rigid, ears pointing: Fetch, he said, and the dog flung itself into the water. It was back in a minute with the mallard held gently at the shoulder. Stooping, he let the dog put it into his hand, and as he straightened a disturbed sheldrake passed over, gruntling as it flew. It circled the mere twice and came down with a long splash: he had caught a glimpse of the breadth of its wings and had heard its small noise, for the wind was dying now, and he was nearly sure that it was a sheldrake. The bird swam close to the butt, safe in its uneatable rankness, so close that he could see the nob on its beak: he was glad to see it, for it would bring the other duck down.

He lit his pipe, crouching in the bottom of the butt, with his head on one side for the sound of wings. Presently they came, a flight of mallard, and above them, close behind, half a dozen sharp-winged widgeon. The mallard came straight down, sweeping right across in front of the butt with their wings held against the wind and their bodies almost upright; they tore up the water, each making a distinct tearing sound, and settled at the far end of the decoy. At once they changed from things of the wind to earth-bound, quacking ducks, awkward and lumpish in the water. The widgeon, more wary, went round high and fast: they seemed to suspect something, but the duck on the water reassured them, and they dropped down, slipping sideways down through the air on stiff, decurved wings, on the one slant and then on the other, like aeroplanes that have come in too high.

They came straight at the butt, as if to skim over it and land the other side. As he brought his gun up for the difficult shot they saw him and lifted: he fired at once. The first barrel jerked the bird a yard higher and clipped feathers from its wing; the second missed altogether. With a loud and rushing noise, the mallard got up. He stared impassively after the flying widgeon, not allowing himself any emotion, for he was a choleric man, and if he let himself start to kick and swear he might carry on and spoil his whole morning with rage, as he had done before.

Automatically he re-loaded, sniffing the sharp, sweet powder smell: the mallard wheeled back over the pond. He took a chance shot at the lowest and winged it. It came down in a long slope into the brushwood on the other side of the decoy. The dog went after it, but could not reach it, for the bird was in a tall, dense thicket of brambles. The dog came back after a long time and stood bowing in deprecation: the air was quite still now, and the mallard could be heard moving over on the other side. He cast a look round the low bowl of the sky, now almost white, and saw no birds: he walked quickly round the mere, for he hated to leave a wounded bird for any length of time. The brambles ripped through to his flesh, but he got the duck and gripped it by the neck. A strong pull, and the bird jerked convulsively and died.

He looked up: three widgeon were coming over, high and fast, with their pointed wings sounding clear. He flung himself on his back in the rushes. They were right over his head as he raised his gun: the movement was plain, in spite of the rushes, and they lifted high. It was too long a shot, but he fired his choke barrel at the middle bird, making great allowance ahead. The bird seemed to fold, to collapse in the air: it fell like a plummet and hit the ground a yard from his feet so hard that he felt it strike. He stared at the duck with an unconscious grin of pleasure; for it was a wonderfully long shot. He picked it up and smoothed its beautiful ruffled breast with his finger. With a sudden, unforeseen leap, the widgeon came back to life; it almost sprang from his loose hands. He killed it and went back to the butt.

It was a bird worthy of a good shot; a fine drake it was, nearly as big as the mallard in the corner. He smoothed its yellow crest: its blue legs and beak were brighter than any he had seen.

Far away there was the deep boom of a punt-gun. That will get them moving, he said, and the dog moved its tail. A big mixed flight came in: with good fortune he got four barrels into them, killing two mallard and a shoveller. He regretted the shoveller, for by his private rules they were not to be shot. There was something about their coral and prussian blue and white bib and tucker that combined with their disproportionate beaks to make them look too much like agreeable toys. But, firing so quickly, he had not distinguished it.

For half an hour after that, while the first rays of the true dawn showed, the duck flighted in great numbers over the marshes. He shot a brace of teal right and left, a feat that consoled him for many bad misses, and he killed another widgeon and three mallard. But he was not shooting well: the duck were moving very fast, and his tired eyes were strained by the changing light. After seven successive misses – one bird carried away a deadly wound – he felt a wretched frustration welling up. By now the watery sun was showing a faint rim over the sea. All at once he felt very weary; unshaved, dirty and weary, with his eyes hot.

A little time passed and the sun came bodily up. The flighting was over, and he bent to his bag. As he stowed each away he smoothed it with care; he put the exquisitely marked teal on the top and strung the bag up. It was barely a quarter full: he had not done at all well. He knew that on such a good day he should have killed many more. He counted the big pile of empty cartridges against his bag, and he thought of the long walk back. He always had a feeling of reaction after he stopped shooting, when the taut excitement died rather ignominiously away, and now there was a strong vexation of spirit upon him as well as that.

'Oh well,' he said, and slung the bag on his back. He could see far and wide over the marsh now; beyond the sea-wall the masts of the fishing boats showed clearly in the sharp air. It was freezing now for sure. Towards the sea he saw a ragged skein of duck weaving and drifting like a cloud: there was none over the marsh. A curlew cried despairingly over his head; breaking its heart, it was.

The wind had quite died. Stiffly, with a lumbering gait, he went back towards the sea-wall with his dog padding quietly after him.

From far away there came a sound over the marsh on the still, frozen air: he looked round and above, but he could see nothing. The sound grew stronger, a rhythmic beating, strangely musical, and he saw three wild swans. The light caught them from below and they flashed white against the cold blue. High up in the air, their great singing wings bore the swans from the north: they flew straight and fast with their long necks stretched before them.

The rhythm changed a little, sighing and poignant, and a leaping exaltation took the man's heart as he gazed up at them, up away in the thin air.

The beat changed more, and now they flew striking all together, so that their wings sung in unison as they went over his head. He stood stock still watching them, and long after they had passed down the sky he stood there, with the noise of their wings about his head.

Not Liking
to Pass the Road Again

THE ROAD LED UPHILL all the way from the village; a long way, in waves, some waves steeper than others but all uphill even where it looked flat between the crests.

There was a tall thick wood on the right hand for the first half: for a long time it had been the place of the Scotch brothers. They were maniacs, carpenters by trade, Baptists; and one had done something horrible to his brother.

I have forgotten now why I thought that only one brother still lived in the wood: perhaps I had been told. I used to throw things into the wood.

At first they were small things, bits of twig or pebbles from the middle of the road, the loose stuff between the wheel tracks; I threw them furtively, surreptitiously, not looking, just into the nut bushes at the edge. Then I took to larger ones, and on some bold days I would stand in an open wide part of the road flinging heavy stones into the wood: they lashed and tore the leaves far within the wood itself. It was a place where there had been a traction engine and where they had left great piles of things for the road.

Quite early in the summer (there were a great many leaves, but they were still fresh and the bark was soft and bright) I was there and I had two old chisels without handles; they were brown and their cutting edges were hacked and as blunt as screw drivers, but their squared angles were still sharp. I had gashed a young tree with one, throwing it; it had taken the green bark clean from the white wood.

I had them purposely this bold day prepared, to throw them

35

in with desperate malice – I was almost afraid of them then. I did not throw them far, but flat and hard and oh God the great bursting crashing in the wood and he came, brutal grunting with speed.

Before my heart had beat I was running. Running, running, running, and running up that dreadful hill that pulled me back so that I was hardly more than walking and my thin legs going weaker and soft inside.

I could not run, and here under my feet was the worst hill beginning. At the gap by the three ashes I jigged to the left, off the road to the meadow: downhill, and I sped (the flying strides) downhill to the old bridge and the stream full-tilt and downhill on the grass.

Into the stream, not over the bridge, into the water where it ran fast over the brown stones: through the tunnel of green up to the falls I knew the dark way. I knew it without thinking, and I did not put a foot on dry ground nor make a noise above the noise of the water until I came to the falls and then I stepped on a dry rock only three times all the way up the wide mouth. It is easier to climb with your hands and feet than to run on a bare road. And I came out into the open for an instant below the culvert on the road, a place where I could look back, back and far down to the smooth green at the foot of the old bridge.

It was still there, casting to and fro like a hound, but with inconceivable rapidity. Halfway up the meadow sometimes to hit back on the line, so eager, then a silent rush to the water's edge and a check as if it had run into a stone wall: then over and over again, the eager ceaseless tracing back and fro. Vague (except in movement), uncoloured, low on the ground.

There was a cart on the road now, well above the ruined cottage, and I went home. I changed my boots without being seen – they had kept the water out for a long time, although I had been up to my knees at once; in the end the water had come in down from my ankles, quite slowly.

That night and afterwards, when I told the thing over to myself I added a piece to make the passing of the road again more bearable. In the added piece my mother came in and said that we were all to be careful when we went out because there was a mad dog. 'Hugh was found on the old bridge,' she said (Hugh was one of the farm boys), 'at the foot of the old bridge, with his face bitten. They have taken him to hospital, but he will not speak yet.'

The Slope of
the High Mountain

SNOW HAD FALLEN in the night and it lay on all the ground above five hundred feet, showing brave in the sun and making the sky so blue that it was a living pleasure to look at it.

To the men walking fast up the Nantmor road the sharp cold was a pleasure too, for their hurry had warmed them to a fine heat. They had already come some miles over the mountains before they had struck the metalled road, along an ancient track that wound among the high bogs, often ambiguous and always hard to be found: they had followed it without losing it, but it had taken time above their allowance. They were hurrying, therefore, with the fear of lateness behind them, and their nailed boots rang quick on the hard road, and they steamed in the frosty air.

It was to a meet of foxhounds that they were hurrying, a meet right under Snowdon, at ten o'clock. Moel Ddu was on their left, and Moel Hebog after it, and the snow lay well down their sides; the men could not see Snowdon yet, for the hills shut in the top of the valley. The cruel black rocks of the Arddu rose sheer on the right hand, and the Nantmor river ran fierce below them. Far along on the road ahead a man was walking fast: he was a dark figure, dressed in black, incongruous among the rocks, and he was singing passionately. It was a hymn in Welsh and he was a shepherd: presently he vanished at a turning in the road, and although they heard his singing high up among the stunted trees they did not see the man again.

The road continued to rise and soon there were no more trees on either hand, and the black rocks showed harsher. The top of the valley was desolate with the gigantic spew of a dead slate quarry, high and lonely on the deserted road. Marching lines of square pillars showed where the aqueduct had run: many of them leaned strangely, and some had fallen. Huge, unprofitable slate rocks lined the road, holding back the black hills of jagged spoil.

The men had spoken little for the last half-hour, but now they said to one another that the road would soon turn to the left, and Gonville began to talk about how birds cannot tell how fast they are going in the air if there is a cloud or no light at all. Brown did not believe what he was told, but he was unable to refute it. Gonville, aware of his disbelief, went on in a dogmatic tone, telling him more about the birds of the air and the way they know nothing except possibly by magnetism. However, Brown did not quarrel with him, and when the road turned to the left all thoughts of wrangling went out of his head.

Right before them was Snowdon, sharp and brilliant in the sky, with Lliwedd jutting fiercely on the right and deep new snow over all, sparkling nobly in the sun. New clean snow, unspoiled by runnels, and Snowdon's eastern face looked smooth by reason of the depth of the snow.

They were looking at Snowdon from a fair height and with a deep valley between: this waste of air below and before them gave the mountain an altitude and a majesty far beyond the amount of its height in feet. The sun was behind them, and it shone on the incisive, spectacular ridge that joins Lliwedd and Snowdon, separating the peaks with a great sweep of hard shadow.

It was a sight to make even a dull man's heart leap and exult, like sudden good news or a lost thing found.

The way was downhill now, down into Nant Gwynant, with the big lakes one on either hand and the river joining them. The hard walking they had done had caught up with the clock, and when they came down into Nant Gwynant, to the Glaslyn and to the gate leading up to the farm of Hafod Llan they were before their time. For all that, anxiety harassed them as they waited by the gate where the milk churn stood, and they discussed the misadventures that might have happened, the possibility of a mistake in the time and of an error in their route – suppose, they said, the Captain has gone up by another way? But when they had been worrying themselves for a quarter of an hour the car and the trailer passed them and swung up the cart track to Hafod Llan. They ran after it and came up as the Master was going into the farmhouse to ask after his fox. There were a few other people, and the farm children stared at them and the hounds.

Eight couples were there, stretching and walking about: there was a strong smell of hounds everywhere. The outraged farm dogs bawled from a distance, but offered nothing more. The hunt terriers ran busily to and fro; all hard-bitten and many with recent scars and bald patches. The hounds were mixed. There were Welsh hounds, fell-hounds, and crosses, and there was an English bitch with a noble, judicious head who looked strange among the slim, fine-boned creatures around her. Benign hounds they were, but not effusive like some; Ranter, Rambler, Ringwood, Driver and Melody, Drummer, Marquis, and Music, the surest of them all.

The Master came out of the farmhouse. He was of an ancient family, and his people had hunted this country above three hundred years. He had a falcon's nose and eye, and his moustache curled with a magnificent arrogance. He wore a very old cloth cap and a torn Burberry which concealed his horn and the whip he carried over the shoulder of his jacket. He spoke to the huntsman in Welsh and they moved off towards the Gallt y Wenallt, the mountain behind the wood.

When they came to a gate at the bottom of the wood the Master turned off downward and the huntsman, with the field and the hounds, went up through the copse. Hounds were soon out of sight among the trees, and Gonville and Brown pushed themselves to keep up with the long-legged huntsman. Soon they reached the snow where it lay thin and melting in the open spaces between the trees: they climbed quickly past the height where it was melting and came out at the top of the wood. As they cleared the trees a hound spoke below them, and they paused for a moment. Hounds passed up through the wood, working intently, but with very little sound; they were moving quite fast, and when another hound spoke – a deep-mouthed hound it was – they were far along.

The men had reached a path, and they followed it. It ran up from the wood to the top of a bluff, an almost sheer cliff that rose high above the woods. They could see hounds below them when they reached the top of this bluff and they stopped in a sheltered place – sheltered, because the wind, a small wind that came off the snow, bit very sharp and hard, they being in a sweat with the hurry.

They had come round the shoulder of the Gallt y Wenallt out of the sun, and here it was much colder. The face of Wenallt, running steeply down to Llyn Gwynant, was on their left: below them, at the bottom of the mountain, was a deep belt of trees; above the trees, a long sloping scree that stretched up to the foot of the cliff. Below the wood was the still lake and its river, and beyond the lake the ranks of bare mountains marching away one behind the other.

Hounds were working across the scree just below the snow; they were coming slowly up, and dubiously. However, they puzzled it out across the rocks, up through the heather in the face of the cliff, for the scent lay there, and up almost to the men crouched in their bit of lee.

Now they were hunting more confidently, and it was a rare delight to watch them packed close together with their heads down and almost touching and their backsides wriggling as they carried the line over the hard places, and how they ran streaming out over the easy ones. Down they went again, much faster than they had come up, down and into the wood.

Then the waiting men heard no more for a long time, nor saw anything. Brown talked to the huntsman, a young, tall Welshman who swore in English; he had most of the terriers with him, and the old white bitch nipped precisely into Brown's lap. The other terriers crawled in the snow, for the pleasure of scratching their bellies against its crust. The huntsman carried a long pole and he wore old blue breeches: he told Brown that the Master would be below the wood, and that if the fox were a Cwm Dyli fox, as

he supposed – but as he was speaking there was a crash of savage
music in the wood. They all stood up in silence, and directly
hounds were speaking again, singly and in a choir. They were
running fast. In a minute or two the huntsman said that they
had either got him going or they were very near to him, and in
that moment the fox came up out of the wood, up to the clear
edge of it. A dark brown fox was he, big and rangy, a long-legged
fox. He looked up at the men far above him, and plainly they
could see him deliberate as he stood there, looking up and
damning their eyes. The fox looked down and trotted away along
the top of the wood, inclining rather upward to the mountain –
a low-pitched diagonal up the great sloping apron of Wenallt.

As the fox went away clear of the wood the huntsman sprang
down the face of the cliff and holloed him away with great shrieking hooicks: he went down with a wonderful agility, going too
fast to fall, and the snow flew up from his feet. The fox did not
hurry for all that, but went steadily on: the men could see him
between the rocks and low pieces of broken wall, and once or
twice he looked up with a fleeting glance. The huntsman was
crying to his hounds to lay them on, but they came up rather
slowly, and by the time they were running on the line the fox
was farther away than a man would have supposed possible.

He was going toward Cwm Dyli, it appeared, Cwm Dyli, far
up at the top of Nant Gwynant, higher up than Llyn Gwynant,
and right round the whole mass of the Gallt y Wenallt the men
must go to get there.

This mountain, this Wenallt, is the end of the mass of Snowdon
on the Nant Gwynant side – the deep valley and the lake define
the mass. The mountain faces the lake squarely. Its top part is
craggy, but not pointed: two arms run down from the top, arms
that would embrace the lake if they ran further, but the one that
shelters Hafod Llan is broken by the cliff and the wood swallows
it, and the other, the far one towards the top of Nant Gwynant,
peters out in the dead ground at the marshy top of the lake.
Between these arms and below the crags of the top is a vast
stretch of ground, a table tilted to an angle of fifty-five degrees
and more. The men must cross this stretch. They were already

about two-thirds of the way up it, and the intention of the first man was plainly to go straight across. The rest of the field followed, for he knew the country well. As soon as they left the rock of the cliff they found the going very hard. The sloping face was covered with thin wiry grass growing in shallow soil, and the grass lay under an inch or two of snow. Everywhere there were rocks and stones, nearly all on the surface, and none to be relied upon for a handhold. The snow was too shallow to tread into steps, and it was of that coarse, crystalline sort that makes a foot slip as ice does; much of the stuff was hail. The grass was no help either; the way it lay was all downhill, so it would not hold a foot up, and its roots were so poor in the red scratching of soil that a very little pull brought the whole handful up.

They came to a wall, a wall that ran down the mountain to the wood, one of the innumerable walls that intersect the summer sheep-walks there; it accentuated the angle of the slope, and if Brown had not heard the cry of hounds in front of him he would not have followed the leader over the wall, but would have looked for another way.

It was worse the other side. Brown had not brought a stick – he preferred to have both hands free for climbing – and he missed it sorely now. Gonville was a little way behind him; they were too far apart to talk, and even if they had been closer the difficulty of their way and their hurry would have kept them silent.

For a little way there was the likeness of a path, but this vanished after it had led them well out on to the face of Wenallt. The slope grew a few degrees steeper now, and now they crept painfully and slow. It was a cruel slope: a man could hardly keep his feet standing quite still on it.

From time to time Brown looked down to the distant wood, over the great sheet of white, a sheet that he could now see to be full of boulders that jutted sharply from its surface.

They were all crawling along with their left hands to the snow, sometimes with their whole bodies pressed to it, all with a strong uneasiness. The real present fear, with no interposing doubts or comforting illusions, did not strike into Brown's heart until he saw a flat stone that the man in front of him had dislodged go

43

sliding easily down, easily and then faster, throwing snow from it like a ski, and at last crashing into an ugly great black rock far, far down. Just after this the man in front turned left-handed directly up the mountain, going up a gully with the help of his iron-pointed stick: he was aiming for a saddle that led behind the rounded brow of the peak. He did not speak to Brown – he was too much occupied for that – and Brown stood considering. He did not like the look of the way up. He kicked the rounded clogs of rammed snow from his boots; they clogged every few steps in this stuff. He looked forward, and again the cry of hounds raised his heart: the slope was surely easier in front, and indeed he must have come over the worst, and by God there was no going back over that stretch. Below him, a great way down, he saw a figure at the far end of the wood; it was the Master, and he was looking steadfastly up to a point on the other side of the shoulder of Wenallt that was in front of Brown.

If they have run him in round there, said Brown, I shall be the first up. He looked round before he started forward and saw Gonville spread-eagled in a bad place; another man was holding out his stick for him to grasp, and it was obvious that they were going back. Brown waved; he felt secretly rather pleased. His fear had receded, and although he knew, with his head, that he was in danger, the real starkness of it had gone. I may slip or fall, he said in effect, and that could be fatal – probably would be – but these are things that happen to other people.

The first ten paces were easy and the next quite plain, but then he saw bad ground ahead and he judged that he must go down a little to get along at all. The huntsman came into sight just below the snow; he was walking with the terriers along the diagonal line the fox had taken. He had been hidden for most of the time by a drop of ground that did not show from above. This confirmed Brown in his plan, and he decided to go down to the good ground and then across to intercept the huntsman's path as he crossed the far arm of Wenallt. Just at this point the ground went down in steps, still grass-covered: these he negotiated, with his face downward. Below the steps the slope was terrible, but there was no retreat. It had looked just the same, or better, from above. I will go down on my bottom, he said; a little farther down and then across. The immensity of the stretch below him, the snow ending in shale and the far, far trees; the huge sweep sickened him.

He shuffled down – come, it's not too bad, he said, but while the words were still in him, and he in an awkward position with his legs stretched out and his weight on his elbows and heels, he began to slip. With a furious, controlled energy he gripped into the grass and earth. It tore away without hesitation. Flat on his back, he went; he went with his arms out and his crooked, tense hands scrabbling for a hold, failing, then pressing fiercely on the sliding snow, stemming, breaking, but impotently and in vain, for he was going faster. Faster: with a terrible certainty the momentum increased: the seconds of controllable speed had passed. It is happening to me, he said: and Now for it, he said, as he passed into a hurtling rush down; but still he hunched his shoulders to protect his head and forced his hands into the snow. The sense of responsibility was gone and with it his fear: he expected one dark blow, a smashing blow and the end, but not without a certain constancy of mind.

His feet were against a rock, a firm rock. It was all over; and he was still, unmoving and unhurt. He lay for a moment, for some minutes, breathing and looking at the sky. He was wet, soaked through and through; the whole of his back was wet through and the caked snow was forced into his clothes. Was he hurt? No, he was not hurt. His hands were strange to him, but he was not hurt – all whole. He got up, trembling and shaken: he did not think very clearly now, in this strong reaction.

The trees were a good deal nearer: Brown was halfway down the mountain-face. He could not see the others when he looked up, nor could he be sure of the place where he had started. He looked down, but the huntsman was no longer to be seen.

He felt that there was a strong necessity to go on, not to stop, not to make anything of it. He thought slowly: perhaps he had been stunned, had been unconscious for a while without knowing it? How otherwise could Emrys have vanished like that?

He went on a few steps farther down to look from side to side:

no man could he see, but there was a neat precipice, only fifteen or twenty feet deep, but sheer, and if he had not fetched up where he did he would have gone over it without any sort of doubt. This shocked him unreasonably and he turned his face to the dark crags above him. How he longed for the rough, strong rocks, firm and true: their steepness was nothing, he said inwardly, for they were reft and fissured and it was like going up a ladder.

Without thinking any more he started to move up. From where he was the crags seemed continuous right from where the grass ended to the very top, and once the rock was gained it did not look at all difficult to go up over the summit of Wenallt.

His new way was easier than creeping sideways across the mountain, but it meant going on all fours, and soon the snow had so numbed his battered hands that all the strength left them. They would hardly even open and close, so when he reached the first of the rocks he could not go up. He rested a long while before they recovered, and in a few minutes that he took in climbing the first stretch their strength went again. Again he rested, this time under an overhanging rock where sheep had stood years beyond counting in hard weather. By some freak his sandwiches had escaped being crushed into a mess, and eating them brought Brown back to common things and to a comforting sense of ordinariness – a feeling that had been quite stripped from him for some time before. He was shivering in his soaked clothes, soaked in front now as well as behind, for he had groped upward through deeper snow on his hands and knees; but his courage was fairly well as he came out of the sheep's place.

He could see three separate masses of rock above him, and no more: he would be climbing them, he could see, in the right direction – that is, his path would carry him over toward Cwm Dyli, and he reckoned that from the top of the third crag he would see round into the valley on the other side.

The first crag was steady, exhausting climbing, not difficult, but needing continual strong effort. At the top of it was a stretch of open shale before the foot of the next crag. This was anxious going, very, for the snow was far thicker at this height, and it was not a pretty task to creep over unseen shale pitched at that angle and with that vast amount of world below. Brown set himself to it, and worked up along the edge of the scree, where he knew the bigger stones would be lying under the snow.

His good fortune brought him up to the top, under the second crag, trembling with the effort. He had to wait for his hands again, and now for the first time, as he squatted out of the way of the little breeze, cramps seized him with force and anguish, so that he grunted aloud. Now his heart began to falter a little, less at the pain and the fear that they might grasp him again when he was crucified on a rock than at the new appearance of the crag above him: rocks that had appeared to be joined when he decided to climb them now had showed themselves to be far apart, separated by stretches of snow that might conceal anything, stretches that tilted shockingly, so that some of them looked almost vertical.

However, he hoisted himself up the nearest rock, and reached for the next handhold; it was a high, flat rock-face that he was going up now, and he had to walk up it with his feet while he held on with both hands. As he looked down to see whether his right foot was well placed, looking down with his chin in his chest, he saw beyond his foot black rock and snow stretching down forever, then that horrible plane slope, and infinitely far away the trees and the lake. These he saw upside down, and he sickened at the sight. With a convulsive, wasteful effort he struggled to the top and lay there. He knew that he must not look down any more, for his courage was beginning to go, and with it his freedom from the terror of height.

It was while he was on the third mass of rock, worming himself across a gully to a climbable rock, that he came face to face with a hound. It was Ringwood, obviously coming down from the top. He was followed by others: they looked momentarily at Brown and went on. Even with four legs they found it hard, and one slipped twenty feet and more while Brown watched them. He no longer minded about hounds: all that he wanted, and the huge want filled him to the exclusion of all else, was firm ground, level ground, under his feet and the sky in its right place over his head.

The topmost piece of the third crag was an ugly, out-leaning breast of rock with a narrow cleft in it. The strength of his hands was gone again, and as he stood wedged in this cleft he thought he was going to fall at last. He did not fall, though he swayed backward; his elbow held, and with his chin ground down to the top of the rock and a chance grip for his knee he came up to the top. Kneeling there, almost sick with the muscular effort, he saw that what he had climbed was a false crest. Beyond and above him stretched three hundred feet of nearly perpendicular rock, interspersed with gullies and patches of shale. A wide tract of flattish ground that led back from the top of the false peak had hidden all this from him as he stood below: even now what he saw as the top might not be the real summit.

Without allowing himself to formulate anything about this, Brown began to walk across the dead ground. The gesture was very well, but after he had climbed a little way cold despair overtook him. This was worse than the mountain below: the rocks were farther apart, the bare, smooth slopes steeper and wider. It was unclimbable; his strength was almost gone and there was no way down.

When he came to a platform with a sheltering slab over it Brown stopped. The last phase of climbing had had a nightmarish quality; not daring to look down any more, he had won the last fifty feet at the cost of cruel labour and intense apprehension with each movement. All the time stark, naked fear had been on him, and it was on him now, and he knew that it was a rightful fear.

For a long time he squatted, inert and unfeeling. A cramp revived him and he noticed that the sun had come round the edge of the mountain. The sky was still the same unclouded perfection of a sky that it had been in the morning. He did not know the time – could not guess it, either. His watch had stopped when he had gone down.

Now that he was wholly determined not to go on he felt better. He looked down, pressing his back against the firm rock, and he experienced that sense of flying that comes with some kinds of giddiness. This passed, and he surveyed the country below him.

He had come a long way: the trees were even more distant. A feeling of utter, desolate remoteness filled him: he seemed quite cut off from the world. But so long as he was no longer going to drive himself up he did not mind very actively: no more fruitless crawling up, with knees and hands slipping and every movement perilous, arduous beyond bearing: to be left alone, that was the thing.

How kind the weather has been, he said after a great timeless pause; if it had blown hard or snowed some more I should have gone before now. How long would it be? he asked; but made no reply.

Far, far down, a little above the wood there was Gonville running with the immense strides of a man going downhill; he was crossing from right to left. Brown could recognize him by the yellow waterproof jacket that he was wearing. He ran to the wall at the end of the wood and stood by the gate.

Brown's heart went out to him in a kind of envy and a desperate longing to be down there. The thought of shouting came to his mind: on a still day like this he might make himself heard down there. But he dismissed the thought, and in a few moments the whole pack came running fast along the wall toward Gonville; Brown flushed at the sight and stood up to watch them tear along the top of the wood and vanish on his right. By the time he sat down again Gonville had disappeared.

He relapsed into the same dull, marooned feeling; he repeated that it would not be possible to go down the way he had come up, but he did not care very much. Time dropped slowly on and on, and nothing at all happened: no change, no movement.

Two ravens flew out above him from Lliwedd over the lake, flying with steady wing-beats whose sound came down to him. The front one was almost silent, but the second bird spoke all the time in a guttural monotone, *gaak gaak gaak*: occasionally the front bird replied, deeply, *gaak*. They flew straight away from him in an undeviating line for his home.

The warmth of the sun was grateful to him: in spite of the sodden coldness of his clothes his spirits rose under it, and presently he was aware of being alive again, with an active mind and his apathy gone.

When he made his great discovery he felt a fool; he could have blushed for it. Ever since the sun had come round the shoulder of Wenallt it had been melting the snow fast. The snow-line on the horrible slope, his chief dread, had been retreating steadily for a great deal of the time that he had been climbing – had crept up after him. Inexplicably, when he had looked down he had never looked for it nor seen it. But by now the slope was free from snow almost to the foot of the crags. A vast sense of relief, of ignominious anticlimax filled him. Without waiting, he let himself down from his place, he let himself down like a sack and he fell safely. He slid and scrambled recklessly down the shale and it submitted to this. He defied the black rocks now and in minutes he threw away the height that he had won with such pain. Twice he slid deliberately down long stretches of snow, squatting on his two feet; the first time he pulled himself up on a rock on the calculated edge of destruction; the second time he let himself go down the last snow of the horrible slope and did not stop until he was on the clean grass. He kicked the last snow from under his boots and ran down the grassy innocent slope laughing like a boy, down to the thorn trees and down safe and happier than Lazarus to the lovely wood and the lake with the blue sky over them, and in ten minutes the real knowledge of naked fear had left him again.

The Little Death

HE HAD NEVER FELT that sense of having been there before so strongly: climbing up the ladder to the platform, he knew perfectly well that the top rungs would be scaly and harsh, and that there would be a box, a dark green box on top of it.

There was no box.

He pushed up the trap door at the top and awkwardly, holding the gun in his left hand, clawed up on to the bare rectangle of planks: there was no box. However, the newness of being up there carried his mind directly on, and he looked eagerly about.

For years he had wanted to see what it would be like from the platform, and it was pleasant to find that the reality surpassed his old expectation. He was among the tree tops, up in the delicate, gently waving part of the trees, and all the branches tended up, reaching towards him. There, to his right, was the sharp white ribbon of the road seen at intervals through the dark pines, and there was the shooting-brake in the gateway: on his left were the ordinary trees of the wood; some, like the birches immediately under him, were shorter than the truncated pine that supported his stand, and these he could see from top to bottom, wonderfully graceful and delicate, although their leaves were going. Most of the trees on the left hand were about the same height as the platform, or a little higher, but here and there a tall beech or one of the noble ashes for which the wood was named rose high above the rest.

He stepped to the edge of the unrailed platform, and, repressing a first hint of vertigo (the platform was in gentle motion), he looked over the edge to the shadows, where the keeper still stood, the white of his upturned face showing far below: forty feet, or was it sixty? These heights were very difficult to judge: at any rate, it was high enough for the man's face to be small, like an egg, and for his voice to come floating up strangely.

'Mr. Grattan? The horse is under the far side.'

'Under the far side, is it?' He did not know at all what the keeper meant, but he was not going to show his ignorance: the keeper had already glanced at his gun, an old common, long-barrelled hammer-gun it was, of Belgian make.

There were two big hooks fixed underneath, and groping under the platform Grattan found a trestle – obviously a thing to sit upon. He pulled it up, and he was setting it square on its feet when the keeper called again, telling him that the pigeons usually came in from the right. Grattan thanked him, and watched him go away: for a few paces he could see the keeper's feet before his head and behind, fore and aft, a queer, long stride it looked, before he was under the trees and out of sight.

The trunk of the pine ran up three or four feet above the stand, and it was pleasant to have it for his back as he sat upon the trestle. The sound of the keeper's going died away, and the returning quiet brought back with it that remoteness that had been with Grattan all day, that feeling of being at one remove from life, or rather from one's surroundings, so that they look as little real as the back-cloth of a pantomime, and it would not be surprising if they were to sway gently with a bellying wave from behind. It was something remotely like one of the stages of drunkenness when a man seems to stand a little to one side of himself, listening to what he says and watching him, but without a great deal of interest.

All day it had been with him, but that was not remarkable for it had waited upon him now and then from boyhood, and since he had come home from the war it had been at his elbow most of the time. Nobody knew about it: he had not told anybody, and indeed if he had wanted to he would have found it very difficult to describe what it was, the thing that interposed itself between him and ordinary life, so that with an indifferent eye he saw everything strange, so that sounds and impressions came through to him as if they travelled more slowly: the something that gave him an inner life of far greater reality than that which went on around him at the same time and in which he took part with the rest of him. It was not to be defined, this inner life; it had little to do with conscious thought; it was a kind of awareness and a withdrawal to another plane of existence. And always, from the very first time that he had known it, a boy walking along the tow-path on a summer's evening in the shadow of the heavy, dusty green of the trees, twenty years ago, always there had been something of anticipation in it. In the last year this had increased, and now, today more than ever, it was a sense of growing, inevitable crisis – something outside himself for which he was waiting. It was something that he awaited calmly, for in this everything was slow and calm, but it was of vast importance and his being was keyed up and up for it.

He could not, on the few occasions when he had (almost impiously, it seemed) tried to formulate some ideas upon it, he could not even put any name to its nature, but today he was more certain than ever of its imminence. It would happen to him without any doing on his part: it was at once desirable and terrible.

The existence of this more real life did not prevent him – never had prevented him – from living at his common level: this very afternoon he had felt a strong inclination to decline the brown holland bag that his aunt had lovingly made him for his cartridges, as a surprise; and he had been ashamed of the appearance of his gun among the lovely hammerless ejectors carried by the other guests. However, he had neither put the cloth bag down nor concealed it in his pocket, and as a penance for these impulses he had worn it until he had forgotten it. Nowadays he forgot things very quickly; even the excitement of this invitation to Langton and the near-certainty of a job on the estate, which had made such a flutter at home, had left him almost unmoved after half an hour, although but a few years ago it would have kept him in a turmoil, partly pleasant, but increasingly alarming as the day grew nearer: for Mr. Clifton's Langton was a very grand place indeed, quite the grandest in a county full of big estates. His uncle and his three aunts (dear, kind people: he had lived in their celibate house nearly all his life) had always talked, interminably and vaguely, of great things for him; they had foreseen, foreseen. Entirely without influence themselves they attributed to it a mystic value. With significant, worldly nods they had approved his first boyish acquaintance with the children of the local magnates. 'So *suitable*,' they said to one another, pluming and settling in their upright armchairs. Few things had given them greater pleasure than the chance that made their nephew a friend of young Clifton: they had served in the same squadron, and in the short time before Clifton had been killed they had grown very much attached to one another. The invitation to shoot pigeons at Langton and the offer of some as yet undefined employment with the old agent were consequences of their friendship: the old aunts had seen it as an opening of long-closed doors.

But all this was wonderfully remote now: Barringham and Langton seen through the wrong end of a telescope, wonderfully remote; the aunts and his uncle and the garden, little moving figures in the garden with no meaning, hardly names even. And the quiet flooded back into the wood, and his mind retreated, moved back and back and back. He sat bowed on the trestle, with his mouth open, with his eyes – wide, staring eyes – fixed on a knot: his gun lay across his knees, held inertly by a passive hand.

There was so much quiet in the High Ash wood that even the bang of a gun away before him did not dispel it, nor the quick left and right behind. The creaking flutter of two wood-pigeons coming in to the dark pine just to the right of him pierced through to his mind, but it made no impression: the birds settled noisily, with the trunk between them and him. He was quite still, his breathing slow and shallow: his eyes did not move from the knot.

The dusk gathered under the trees, dark pools where the peeling birch trunks showed white. They were having good sport along the edge of the wood, just inside the belt of pines, and the guns were going fast: the pigeons were moving continually up and down the long, dark tract, uneasily in flocks and swift single birds clipping fast to their night's rest. They were filling the trees all around Grattan, heavy, fat birds that looked too big for the twigs they landed on, fat heavy wood-pigeons that walked, hopped, flapping among the twigs and branches to solid perches, and smaller stock-doves with them, many in the trees and many passing overhead.

In some part of Grattan's bowed head there was a picture of a pale, clear sky, quite clear above an unending floor of white cloud, and in the sky was an aeroplane falling and falling, falling for ever. It turned as it fell in its dying, broken fall, and each time it turned full to him he saw the Hackenkreuz on its wings. He went close to it, and he could see the German's face, expressionless and closed. They were quite alone in the sky. Grattan watched impassively and said, He is not going to bail out. I think he cannot bail out.

A trail of black smoke shot from the Messerschmitt before it plunged into the white floor of cloud, and the black plume stood, poised on a narrow foot that stayed momentarily firm in the sudden vortex of the swirling white, after the machine had disappeared; and he was saying aloud, While I live I shall never kill another living thing.

But all this was only in the forefront of his mind; behind it he was withdrawn, and there was a very slow current of thought going on between the two: up there, above the cloud, he had known that he had been there before, knew just what the black smoke would look like over the billowing hole in the cumulus. The very words that he had said had had a used feeling and an accustomed sound: they had been formulated, like a prayer. Here, on the platform, he had known what it was going to be like. There was no box, of course; but the box had been there once. If he got up he would see the place where it had stood. But that was by the way: the *déjà-vu*, which had once made him so uneasy, was only a side issue, something that came at the same time as the withdrawal: all that mattered was what was coming.

As he stirred unconsciously he made the legs of the trestle grate on the platform: now a fat wood-pigeon was staring and bending, peering at him with a round eye, bowing and staring like an alderman about to cross a road. The bird's suspicions were confirmed, and it clattered out of the tree, followed by a cloud of others: the noise jerked Grattan into the living present, and he stood tense on the platform, with his gun ready to spring up. The light was almost gone: he could not see the tiny disturbed goldcrest that went Tzee tzee so loudly in a branch within his hand's reach.

A returning pigeon – some had not believed, and had only circled once – fluttered against the clear sky at the very top of a tree right before him. He had cocked his gun automatically as he stood; now he pulled both triggers, firing down into the dark shadows, and watched the horrified bird flash dodging away. The scent, delightful from old association, the scent of the powder came up as he broke the gun and dropped the smoking empty shells on the stand, stopping them from rolling off with his foot. Then he fired another two barrels, and did the same: That should do for the keeper, he said, and sat down again.

Again the quiet came back, the curtain dropped fast, and now his mind was glowing with active suspense: it even invaded his body: his heart beat and his stomach was constrained just as it had been with him and he a young boy in his first love. Now it was here, here and coming on him.

He stood up slowly, with his gun hanging open in his right hand and his left hand wavering to his lips.

But it did not come. There was only the soft wind and the far-off voice of old Mr. Clifton: 'Grattan, we're going along now.' The words drawn out, calling to carry, and the lights and the gentle whine of the car, that died to a throb.

He made no reply, but turned in the darkness.

The Passeur

BEHIND THE TOWN there was a hill, behind the hill a mountain range; behind the range another range, behind that range an ancient wood, and in that wood there was a man.

The little rosy town, tight like a swarm of bees, with its roofs touching everywhere and not a foot of ground to be seen from above except in the great drum of the bull-ring, all this and the brilliant sea, the pure curve of the harbour and the row of fishing boats, has been described so often that there is nothing new to say.

The hill – the hills – behind, these too are so well known: the terraced vines, black gnarled points on a contoured, modelled chocolate pattern, a green blush, a blue-green incipient flood when they are sprayed, a full green solid mass, then gold and crimson on the hills according to the season: the olives and the pines: the gardens, flat with rigid squares wherever there are streams – the gardens with their peach trees and their apricots in the beds of green; trees like trees in samplers or on stocking legs, neat, trim, precise – these too are full of people and well known. Beyond the utmost limit of the vines, the garrigues covered with cistus and myrtle and Spanish broom, false lavender and asphodel, carpeted with thyme, dry, arid, wrecked by goats; here still there are people: the garrigues are known, known as well as the cork-oak groves that stand so nobly on the higher ground, crimson-lake when the cork has left their trunks. The trees are orderly, arranged in quincunxes and numbered in white paint: men are there, if it is only twice in a year. Even beyond them, in the barren country, a few parched farmhouses keep their hordes of goats and walk them on the nearer mountain range: and that is not the end, for on the mountain live the cattle,

57

PATRICK O'BRIAN

belled but savage, and they wander free, bulls, cows and heifers,
steers and calves, the whole crest of the nearer range is theirs,
and the other side to the very edge of the unknown country.

This country starts with the second mountain range. The two
are separated by a scorched and naked valley, wide and deep
with sides that sheer abruptly into overhanging crags: for here
the rock is granite. The harsh, crumbling micaceous schists are
left behind, and with them that acid, chemical, volcanic sterility
that brings to mind a slag heap, the poisoned wasteland of an
industrial town. With the change of rock comes a change in
vegetation; it is much richer, far more gracious. It is a country
of forest trees except on the higher land where, when even the
low holly and the dwarf juniper can no longer hold out against
the wind, there is sweet turf like a lawn, covered with flowers.
You would gasp to see them in an alpine garden, but here they
are in such profusion that you cannot walk without treading
on them; and then, wherever the gray and lichened rock shows
through, or where the huge boulders stand uncovered, everywhere there are saxifrages crowding, cushions of delicate pink
flowers, tight rows encrusting the gentle rock where they can
hold a footing.

Here, in this intervening valley, there were no trees, however:
the whole of it had been ravaged by a fire that burnt not only
the undergrowth, the trees and every living thing that moved,
but even the earth itself, searing it to the bare rock: and so it
remains. The prevailing wind, the tramontane, swept over the
distant ridge for all the days of the fire, and preserved the farther
trees – prevented the fire from crossing the mountain. The forest
reaches the top, therefore, and can be seen between the naked
peaks, just overlapping into view.

The ravaged valley must be crossed: hours of break-neck
scrambling and sliding down; a long traverse over the bottom;
hours and hours of climbing up the other side. There is nothing
but charred wood and ruin: a few blackened trees still stand, and
where there is some trace of fertility left in the soil, there are blue
thistles. Some wandering birds are there, that hurry through, and
a few large green lizards; nothing else. But at the crest suddenly

58

the new country shows itself and unfolds in a series of high, cut-off, unsystematic valleys, with the forest spread over all of them and running up and over all the peaks and ridges except the highest. It runs on and on, a dark green that smooths all angularities, on and away until the trees appear no larger than the smallest bushes seen from a distance; and in the end, before they are lost behind the higher mountains, they might be no more than a crop of darker grass, so uniform they are, and so united.

Once across the ridge you cannot look back and see the sea any more: it is the unknown country, and everything behind and known is cut off. There are trees before you, and on each side trees: and already you are among the first of the trees. This is the wood.

The man in the wood had crossed over the ridge that afternoon, bleeding from the thistles on his legs, striped with black where he had pushed through the rigid, scorched, dead trees, and choked with the black dust. On the ridge the trees stood wide on the turf – oak trees here – and he passed through them and down the slope, being swallowed by the wood almost before he realized that he was well in it.

He made his way down, where the oaks were thick and smaller on the steep slope, low, almost bushes, down, across the brown stream, and up again through the tall trees to the first of the downland crests, where the high timber stopped, diminished to a border of strong hollies, and those to low, neat, prickly bushes, as trim as if they had been shorn. There were little silvered junipers on the clean turf, and flowers everywhere – tiny yellow rose-shaped flowers. He had stayed up there for half an hour, standing exposed on a certain rock, and then returning he had plunged into the trees again.

He sat now on a slope above the stream, a little way inside the wood. Here it was beech wood, all beeches except for a few spindling hollies and one prodigious oak. The upper edge of the wood, with its belt of hollies and mixed lower trees was dark behind him, and in front the wood was gray.

When first he had passed through the sunlight had dappled

59

the ground, and in the stronger light the carpet of dead brown leaves – no undergrowth, but only leaves – had shown red and umber, and a lively green had filtered through. Now the shadow of the mountainside had swept across the wood: it was light still, but the night had never wholly left the wood and by the stream it gathered there again.

It was not a deep, a thick, wood, obscure or hard to penetrate: far on each side of him the gray trunks rose solemn to an unseen burst of green, but its gray silence was quadrupled by the dead trees that stood; still stood, though dead. From the hump of moss on which he sat it seemed to him that half the company was dead: it was not so, but dead trees stood on every hand. Some lay, felled by the wind, and many were there, flayed white and blackened by the lightning blast. On the ground, covering it high in some places, the branches lay, some moldering to their last decay, some fresh, but all pale: in the living trees too there were dead branches, diseased limbs of their own or the arms of other trees which, falling, had caught and had not reached the ground, huge gaunt bones hung up in chains.

It was a wood in as natural a state as it could be, for no one had cut it, planted or touched it: it was too far, too isolated by the rocks and precipices for the charcoal burners even. But to him it looked unnatural, a wan Golgotha of a wood.

There were ancient trees that had died where they stood, and some had fallen, bringing down others: there were ancient trees that still lived, enormous slow eruptions that had been glorious but that now were three parts dead, massive limbs that towered up beyond the screen of leaves, dead and naked in the sea of green. There were very few young trees, and even those few were gray: everything was gray now, beneath the barrier of the leaves.

At the bottom of the slope, far down, a cataract in the stream sent up a continuous noise that made the silence stronger. He sat there, wondering if he would ever *hear* the trees, and he sat comfortably on his moss-buried rock, quite relaxed, leaning his head back against the broad stone, slowly drawing in fresh strength (it had been a cruel journey). His mind wandered at large; but it did not wander far, not so far that it did not return with an instant spasm when there was a sound behind him.

It was to his left, in the higher wood behind him. With his neck rigid he kept his head still; a movement is seen when stillness is not. And the sound was crossing behind him.

There are sounds made in spite of an intention to make no sound: they are not like common noises. There are small sounds made by large things, and they are different: a blackbird scuffling in dead leaves may make more noise, but it is not the same.

Now it was directly behind him: it must be nearly by the hollies, he said, with all his senses sharpened to the last degree, but strained backwards and his useless eyes unseeing. His mouth was half open, and his nostrils flared; he breathed, but very faintly.

The noise stopped. He grew more rigid, and his right hand, poised above his knee, slowly clenched to. From the first second he had known that something was in presence: now *it* knew; and this was the crisis now.

Then from the centre to the right, faster, and more quietly now: it was on his right side and his eyes, forced to the corner (but his head quite rigid still) pierced with all their force. The sound, now stronger, and his head jerked round; and there fleeting among the trees, the glimpse of a tall gray form, far bigger than the dog he feared.

Breathing normally again, and easy now against his rock, he closed his mouth: the tension died all over his body.

Cold: it was growing cold, and he gathered in his warmth, sitting closer, buttoned up his coat. With the creeping shadows the naked trunks stood barer still, with a light of their own under the darkening canopy.

Now he was leaning forwards, waiting actively: it was nearly time. He caught it at once, the low far whistle away on the right hand: he was half up, and across his field of view the tall gray wolf ran back through the trees, headed, fast but unhurried, almost noiseless.

The whistle again, and he answered; a clear, true whistle. A distant voice, well known, carried across on the silent air. 'Aa-oo, aa-oo,' and 'Aa-oo, aa-oo,' he answered.

Leaning on the silence he waited, and the words came clear, calling over the distance, 'Come back again, man: come back at the dark of the moon.'

The Tunnel at the Frontier

LOOKING UP he saw the sea at the end of the tunnel, the line of the horizon sharp, dividing the round mouth. On the sea, brilliant light, and a boat with a man in it, doing something with a net over the edge. Outside the tunnel the world was blazing with a white glare, but inside he could hardly see: there was a dull, sweating concrete path, and the walls curved, arching overhead.

What the devil was the sea doing at the end of that tunnel? The *sea*? From that he asked himself What tunnel? and he paused, walked slower, coming up from the abstraction into which he had sunk. The tunnel must have been familiar, or he would not have wondered about the sea. Did he usually walk along it the other way?

He recalled getting off the train, with a crowd of other people, their noise as they hurried through the tunnel with their feet echoing and flapping. They had hurried intently past him, although at first he had gone fast, imitating them. Now they had all gone and alone he went slowly: lagging still in his ear was the sound of the last people, their resonant feet before they left the tunnel to him.

It was like waking up from a strong dream, one so strong that for minutes you lie on the borders of the dream and reality and wonder which is which. But it did not clear: there at the end of the tunnel was the sea, stretched tight, the flood of sunlit air, and all enclosed by the mouth of the tube, a round patch of another world, infinitely remote, and unreal – not so much distance (though the tunnel was still long before him) as on another plane.

Slowly he went now, very slowly, his feet going of themselves.

63

His mind was still heavy, turning slowly. It had been warm in the train: and everybody had got out.

There were books under his arm; it was cramped with carrying them. He had been reading a book in the train, wedged in the blind corner by the corridor: people were standing all the way; he had not been able to see out. He must have been reading a long time before he went off into this meditation. The book had been about a man – he moved his hand to look at the book's title, but it was much too dark in the tunnel. It had been about a man who had loved a woman and had married her, and they had lived very happily, part of one another for years and years, and she had died. She had been killed in the war: or had she died? Was he confusing it again?

She had died. That was why he was so unhappy, because he had felt for this man and woman in the book, and he had caught the desperate, everlasting sorrow of the man, the dreadful unhappiness that was with him all the time and when he woke in the morning instead of a real life this man awoke to a silent blank, an emptiness that filled instantly with the realization, fresh each morning after the interval of sleep, and the sorrow welling blotted out each fresh day. This man had no comfort, because he did not believe in a future life; no hope, and he could not be a coward now and cheat and alter the order of his mind. He lived in the same house and all day her things were round him: there was nothing in his life that they had not done together.

He had never liked other people much; they were so imperfect and dull by the side of her. But in a hateful world, with war and the threat of war every day at every turn, and tyranny, misery and oppression and grinding poverty of the spirit, he had been happy: and he was lost now, alone in it. Job had been blasted: but Job had a God. This man was quite alone. He had only his virtue and his courage, and his virtue and his courage were ebbing fast away.

They had been very poor, and the dreadful details had piled on him. When there is a body in your bed, do you lie with it or stretch out on the floor; when the body is the corpse of your love, I mean? He could not do what they had always said they would do: she was buried roughly by officials, casual, hard, inimical municipal employees, and his hate for them had kept him alive for days and days. But it sagged, flagged away, and he had to simulate the motions of rage to feel it at the last.

That was the book. That was the book: it had made him so unhappy.

He stopped dead, and the sound of his feet echoed as he stood still, staring at the sea, far sea. That was the book? Irresolutely he put his free hand to his eyes, wavered. That was the *book*?

He turned his back to the light and hurried back into the gloom, faster and faster, his feet alone and hurrying, faster until the echoes were confounded into the one dull noise of his flight.

The Path

I FORGET NOW why I went down the track alone: but I did, and Mary and my sister, the Franciscan nun, were to follow me in half an hour.

It was a poor little brown track, nothing more than foot-worn, which was surprising for so important a frontier. The frontier itself was one of those noble, striking barriers between one country and another; a high, long mountain up whose farther side we had toiled, insect-small and hardly moving in the vastness of the landscape, all the morning. Then there was the top with a breathing of new air coming over it, a new sky, and stretching indefinitely below, another world, vague and indeterminate in the haze so far below, stretching away forever.

In this middle state we could look back to see where the cities in the plain stood one behind the other, each with its pall of smoke, and from them every now and then a gleam of light flashing back from the glass of a moving car. But we were not much concerned with what we had left: it was what was to come that absorbed our whole attention. And yet I went on alone: I cannot think why; but no doubt we thought it best at that time.

We said that we would meet again in the town. We none of us knew the town, and it appears now to be a hare-brained arrangement – so many opportunities for confusion, missing one another.

The path, as I have said, was a narrow track, winding and easy to lose at first on the bare mountainside, so very strange and foreign, so very unlike the farther slope. I had not expected this at all. However, I was too much occupied with the little, immediate details of our journey to take in more than the general impression of it, and now I have only a confused recollection of

brownness, a warm and naked descent over a rolling mountainside, immense on either hand.

We had not been able to see the customshouse from up there,
nor the town below, because of the fold of the mountain, but I
had no doubt of the way. Though perhaps it is not exact to say
that I had no doubt, because I was fortified and reassured when
in a little while the path led between two embanked walls –
obviously a road, constructed at one time with great labour, but
never finished or carried up to the frontier itself.

I was carrying the pack, as I should have said before: and
because the distance to the customshouse was not very great I
had not troubled to swing it on to my galled back again; I carried
it in my arms, like a baby. It was very inconvenient; it had
always been too heavy – in all the upward climb it had grown
heavier – and now it hampered me intolerably. I continually
shifted my grip, but nothing would do: it would not rest easy,
and when I came in sight of the customshouse and saw that they
were closing I cursed the wretched burden, cursed it with all my
heart.

By the time I reached the building all the doors were shut but
one, a little side door probably meant for officials. I went through
it without much hope, but nobody appeared to notice me and
inside there was a scene of great activity. It was a very large
shed with people in every direction, and I stood undecided for
a time, not knowing what to do or where to go. Quite near me,
on my left, was a kiosk, not unlike a paybox. It stood isolated
there on the floor of the shed, and it drew my attention.

There was a priest in the kiosk, a big, pink-faced man with
barely room to sort his forms and papers. I was in such a hurry
of spirits that it hardly seemed extraordinary to see him there,
nor was it very strange that at the sight of my passport he should
speak to me in English. A part of the reason for my confusion
and trouble of mind was that I had stupidly brought the other
two passports with me instead of leaving them with my wife and
my sister: I had been worrying about the necessity for expla-
nations and the difficulty of them, and I was in a miserable state
of indecision. He was so very helpful and unofficial that before

we had exchanged half a dozen words I had shifted the whole problem on to him. He did not appear to find that there was any difficulty at all. As he turned the pages of the passports he said, looking at my sister's face, that he had often seen her; not in the flesh, he added, but in the papers – which, considering the universal spreading of the church, is not astonishing. I was astonished, however, and gratified as well: I felt that I was the better received for it, and that I myself had a certain reflected glory, not without material advantage in so clerical a country.

It was a pity, for the friendliness left his tone. He assured me that he would look after them when they came through, and towards them his voice was cordial: but for me he was no more than polite, and when I took my heavy pack to the inspectors I felt him looking after me.

Now the confusion again and the hurry: I must pass over this, and the bad revelations of my pack, so exactly rifled, turned inside out by expert searchers. (They were perfectly correct, always civil – I could not complain – and everyone was searched.) All that my head cannot recall precisely now: indeed, I must quite soon have lost the sequence of happenings and the thread – it was all so very important, and because I was so conscious of it I foundered in a welter of explanation, doubt, uncertainty – worry and confusion that did not clear (and will not clear now, at this great interval of time) until I was free on the mountain again.

From that time on, or rather from that *place* on, I have everything straight. It has been, after all, plain enough, uncomplicated.

There is this path, brown in an uncoloured world of hills: it is halfway up the side, running straight, never rising much or falling. It is trodden into the side of the hill and it winds continually as it follows the swell and curve of the mountain.

She started before me along this path, and I hurry to catch her up. It is easy walking, neither hot nor cold, and I go with long strides, fast and pursuing. I shall never catch her: I know that. I shall never catch her, however much I hurry – and I do hurry, press on hard without a moment's slackening of the strongest continual effort; and I go fast, for all the weight of my pack.

I shall never catch her: but I have this, that I am on the ground that she has travelled. The 'never catching', that is less important now: we are divided by the distance, but the path is our connection; and I shall never let the distance grow.

The Walker

IN THE COUNTRY around this village it is not as simple as one could wish to find a pleasant, easy path for walking. The roads inland are all uphill, and although it is true that they lead through magnificent, dramatic country – bold, falling rock with terraces of vines and olive trees standing among the dried-up, barren mountains – they are roads that have to be climbed with attention: the landscape makes continual demands upon one; the winding, rock-strewn paths need perpetual care, and both these things interfere with the real aim of a walk, which for me is a half-conscious gentle physical exercise, the perfect accompaniment to reflection. I do not say that the countryside is anything but superb, and for one who walks to see magnificence these paths are ideal: but that is not my aim, and sometimes I long for an ordinary sober country lane, a way through the level corn-fields or a towpath along a quiet river or a sea wall between salt flats and a marsh. Then there is the heat: for a big, heavy man that is important, and in the summer (it lasts from April to November here) all these roads are tilted to the blazing sun throughout the day.

The alternative is to walk along the sea. It is fresher in the summer, but there again it is not the kind of walking that I like best, for the sea is bordered by high cliffs: the sea comes right to their feet, and there is no way along the shore; one must be climbing or descending all the time.

When I was a little boy I lived for a time in a place where there was an immense stretch of sand, hard, pounded sand upon which you could walk for miles and miles. You never had to watch your feet on the level sand: walking was effortless, and the rhythm of your steps and the half-heard incessant thunder of the

70

sea induced that trance in which one can go on and on for ever, singing perhaps, or talking to the air. There were shells, too, far better than the shells are here, delicately stranded at the watermark, and all kinds of sea-wrecked things, trawlers' floats, kelp, sea purses, spindrift, tarred or whitened planks of wood.

That is the sort of beach or strand that is lacking here; for here, as I say, there is no way along the sea except by the cliffs, and although they do sometimes go down to a little bay of shingle, it is only to rise again abruptly within a hundred yards. It is not a coast for general wandering: it is not a shore where one can stroll at all, and that is my only complaint against this place. I have no others. My lodgings are clean and orderly, the people are used to me, they are quiet and civil, and nobody interferes with my work or my set habits.

However, there is one walk that is neither violent nor exhausting. It is not a very good walk: it is an illogical, synthetic walk, but it is the best that I have been able to find and I have gone over the paths of it so often now that my feet find their way by themselves, leaving my mind free, to meditate or drift in vacancy, just as it pleases; and that is all that one can ask.

I go out of the back of the village, past the fort: for this is a bad part, for the quarter's rubbish dump is by the fort, and there is always a carrion smell and the thin dogs hunt about in shameful, mean-looking bands. The rubbish is supposed to be burned in that square concrete box, but although a cloud of stinking smoke drifts over it, the amount is never the less. I pass it and hurry over the bare drying-ground: the wind is almost always in the right direction, and as soon as I am on the level field the reek is blown away, so by the time I am halfway over it the unpleasant feeling has quite gone. This is the place where the women spread their washing out to dry, and in certain months of the year the men bring their nets to lie in the sun.

Beyond the drying field one must branch off to the left, to the main road and follow it to the entrance of a broad cart track: this is where the walk begins. The track dips down between high banks, and very soon there are hedges on either side. These are the only hedges for miles around, and if it were not for the prickly pears that show here and there and the pomegranates that form part of the hedge itself, one might suppose the track an English lane. On the far side there are orange trees and vines, which destroy the effect, but all around the farmhouse that stands on the downward slope an ordinary market garden gives the green in ordered rows again – broad beans, cauliflowers and cabbages, lettuce, carrots, familiar plants. Farther down, the bushes close overhead and the lane becomes a tunnel through the green; then at the bottom there is the river. For nearly all the year the bed is dry, and even when there is some water flowing it is always possible to cross dry-shod. Now I turn to the right and follow the path downstream. Here there are laurels, a few willows, tamarisks and those tall, thin bushes that have purple sprays of flowers – the kind that bloom in the late summer and draw flights of peacock butterflies.

Among the bushes there are dragonflies, for the river, flowing underground, leaves stagnant pools in the hollows: and up and down the river bed, low under the trees, innumerable swallows dash through the light; there are martins, too, and in the evening, when the bats are out and the swallows are no more than dark blurs, more sensed than seen, the white bottoms of the martins show, disembodied, weaving up and down.

I follow the river then, and come to its mouth. This is in one of the little bays that I have mentioned: it stands between the cliffs on either hand, a half-moon of shingle, with tall reeds at the back of it and behind them an orchard of fig and orange trees. The river, when it is flowing, hugs the right-hand side, cutting along at the foot of the cliff itself, and the beach shows no sign of having a river in it at all.

It is a shingle beach, with large pebbles at the back and small ones by the sea. Nearly always there is a high-water mark of broken reeds, bushes, driftwood and grass-like seaweed: this line of vegetable rubbish (it is as much as two feet high sometimes) stays unmoved from one big storm to another. Only at the equinox, when the wind comes straight in from the sea, do the waves beat in so far, and then there is nearly always rain inland, so that the river brings down more dead reeds and bushes, and these, being unable to drive out to sea, drift in the little bay and are thrown in to the same high-water mark.

It is only at these times, too, that the one boat that lives on that beach is hauled up far from the sea. It is a blue boat, shaped like those one made from paper as a child; the old man of the orchard uses it to fish for congers. He spends more time in his boat than working on his land, and it is said that he knows the rocks at the bottom of that bay better than most men know the rooms of the house they live in. But he is a savage old man, a solitary, and I do not speak to him nor he to me.

When I am on the beach I usually walk up and down it. It is not that it is agreeable to walk upon – the shingle is so loose and shifting that one's feet plunge deep and walking is painful – but it is the end of my walk. One must either go back the way one came (an unsatisfactory retreat) or else climb up the cliff, which is not walking any more. It is the cliff path that I nearly always take, up past the destroyed German searchlight and to the huge domed gun-emplacements home; but I walk up and down first to consider it.

I walk, naturally, by whatever water mark there may be. Not the high ridge-like mark of the great storms, for that so rarely changes, but by the sea itself; and sometimes, when there has been a swell, or a storm in Africa, there are shells or wreckage on the beach.

Once I found a wet brass ring. It had just arrived from who knows what rolling in the sea. It was a cheap ring, the kind that is sold in fairs: the sea had pitted it with eatings-out and dents, which gave it the look of vast antiquity. But in low relief on the flat part of it there was a swastika, and no doubt it had belonged to one of the Germans drowned here in the war. The ring filled me with repulsion, like a thing unclean: the round was so much the answering shape to the finger that had fitted it that I shuddered and threw it far into the sea, wiping my hands on the pebbles afterward. A human finger, by itself without a hand, is a disgusting thing. A human finger in the sea.

The pelvis that I found did not have the same effect. It was not long after the ring, and it lay within a yard or two of the place where I had picked it up: but I did not connect it with the Germans drowned – nor, indeed, with mankind at all.

It was by itself, white, dry and smooth, symmetrical and polished to inhumanity by the sea. It was only by a conscious effort that I could feel that this had been a piece of a man – only by running my hand round my own hip to my spine and tracing the same rise and curve that I saw on the bleached and diagrammatic bone in front of me. It had been in some way human, that was true; but is a shell the shellfish? This pelvis was very like a shell. Ordinarily, I suppose, a human bone would raise some emotion, some emotion resembling piety; it would be a disturbance of decency, a kind of profanation on the shore. But I felt no such emotion as I sat looking at this bone: I connected it with death, but with no particular death. A specimen in an anatomical museum could more easily have been clothed with living flesh than this white basin in the sun.

One's mental processes, and especially the wandering fantasies that pass through one's mind as one walks, are linked by a chain of association so slight that it usually cannot be traced. A bramble will claw out from a thicket: one pushes on automatically, and then in half an hour one will find that one has been dwelling on the Passion for the last mile of the road. That is why I speak of this bone: it provides the obvious and unfortuitous start for the recollections that unfolded in my head as I walked up the cliff path and high along the edge of the sea to the ruined batteries, where the camouflaged concrete still lies among the thistles and the asphodel, with its reinforcing steel rods all standing like the prickles of some prodigious monster of the earth.

When first I came to this village I lodged in a house belonging to an elderly couple named Joseph and Martine Albère. It was a large house, but I was the only lodger: it was a tall, gaunt place, always cold and damp, even in the height of the summer, and from the outside you would have said that it was uninhabited. But it was in good repair, a solid, middle-class house, much richer than the terrace-cottages in which most of the villagers lived: only the presbytery and the doctor's house were better; and from this I judged that the owner would be a man of some standing in the village. I learned, too, that my landlord was the owner and the equipper, the *armateur*, as they say, of three fishing boats: his boats, then, were the direct means of livelihood for nearly forty of the men of the place – a considerable proportion of the working inhabitants.

However, I soon gathered the impression that Albère was not a man of high standing. It is difficult to say how one forms an impression of this nature: it is built up of so many little things – gestures, tones of voice, a look cast backward, an avoiding eye – but in the end it grows into certainty. On the concrete, demonstrable side there was the fact that he never ran for municipal office, that he was president of none of the many co-operative or political associations and that he never appeared at any of the funerals or public feasts.

He seemed to be rich but unconsidered: a contradiction of common experience. At one time I asked myself whether in fact he was rich. Would a rich man take in a lodger? He did not seem to like letting the room I had; but when upon some trifling disagreement (he did not allow his lodgers the front-door key) I suggested that I should find a room elsewhere, he showed so much concern that I could not but suppose he was in earnest. He at once proposed a much lower rent if I would give up my point, and after a little more discussion I agreed to stay. This caused him a disproportionate satisfaction.

Then I learned that he had a fourth boat building on the stocks, which disposed of my idea that he was poor, for at that time a new boat was a very costly undertaking. As for the letting of rooms, that might indicate much or little: after all, in a big house one might let rooms to keep the house lived in, simply to prevent that decay that always comes in an empty place.

But still he remained a curious man to me. He did not like me, and he did not like having me in the house: yet he did not want me to leave it. The rent that I paid was a trifle to him even before he reduced it, yet he forced himself to be amiable to me, provided my room with the meagre best of the furniture in the house, and waited up every night to let me in after my evening walk.

He was a small, dark man, about sixty-five years of age: he was always carelessly dressed, dirty and unshaved, and his air of brutality contrasted strangely with the house he lived in. How did this brutal air appear? He was not obviously vicious: he spoke politely enough to me (though it was patently constrained) and I can only say that it must have been his lurching walk, the set expression on his face and the way he terrorized his wife that made me think, 'Albère? A brutish man.' His wife I hardly saw: she was utterly effaced, and she moved about the darkened house furtively, with the sound of a person who is trying to make no noise – this was when she was going about her obvious, everyday duties. She was much more like an imprisoned servant than the mistress of the house. Whenever she spoke to me he would appear and, whatever she was saying, she would stop and hurry downstairs. Yet I had the impression, that in spite of this domination they were allies. Sometimes, in the dead quiet of night, I would hear them talking, two whispers, urgent and hurrying, that would answer one to the other in the basement of the house. They slept in the kitchen, and I do not think they ever used any other room.

When I had been there some time I learnt something of their habits. They did not sleep very much, and every few hours one or another of them (or sometimes both) would creep up to the top of the house, along the passage that traversed its length, opening every door softly and softly closing it again, then down the stairs to the middle landing, very silently past my door to the room beyond, and there they would pause, perhaps for as long as half an hour, before coming out, crossing quietly to the other side of the house, back to the stairs, and so down again to the hall and their kitchen.

But I have my nocturnal habits, too: and more than once I have been there before them, fixed silent in a corner just off their trodden beat (for their patrol was so settled by long routine that their feet stepped in exactly the same places night after night), silent and unbreathing, watching their shadows.

However, this was much later: at first I merely noted that they never left the house together, and that when one was gone the other always waited in the hall or near it to open the door.

They appeared to have no relations. At least nobody ever came to visit them; and as far as I could see they were always in the house except when Albère was on the beach, conducting his business with the crews of his boats or when the woman was out for shopping. She never went to church: nor, of course, did he.

I had been there a long time before I found out what was the matter with them. It was a long time, for there were two difficulties in my way: the one was that the people of the village were not unduly open – they may know for generations, but they will not go out of their way to tell strangers – and the other, that I do not talk readily either. I do not go to cafés nor make acquaintance with the loungers on the quay. My form of recreation after my work is to walk. I like to go for long, uninterrupted walks.

Eventually it was a Dutch painter who told me what I had to know. He was a fat, exuberant man – spoke the language perfectly, having been brought up in Rheims – and he almost forced himself upon me. All he wanted was an audience: he loved to talk, and the smallest word of attention would keep him talking on the quay for hours. He was not my idea of a Dutchman. He knew all the fishermen and all the shopkeepers: he was hail-fellow-well-met with all of them before he had been here a month, and he stayed for a long time. It was a local man who told him about Albère: or perhaps 'local man' is inexact, for he was a waiter who had married a local girl and settled down here: he did not have the same sense of a closed community. The facts were common knowledge, and I often came across references to them afterwards. Albère was originally a sailor, a seaman employed on the packet boats that run between France and North Africa. On his ship, the *Jules-Bastide*, there were two other men from this village.

One night, about thirty years ago, the *Jules-Bastide* put out from Marseilles in a black gale of wind: there were very few passengers, for it was mid-winter, and most of those few went straight to their cabins. Only a few Algerian deck passengers huddled on the fo'c'sle, and one solitary priest, indifferent to the weather, stayed on the afterdeck. He carried a black valise wherever he went. When he went below for dinner he kept it

with him, and afterwards, when he returned to the deck, in spite
of the wild seas, he carried it still. He paced up and down in the
gale, always carrying this valise. There were three men on duty
on this part of the ship at this particular time, Albère and his
two fellow-villagers.

In the morning the priest was missing. Nobody knew anything
about it: the official inquiry revealed nothing whatever. There
was even some mystery about the identity of the priest, as there
had been a mistake in the list of passengers, and the person who
had arranged for the priest's ticket could not be traced.

Shortly afterwards the three men left the sea. One bought a
café in the town ten miles up the coast: the second took an
important farm some way inland; and Albère bought the house
where I was staying and the three fishing boats.

Within a year the first man and his wife were burned alive in
a fire that destroyed their house and café. Two years later the
second man, already overcome by misfortune in all his enterprises, lost his only son: the boy was killed riding a motor bicycle
that his father had bought him. The man returned to this village
by foot, walked to the graveyard, and hanged himself in the
daylight.

Ever since, the Albères had been waiting for their turn. They
had taken me in as some kind of protection (the lightning, they
thought, would not strike a house where a just man lived) but
still they did not think that my presence was enough: they were
still in dread, and I remembered how one night, early in my
stay, I had gone out about three in the morning (I had thought
that it might be the beginning of the day of wrath, but when I
looked at the stars I found that I was wrong: I had been unable
to move Aldebaran) and I had unbolted the door without a
sound. When I came back and closed it after me, I heard the
stifled gasp that Albère made as he stood silently behind the
door, and in the moonlight from the landing window I saw that
he had a gun. He muttered something about thieves, but, as I
thought at the time, you shoot thieves down. Thieves had their
hands cut off in former days; they were also stoned to death.
Some thieves were nailed and hung up alive.

Nothing has ever given me a livelier pleasure than my realization that they had taken me in as a protection. And it came to me quite slowly, as I was walking by the river, that once again I had been chosen as the hand of God. After such a long time it had come again: all my anxious waiting was rewarded. The wickedness of my doubt was overlooked – for at times I had wavered – and now once again I was the elected vessel. I had hoped for so long: and to hope for such an election twice in one lifetime seemed presumptuous indeed. But now I was the hand of God again; the wrath of a jealous God Who spoke through the prophet and ploughed the Amalekites into the ground. And without any knowledge I had been set there in my place for a long year past: oh, it was the sweetest realization in the world, this kindness done to me.

Clearly I knew that it was not for the murder I had been sent: no, no; it was for accidie. These wicked people had despaired of all forgiveness: they had hardened their hearts, and for that last wickedness they were to be destroyed in this world as they were already damned in the next.

I waited for the dream that would direct my hand: it had been so clear before. It had been so clear and explicit, and twice repeated, on the last occasion, the sawing of the blasphemer in Newtownards. But it did not come at once this time, and in my lightness of spirits I could not sleep. Between half-past three and four o'clock they were on the upper corridor, together; and the spirit of delight was so strong in me that I could not resist the pleasure of running out with my black coat over my nakedness, barefoot up behind them. They were in the far room, listening; I was fast in the black shadow of the corner, and as they crept by I sprang on them shrieking, 'The priest, the valise, the priest, ha ha ha ha ha.' I leaped and sprang, but with the shrieking and the laughter I could hardly run as fast as they did. They were some way ahead, the man before the woman, and I am a very big, heavy man; but I cut them off at the head of the stairs and hunted them into the farthest room: I howled and howled in the room. And I let them escape me there while I ran to leap and shriek all through the house. Then I had them on the stairs half down, the man dragging the woman by the arm. They were trying to reach the door, and the laughing nearly choked my breath. From up there I flew, I say I *flew*, and smashed them down on to the far stone floor.

But it was finished then. It was finished almost before it had begun. I had meant a full night's inspired, enormous ecstasy, and I had wasted it in half an hour. Before it had started it was done: they had died without a mark; and I had not set the sign.

The Soul

WITH THE FULL MOON hidden, but only just hidden, the world was lit by a gentle light, enough to see the great features of the land, the rocks, the line of wild mountains, and the shape of the coast. There was no wind, no wind at all, and the soft clouds hung low, smooth, united and unmoving; they never parted for the stars to shine through, but it would not have been called a *cloudy* night; they were not positive enough for that. The warmth came up from the ground, from the side of the hill, from all around, an enveloping warmth in that still air.

As she had but just left the cemetery, where the cold lingered among the cypresses, among the angular white tombs and the high pigeonholes where the poor dead lay, she rested on the wall above the cliff and let the grateful warmth soak in.

This, she thought, must be very like what the ancients believed the end of the world to be – the flat world, that had an end. The dark cliff dropped a hundred feet, perhaps two hundred, to an unmoving sea: on the water there was no reflection; a faint haze deadened it, and no sound came up. There was no horizon. The sea and the sky joined perhaps, but they were lost.

It was as if she looked into *nothing*, into infinity. Only a light far out, a round light with no path on the sea, and that gave even more the impression of unending waste beyond.

A poor soul, she thought, would have to go down the path that was before her, the cliff path, and walk out over that space to the light, beyond all words remote. It would be a perfectly smooth desert, and your feet would not find a surface, not a hard surface. Perhaps for some distance you could walk easily, but then for an unmeasurable time you would labour – dream-walking – with a huge mental effort for no gain.

Although it was so empty from here, you might pass a silent, pale soul working out some cruel meanness, some tyranny that had not been paid for with more than a moment's uneasiness before. You might pass: but was there anyone she could pass?

The light was infinitely remote. But it was no good waiting: all the hope that there could be was in the traject; and in the faint light she bent to see the winding of the path.

Lying in the Sun

WITH HIS FACE CRADLED in the soft bend of his arm he could see nothing: but the strong glare of the sun filtered through the crook of his elbow and through his closed eyelids, filling his head with a red light. Behind him, or rather beyond his feet since he was lying on a beach, there was the faint and intermittent murmur of the sea, very small waves that curled and hissed a few inches up the pebbled shore. Above him and all round on every side the dome of the sky pressed down, hemming in and confining this world of brilliant light; there was no room for any air to move and even the sea was flattened by the weight of the day.

Some of the other people on the beach, however, were not conscious of the weight. They bathed, splashing, and ran about with cries; beyond his right shoulder, ten yards farther up the slope, a family of French women under parasols untiringly discussed their concierge, two or three of them talking at once. From time to time they shrieked orders to their children not to go too far, not to wet themselves, to keep their heads covered, and out of the medley of sound the children shouted back.

But the French voices pierced through indistinctly from a very distant world, remote in every way; and the only sound that he heard and accepted was the lapping of the sea.

If he were to raise his head a little and turn it he would be able to breathe more easily; but then the light would change to yellow, and he did not want that. He preferred the dim red, and he nuzzled his face a little deeper into his arms; the redness surged and for a time it was branched through and through with orange streaks. It settled, and he sank farther into his isolation.

This was like swimming in a tide of blood, he thought; or not so much swimming as having one's being in it. This would be the life of a foetus, bathed in dark redness and safe; the only sound in its world would be the throb of the blood, like the waves that he heard now, weak and faint but always there and always prevailing against the irrelevant shouts, the crunch of feet on pebbles, the women gabbling, the ice-cream seller's raucous voice, the thrum of the diving board and the splash of the divers.

Those sounds were all so faint, dream-like and unreal; they did not impinge upon his inner world at all, so long as he kept his head right down. So long as he kept his head down he was safe; his limits were drawn in to the sound of the waves in his ears; the ball of red light in his head, and the feel of his forearm across the bridge of his nose – his world was contained by these three things, and it did not extend even to his body, sprawling there on the stones and slowly roasting under the sun.

But it was such a feeble refuge. He was so vulnerable in it, and he had no defence except pertinacity against such things as the gravel sprayed by running children. The children, the voices, the madly yapping, scurrying dog, they were all able to break in; yet he could defend himself to some extent – against those there was the barrier of numb remoteness and self-removal. The far more dangerous enemy, the enemy against whom he had no defence at all, lay just there on his left.

If he were to stretch out his hand, and not to the full stretch either but only half a foot, he would touch her side. Her right shoulder, probably, for she had turned over some time ago to 'do her front'.

She had only to move, to say, 'Darling, you aren't burning, are you?' to smash straight in. She possessed that power, was entitled to it, and several times already she had used it; once she had asked him to oil her back, once she had said that it was getting hot, and another time, having seen a French couple pub-licly embracing a little way along the beach, she had thought it would be fun and very 'Continental' to imitate them.

But it was a long time now since she had moved or spoken. She was taking her sun-bathing very seriously; as she said, they had so few days left now that unless they wanted to go home without a tan they should spend every hour they could upon the beach.

The time was short indeed. She had prolonged it twice already in spite of protests from her home; but for all that there would be little time now for lying in the sun. They had arrived at the hotel within a day of each other, in the same storm of wind and driven rain. This had been going on, said the despondent guests, since Tuesday; on Friday, when he arrived, it had never seemed likely to stop, and on Saturday, when the girl came dripping from the station, it appeared to be set to foul for ever. The people of the town said that there would be no grapes at all that year – mildew in the vines and the cold rain-bearing wind blowing perpetually from the sea.

The rain poured from the gutters of the roof. Cactuses and palms glistened in the wet; the pomegranate flowers lay beaten in the mud. The hotel was not designed for indoor life; it was meant for sleeping in and eating meals. There was no sitting room and in the bedrooms the hard wooden chairs were shaped for holding bags and clothes. The inhabitants of the town, amazed by this weather (although they had it nearly every year), clustered in the cafés with their friends and stared at the racing sky or repaired their wine barrels and their fishing gear; but for the people in the hotel there was nothing to do at all. Those who spoke French joined together in sudden intimacy and talked with strange, compulsive freedom of their affairs, but these two spoke no French and obviously they were thrown one upon the other; and he, from idleness, boredom, and a feeling that it was 'the thing to do', had seduced her.

That is to say, he had adopted a gallant attitude, and very quickly he had been hurried by circumstances, by an untimely consideration for her feelings (for she was as serious as she was plain), by moral cowardice and by the utter impossibility of getting away, into making declarations that he did not mean and into doing – *doing*, that was the inescapable fact – that which he had only the faintest desire to do.

If only the rain had stopped one day earlier . . . the recollection of that unhappy, intensely self-conscious grappling made him sweat, and echoing in his head there came her words, 'When we are married, darling, we will read psychology together.' The echo exactly reproduced the mincing refinement of her voice, and the curiously artificial sound of 'darling'.

She knew all about psychology; she had 'done' psychology. She was a schoolmistress. She wore spectacles. She was what they called 'one of the quiet ones', and her convulsive ardours daunted him. She went a queer, mad colour when she was moved; a whiteness appeared about her nose and her lips went blue; it seemed that her heart was weak. She was awkward and super-ficially timid; but she had an astonishingly high opinion of her own abilities and she would recount, with satisfaction, the names of the diplomas that she had won; she was also persuaded that men found her irresistibly attractive and she said that she found travelling alone a great trial because of their attentions.

If only she would go away he would be quite fond of her; he would indeed, and he would do all he possibly could to be agree-able by post. But she would not go away. Not in this life. He would have to kill her to make her go away. If he were to reach out now he would feel her there, and if he were to look sideways he would see her, fixed there and immovable.

He would see her round and satisfied face, her somewhat posi-tive expression fixed by years of her calling into a didactic right-ness that would nevertheless melt into a tender leer when she saw him looking – a tenderness that would appear intolerably simpering and affected to his hostile eye. Or worse, an arch coquetry, a privy beam of concupiscence. At all events, he would see this red and peeling face with its cardboard nose-guard against the sun and he would either smirk back at it or commit a horrible brutality; her confidence was spectacular enough, but it was so insecurely based.

Above the face he would see the bright cotton square – 'Real peasant-craft, with such a merry, sincere mood . . . don't you *feel* it, darling?' – and below it the long, thick expanse of body, somehow improperly exposed in a bathing-dress, not deformed in any way yet giving the impression of indecency; then the short, powerful legs, close-shaven and terminating in espadrilles made by 'such a simple, friendly peasant-body – so direct and uncomplicated – at one with the sea, the sun and the vineyards'. Those dreadful, carefully enunciated phrases, how easily they came tripping out and how complacently. 'Oh darling,' she had said when he had given her the monstrous little coral and cameo heart-shaped gawd, 'What a definitely *genuine* mood it has – and the lovely, lovely symbolism of the piece of coral – (solemnly) darling, what a wonderful person you are.' Then archly, winsomely, 'And is it really all for poor me, he, he?' And solemnly again, 'I will keep it for ever. It must have been made by some little sunny artisan who loved it. Wherever did you find it?'

He had found it under the paper that lined the cupboard by his bed, and Heaven only knew what uses it had served before; he had felt ashamed the moment he had given it, uneasy, irritated, and ashamed; it was so tawdry and her enthusiasm was so silly, and yet when she said, 'I will keep it for ever' there was so much true and human feeling rising painfully through all the nonsense that it had stabbed his conscience hard.

If only she would go away. . . . But she would never go away. And if he looked sideways she would be there, holding her brooch, her damned 'for ever' brooch.

Yet perhaps if he looked sideways, if he looked sideways in point of fact he would not see the change he imagined; there would be no hurried rearrangement of the features into a romantic shape. Nor, if he reached out his hand, would he feel an answering reaction from her flesh. For nearly an hour ago her heart had given an odd triple beat and had then stopped. She had felt a confused exaltation which she had supposed to be a part of her radiant nervous state, something between sleep and dreaming, and she had never heard the guttural murmur that her dying throat had whispered out. Her right arm and leg had contracted momentarily, almost touching him; but they had relaxed at once.

Her body now lay under the sun much as it had done before. Her mouth gaped a little more than usual and her eyes were staring wide behind her sun-glasses. If he looked at her closely he would see the blueness of her lips, but he was familiar with that and it would not strike him; he would also be deceived by the oil and the tan that she had already acquired – by the oil particularly because it gave a superficial gleam and because in places it had caught the dust (this tideless beach was very dusty) and that made the skin look inhuman anyhow.

And if he touched her he might still suppose her to be asleep. She was not rigid yet; and the sun still gave her warmth.

But cradled in his red dark secret world he did neither of these things. Although he knew that by now his back must be burning he lay there motionless, retracted and curled up.

The metallic voices of the large family to the right were now discussing lunch; they were calling the children with threats. There was a noise of furling parasols and the grind of their retreating steps at last. Now the chief sound in the forefront of the general, though diminished, clamour was a long stream of words in some Scandinavian language, all delivered at the same high, even pitch – a young man reading to his mother from a book.

From time to time all this seeped in, together with the sound of leaving feet, the long, sad whistle of the train far off – that must be the big express – and oddments of sound like the splashing of a stone or an isolated cry.

He went far, far down into his retreat, but all the time there was a part of his mind that was recording the noises by the sea and when he came near to the surface again he was in possession of two facts. One was that the beach was nearly empty now; the other, that she had not moved for such a very long while that she too must be burning in the sun.

She would certainly move quite soon. She would think he was asleep; she would pat him, and in a deliberately musical voice she would cry, 'Billy! Wake up darling!' She called him Billy, or Billy-boy; and his name was Hugh.

Yet on the other hand, if he raised his head and himself dispelled his safety, she could not break in. There would be nothing to break into. He began to count; he would reach a thousand slowly.

Away down the beach there was a grating sound as the rich

people with the villa across the bay launched their boat – the grating and then the hiss as it took the sea. It was a huge silence after that.

At seven hundred and thirty-two he stopped, stopped instantly and flushed. His counting flew to the winds and he found that he was tingling all over with anticipation. Quite deliberately he raised his head, holding his breath and already straining his eyes round under his closed eyelids. He felt the crinkling of the burnt skin on his neck and then an intolerably brilliant flood of light blinded his opening eyes; they were distorted from his long pressing on them and all he could see as he peered so intently was a dark shadow by his side.

The long beach stretched away on either hand. There was nothing alive but a solitary gull, immobile at the farther end; in the dead stillness the sea was flatter still, and only once a single ripple made the faintest sighing on the stones.

He did not look again until his view was clear. There was nothing at his side. With a violent emotion that he could not define he saw that there was nothing, nothing but his own shadow and the hollow where she had lain, and in the hollow the cameo and coral brooch surrounded by a little heart of stones.

He leant over it, observed mechanically that it was flecked with salt, and furtively he picked up his clothes. With a bowed head he hurried silently across the burning shingle to the road; he was aware of no emotion clear in words, but as he reached the steps he realized with horror that his face was streaming with tears, and that as they fell upon the stone they dried there in little rounds.

Billabillian

CORNELIUS O'LEARY slid the last ten pieces of eight into the canvas bag and put it down again under the table with a grunt. The total was the same as before, when he had checked and re-checked it; but he was glad to have the confirmation fresh in his mind: it would not do to make a mistake.

He sat down in front of the neat arrangement of papers and reviewed them anxiously: there was nothing missing, and he could find but one thing to do – he ranged the row of weights on the right-hand edge of the table in a still more exact line of descending size. He wished the captain would come, but he knew very well that a good half-hour must elapse before he heard his step on the companionway. Cornelius had begun his preparations far too soon: even before the anchor had roared out in Sumbawa Road at dawn he had started laying out his bills of lading, cargo lists, and books. The ship, the *Trade's Increase*, lay under the shelter of Bloody Point, cut off from the ocean swell, and for once the wide, brass-bound table held his ranks of weights, his piles of coin, his strings of cash, his rulers, and his pens as firmly and as solidly as though it had been on dry land. It was all ready, and he wished the captain would come.

It had been a long voyage, a hundred and eighty-three days from the Pool of London, and Cornelius was burning to be ashore: but he knew that he must not move from the cabin until the captain had come below to inspect his papers, and until between them they had concluded the payment of the billabillian with the captain of the port. He averted his gaze from the porthole and began to repeat his tables again. 'Ten pecooes, one laxsan; ten laxsans, one cattee; ten cattees, one uta; ten utas, one bahar.'

Yet although he could shut out the sight of the crowded

harbour inshore, with its forest of masts, curving bamboo yards and rattan sails, he could not prevent the warm scent from drifting in and breaking through the dutiful, ordered line of calculations in his head. It was a heavy, indefinable smell: he could distinguish all the spices, but there was the scent of the tropical land, green leaves still wet from the warm rain of the night, and a thousand other things without a name.

They had smelled it first far out to sea. He had come on deck from the stifling cabin where old Mr Swann lay speechless and twitching under his heavy rugs, and in the milk-soft air he noticed it at once. One of the sailors had said, 'Do you smell that? We shall make our landfall in the morning.' And as Cornelius stood leaning on the rail, breathing the clean and scented air and watching the phosphorescent wave glide smoothly from the bows to the white fire of their wake, the sailor had added ominously, 'The tide is on the make. But it will ebb when the moon dips down: he will not see the light.'

They had buried the old man in sight of land, sewn up in canvas and with heavy shot at his feet: he had slid quietly off the grating and had vanished with hardly a splash in the clear green water, leaving a trail of white bubbles. He had been out of his right wits since they had left the Cargados Shoals, that fetid and toothless old man without a nose, but he had been kind when he was not ill, and Cornelius, thinking of him now as he looked at an entry in the dead man's hand, felt ashamed that he was so cheerful and excited.

A general roar on deck broke across his train of thought: he looked up, and there, framed in the wooden square, was a brown girl, her face and her bare breasts pointing up to the rail. She was holding a basket of fruit to show, and as she stood in the unseen boat, gliding from right to left, the ripple of the water, reflected from the side of the *Trade's Increase*, flickered over her satin body. The crew were shouting a babel of encouragement, praise, and invitation: Cornelius heard the loud smacking noise as one kissed his hand, and the girl's cat face smiled. Cornelius had heard that the heathens went about with almost nothing on, and he was charmed to find it true: he felt the strong stirring of his blood, but as he heard the bellowing of the mate he blushed and restrained himself from going over to the porthole and craning out. There was a padding of bare feet on deck and then the renewed hammering as the men went to work again on the hatches.

He stirred uneasily in his chair. Would the captain never come? Beyond the porthole there was a square of brilliantly sunlit world, all the more dazzling for the darkness of the cabin: the calm dark blue of the road, with the ships lying spaced out; the paler blue of the harbour with the close-packed fleet of junks and proas; the cascade of green on shore, not very far away; and the sun over the whole of it was the sun of the land, warm and golden with dancing motes and heavy with the scent. They had coasted for a week, but still his nose was sharp from months at sea, and he drew in the air with a deep, savouring breath; it was as heady as wine, and it stirred him to the heart. Would the captain ever come?

But he imposed on his face the serious look of a man – a man with great responsibilities – and repeated, 'The Java tael is two and a quarter pieces of eight, and that is two ounces English.' He laid his hand over a paper whose edges were curling in the sun and went on, 'The Malay tael is one ounce and a third: but the China tael is one ounce and a fifth. So the China tael is six-tenths of a Java tael exactly.'

Yes, he had all that by heart. All the currencies, weights and measures of the East Indies and the Spice Islands at his fingertips. And he knew his bills of lading by heart, too: there was no need for this array of papers. He could tell precisely what they had in their cargo and where it was stowed, without his lists. But they had to be there; it was orderly and correct, and their neatness gave him a feeling of solidarity and accomplishment. He was sure that the captain would be pleased. He had seen little of him, but from what he had seen, he knew that the captain liked exactitude: Cornelius had already been commended for knowing how many barrels of powder there were without having to go and count them. That had been a little while after Cornelius had been moved from the *Clove* to the *Trade's Increase* because of

Mr Swann's illness, and just before the captain himself went down with the calenture that, together with scurvy, had attacked the whole ship's company when they were making their northing from the Cape. It had been a sickly ship from the start of this long and dangerous trading voyage, and they had all thought that the captain was going to die. But every morning and every evening, except for the days of the great storm, they had heard the psalms coming from his cabin, and just before old Swann sank for good and all, the captain reappeared on deck, thinner than ever, pale in his black coat, silent, but very much in command. He had at once had the guns run out – they were still a match for any Dutch ship, in spite of their losses – and had had two men flogged who were slow and remiss.

'You are a lucky devil, Teague,' said the mate to Cornelius (the mate was lax in his expressions). 'You have all the luck in this ship, I believe.'

In a way it was true. Both the men over him had died: Wilson of the calenture in Saldanha Bay and at last old Swann; and when their consort the *Clove* had vanished in the storm, Mr Rolfe and the merchants' factor had vanished with her, leaving Cornelius and the mulatto clerk as the only men, under the captain, for the trading, which was the heart and being of the venture.

It was lucky; but it was not entirely unforeseen. 'Old Swann will not last beyond the Cape,' his uncle had said, 'and with any right chance the Dutch will knock one of the others on the head. In three or four voyages you will be on your own, and then, if you have the wit to escape the fever, the Dutch, the Spaniards, the Portuguese, the Sea-Malays and the Java pox, you will make your fortune, if you keep my advice in mind. Then you can sit at your ease like a lord on Fiddlers' Green.'

Cornelius had not looked for his luck; he had been heartily sorry for the occasions of it; yet having it put between his hands, he meant to grasp it. All the way across the Indian Ocean he had conned his instructions, had gone through and through Mr Swann's lists, had counted and re-checked his chests of Spanish silver, his moidores, ducatoons, sequins of Venice and gold mohurs, had dived and wriggled his way through the fantastically mixed cargo in the holds; he had learned all he could from the mulatto, part Malay, part Portuguese, part Javanese; and he had read his uncle's advice until he knew whole paragraphs by rote. But he had not been able to win the confidence of Popery, the mulatto; and he regretted that, for he was a friendly soul. Perhaps if he had made the whole voyage in the *Trade's Increase* he might have done so, but he had sailed beyond Madagascar in the *Clove*; and with the sinking of that ship he had lost most of his intimate friends. It was not that this ship's company was unfriendly or reserved – far from it; but Popery, or Sawney Bean, as some called him, remained aloof, in spite of their common religion; for Cornelius was a Catholic, and that, in a time when it was death for a priest to be found in England, would ordinarily have been a tie. However, Cornelius could not hang out his beliefs aboard an English ship – he had learned that much caution – and perhaps Popery did not know of them: perhaps, too, he resented Cornelius having charge of the papers: he may have hoped for promotion for himself. Perhaps it was just that he was a proud, injurious Portingale.

Again there was a mounting tumult of cries on deck, and Cornelius heard a dull crash on the other side of the thick wooden wall behind him. After a moment of dead silence came the first mate's furious shriek, 'Get your —— boom out of my shrouds, you *whoreson* black ape,' then the captain's cold, harsh voice cutting through the oaths and counter-shouting: 'Mr Williams.'

The mulatto pushed his blue face through the door. 'Captain not coming yet,' he said, and closed it again.

The sound of shoving, fending-off, the orders, the groan of wood and the gurgling of churned water was succeeded by the startlingly close vision of a high, recurved prow in Cornelius' porthole: clinging to the prow were three bearded Arabs, shaking their fists at the deck of the *Trade's Increase*. They were like angry prophets, and they were so close that Cornelius could see their yellow, blood-shot eyes straining from their heads in fury as they shot their stream of words up through the air. There were more prophets in the waist of the dhow, but they were silent: they

glared with dumb rage or watched in motionless indifference as
the dhow laboured past the *Trade's Increase* with her enormous
sweeps. Cornelius noted her armament: only four guns; three
brass serpentines and a demi-culverin: the *Trade's Increase* could
sink her with a single broadside.

The falsetto and the bass of the Arabs died away, to rise again
as the dhow tried to make her way against the tide between two
junks moored inshore: now the shouting was increased by the
shrill howl of Cantonese, but Cornelius' attention was distracted
by a flash of scarlet beyond the junks, a flash of scarlet threading
through the masts of the proas by the landing stage, and the
beating of a drum.

That, he thought, must be the heathen duke: the rajah, as they
called him here. Unless it could be the prince's officers for the
customs. No: the scarlet was on shore, not coming out to sea.
On shore under the palm trees. They were playing a strange,
harsh, screaming music there. Would the captain never come?

Again Cornelius turned his mind from the delights of the
unknown shore to the papers in front of him.

'Some report, these Islands were once in Subjection of the
King of Ternate, but whatever they once were, now they are a
sort of a Common-wealth,' his uncle had written in his clerkly
hand ('No tropes or elegant turns, you understand,' – looking
contentedly at his work before he had handed it over to his
nephew – 'Nothing but a plain, thorough-stitch account. Tropes
are for learned men, not half-merchant, half-sailor, half-witted
swabs like supercargoes.' But he was quite proud of his writing,
nevertheless; Cornelius had little penetration, but he knew that
much.) '. . . sort of Common-wealth; yet there is one Supreme
Officer, whom they call a Subandar, that appears at the Head
of the State, and has the Trouble of Managing, but not the full
Power of Disposing of any Public Affair, without the good Liking,
and intervening Approbation of the People.

'Their way of dealing is by Bahar and Cattee: the small Bahar
is ten Cattees of Mace, and a hundred of Nutmegs; and the great
Bahar a hundred of Mace, and a thousand of Nutmegs. And the
Cattee here is 5 Pound 13 Ounces English; the prices variable.'

This was not Sumbawa: it was Banda, and the *Trade's Increase* would not be there until they had laid in their cargo of pepper; but Cornelius read on.

'The Commodities requested here are Broad Cloth, Stammel, Calicoes black and red, China boxes, Basons without Brims, light colour'd Damasks, Taffatees, Velvets, Gold Chains, Plate Cups gilt, Head-pieces damask'd, Guns, Sword-blades, but not such as are back'd to the Point. There's a great deal of Profit in bringing Gold Coyn hither; for you shall have that for the value of 70 Rials in Gold Coyn, that will cost you 90, if you pay in Rials . . .' Frowning with concentration, Cornelius placed the rimless basins in his mind: they were stowed under the forepeak, beyond the cases with the small blue beads.

'You have at this Place some of the best Benzoin perhaps in the World, and in great Plenty; and the glorious Gems of Pegu shine here likewise. There's vast quantity of Silver in Bullion, that's brought hither from Japan; but Rials of Eight are more in request, and will bring in Bullion ¼ of a Rial Profit. All your broad Stammel Cloth, Iron-works, and fine Looking-Glasses, are things that take exceedingly here, and Saunders, Sapon, Camphire, Amber, Elephants' Teeth, Rhinocero's and Hart's Horn; to which add Honey, Spanish Soap, Sugar Candy, all sorts of Leather, Wax-Candles, and Pictures. Only as to Pictures, the larger they are the better, but they are not so much for Faces, as Landskip, Representations of War, amorous Intrigues, some remarkable Story of comical Fancy, as the Painter's Invention guides him.'

Cornelius turned on: he had all that in his head. At Soocadanna the weights are the mass, the coopang, the boosuck and the pead. At Soocadanna, diamonds. 'They are gotten as Pearls are, by Diving; and the River most celebrated for the Search and Discovery of them is the River Lane; such a one as which any Prince that had it in his Dominions, would not have very much cause to complain, if it yielded the Country no Fish. All the trading Part of Mankind being fond of this precious Commodity, the Place never wants a Crowd of Ships, Praws and Juncks . . . yet the Place is in the height of its charming Lustre in April.'

But one should watch the weighers always, they being Chinese, and apt to favour their own countrymen, in any commodity from rice to dragon's blood.

Cornelius turned back the pages and memorized the piece on civet, bezoars, and musk. 'Musk. There are three Sorts of it, black, brown, and yellow; of which the first is stark naught, the second good, and the third best of all; it ought to be the Colour of the best Spikenard, and of so strong a Scent, as to be rather offensive than otherwise, especially if tasted, when the Fumes of it seem to pierce violently into the Brain, and search the Head at a wonderful Rate.'

His uncle had opened a drawer in the Chinese cabinet and had given him a piece of yellow musk to smell. 'Does that go to your scalp, boy? Does that make your essence quake, eh? Does that clear your intellectuals?'

'Yes, Uncle John, sir.'

'I hope it does, indeed,' – shaking his head doubtfully – 'for I am sure they want a vivifying spark. It's the headpiece that counts, boy,' he had said, patting him on the shoulder, 'You must think judiciously and quick. Tell me now if you remember the customs at Sumbawa.'

Cornelius put his hands behind his back and repeated, 'There is the prince's custom called chukey, which is eight bags upon the hundred, rating pepper at four pieces of eight the sack, whatever price it bears. Then there is the billy, the billy . . .' His voice trailed away.

'Hell and death! The billabillian, moon-calf: the billabillian, you mumchance Tom a'Bedlam brain-sick zany. Swab, to forget the prime foundation of them all. Here, take the page and spell it out.'

' "Then there is the Billabillian," ' read Cornelius, ' "which is this: If any Ship come into the Road laden, the King is to be immediately acquainted with the Sorts, Quantities, and Prices of the Commodities in her, before any part can be landed: upon which he sends his Officers to the Ship to look narrowly into her and takes of all the Sorts what he likes, perhaps at half your Price, or it may be something better, according as you can agree.

So if you lade Pepper, you pay for every 6,000 sacks, 666 Rials, or else are obliged to be the King's Chapman for as many thousand sacks, at one half, or three fourths of a Rial more than the Current Price of the Town. The Dutch indeed go a more com-com –"'

'Compendious, my boy,' said his uncle, nodding pleasantly at the word.

'"The Dutch indeed go a more compendious way to work; and to avoid the trouble of the Duty and the Searching, agree with the Officer so much in the Gross, for the Lading of the Ship, which is generally about seven or eight hundred Rials."'

'Remember that, Cornelius. Remember that, and you will make your fortune yet. It is not your whoreson sixteen shillings a month that will give you all this –' He waved expansively at the comfortable room with its Cordova-leather hangings and its carved plaster ceiling with the Virtues and a Cornucopia; and his wave carried Cornelius' mind beyond the windows to the walled garden with its espaliered fruit trees, and out of the garden to the meadows that sloped gently down to the Thames, where his uncle would sit with his pipe in one hand and a glass in the other, watching the ships going up to London from the sea, or listening to the bells from Dartford over the water, or Gravesend.

'– it is not your whoreson pay: it is the billabillian that you ought to go down on your knees and thank the Lord for. That and your own trading afterwards – afterwards, mind – when the ship has had her due.'

'But Uncle John, sir,' said Cornelius nervously, 'it is – is it quite right?'

'Blood and damnation!' cried the old gentleman, turning from red to blue. 'What have we here? A snuffling, canting, talking-through-the-nose Puritan? A Praise-the-Lord-with-Joyfulness Shufflebottom like the poxy, snivelling French dog of a conventicle-haunting text-splitter I kicked out of the Goat and Compasses the other day? Rot the boy. Of course it is quite right. Do you think I would do it if it were not? Blast your eyes.' He fumed in silence for a while; then recovering his good humour and his normal scarlet face he went on, though with still a trace of the exasperation that talking with Cornelius often brought into his voice, 'It is good for the merchants, good for the prince's officers, good for the captain and good for the supercargo. Everybody, apart from a few sickly rogues who should never have seen the light of day, much less been breeched, everybody does it. Why, kiss my hand, I remember Evans, of the *Roebuck*, when he was sent off for cloves to Pulo-Temba, making himself a purse out of the Sabandar's duty there and another out of the rooba at Timor. He kept it close, he and his captain, until he was knocked o' the head in a fight at Jakarta, and then he told us before he died. He was a great man, and his merchants gave him a piece of plate worth fifty pound, as a gratification for looking after their trade so well, in the year 'twenty-three. And he was one of those quiet dogs – no Java girls, no arrack for him – never moved without an Amen in his mouth and the Good Book in his pocket. That's a good man, I believe? He'd bury you a dead seaman as trim as any parson in the land. No, no: you will see old Swann, if he lives the voyage, or Adams if he don't, give the prince's officer, the rajah's Arapotee, as they say in those parts, a round five hundred pieces of eight for the *Clove*'s billabillian. And the prince's officer, this Arapotee, will give him a quittance in his hand for nine hundred, or maybe a thousand clear, and he will share the difference with the captain: you will get a score to yourself if you stand by, and the next voyage you will get more, and more the next after that, until in the end, with God's blessing, you will have it in your own hands to make the shares. Then, if you keep clear of the Dutch in the Sunda Straights, half a dozen voyages will make you, and you can set up for a squire by land.

'Dear Lord,' he said, blowing out a cloud of smoke some minutes later, 'If Captain Johnson of the *Clove* could hear you a-doubting of the billabillian, he would have you overboard when you were five minutes out of soundings, or keep you to sell to the Sultan of Cayalucca. You must indeed want wit, my poor moon-calf nephew, not to understand that it saves the merchants' goods and money. If you open your hatches and break bulk among those land-sharks – for all those heathens are thieves inveterate, knowing no better – you lose a good eighth, seeing they all have twelve hands apiece, like their idols. And at the end of it they give you no thanks for having made them search, and they buy up half your cargo for their king at their own price, which is a sinful waste. No: it saves the merchant's pocket, and it makes a wastrel venture a profitable voyage. It gives the Arapotee a noble present. It gives the captain and the supercargo a rightful bounty on their wages – and nobody, not even the merchants, expects them to wind their way across the world's great sea for hardtack and a few ha-pence. No: they may take the billabillian, and they may trade afterwards once the ship has got her belly full: that's right and just. Don't you be wiser than the rest of the world, Cornelius, and don't you let your captain suspect he's gotten a formal, psalm-singing precisian aboard when you come to be on your own, or by God, it will be the last voyage you ever make.'

He was benign and calm again by now. When he was not blue in the face with rage he was always kind. He had taken in his widowed sister and her little brood of Papists – and a dangerous charge it might always be – and at this very moment, thought Cornelius, working out the change in time for the longitude, he was probably singing all the decent words he knew of a song while Sue and Bridget piped along beside him. He was choleric at times, that could not be denied, and he hated Puritans like poison, though he never went farther into the parish church than the bell-tower; but these were only squalls on a gentle sea. And it was not only a rough, careless, sailor's kindness that bound Cornelius to him; it was much more. For example, he had not only found his nephew his place in the *Clove* and his outfit, but he had spent days and weeks in drawing up his pages of advice: it was the fruit of great experience, and to the day Cornelius sailed he kept adding notes. There was one here now, beautifully written in the margin of the pages about Timor. 'Balee, to the westward of Lambock, in 8 degrees of south Latitude, yields great Plenty of Wax, which is made up in large Cakes, from eighteen to thirty Rials to the Peecul, as the Time serves. There's a great deal of Deceit, very often, in this Commodity; and to be sure that you are not cheated, the best Way is to break it, and see whether it looks agreeable within. The Wares to be carried hither, are Chopping-Knives, China Frying-Pans, China Bells, small Bugles, Porcelains, colour'd Taffatees (but no Blacks), Pieces of Silver beaten flat and thin, and of the breadth of one's Hand; and your Broad Cloth of Venice Red and all your Coromandel Cloths are topping Commodities here; but the most vendible sorts are the Gobarees, the Pintadoes, and the fine Tappies of St. Thomas. There may be good Profit made of the Trade to this Island, in the Teeth of the false Dutch, for the Chinese have given four for one, to some of our English that ventur'd with them thither.'

His uncle had written that in front of the roaring fire at Christmas, but Cornelius, thinking of him now, saw him sitting in his meadow, listening placidly to the Dartford bells and waving the stem of his pipe to count the changes. Then he realized that it was something on shore that had brought this image so sharp and clear into his mind. He raised his head and listened: yes, in that queer, tip-tilted temple under the flaming trees someone was beating on a gong, a rhythmic boom-boom-boom that came echoing over the water like the passing bell at home.

'The Dutch were highly disgusted at our coming hither, and as inquisitive to know who directed us to this Place, threatening all with Plagues and Death,' he read. But he could not keep his mind to his book. He looked out to the brilliant light again, to the diminished world, yet so much more brilliant and animated for its confining frame. The gong in the temple was beating still, and a little wind was moving the palm trees: the splashes of moving colour up behind there must be the market place, where the men from the European ships, the Chinese junks and the Arab dhows met with the Malays, the Formosans, and the Javanese. If only the captain would come he could go ashore. Cornelius had a desperate feeling that tomorrow it might all be gone: he was so longing to be there that he could hardly sit.

'Mr O'Leary,' said the captain, 'have you the lists for the after-hold? And the papers for the customs men? They are putting off from the shore.'

'Yes, sir. Here is the after-hold.' Cornelius dropped it in an excess of zeal: he was nervous of the tall, yellow-faced captain, and he was not used to being called Mr O'Leary.

'Very good, Mr O'Leary,' said the captain, nodding over the list of bales. The mulatto came in and stood by the porthole, looking out and darkening the sun. 'Customs man coming soon,' he said. 'Billabillian.'

The captain did not answer, but looked among the papers for the lading of the *Trade's Increase*.

'Here it is, sir,' cried Cornelius, divining the captain's wish. 'But we will not need it, except for show,' he said, with a laugh and a knowing wag of his head. 'I have put the chief officer's present on the locker sir, and fifty strings of cash for his men.'

'Present?' said the captain. His back was to the light, and Cornelius could not tell from his voice whether he was pleased or not by this display of efficient promptitude.

'Yes, sir, a looking-glass, a case of spirits, and one of the boxes of opium, sir, like Mr Swann said.' He spoke with confidence; he remembered Mr Swann's words exactly. 'That should please the black bastard's heart,' he said, in imitation of Swann.

'Mr O'Leary,' said the captain, sharply.

'I ask pardon, sir,' said Cornelius, going red and drawing the top of his shoe up the calf of his left leg. After a moment he said, 'I drew up this little paper of the billabillian, sir. It should make us four hundred pieces of eight, give or take a score eitherway.'

After the briefest hesitation the captain took the paper in silence: as he looked at it he said nothing.

The awkwardness that had arisen with the captain's 'Mr O'Leary' did not fade away. Cornelius felt it strongly. Had he made the captain's share large enough? Surely: it was twice what Uncle John had said. He was conscious of the mulatto's fixed stare: he said, 'I have counted out the six hundred reals in the two bags under the table.' Then, feeling that he had to say something more, he added, 'They are damnation heavy,' with an embarrassed laugh.

'Mr O'Leary,' said the captain again, but automatically, without meaning. He had turned a little to the light, and Cornelius could see that his little deep-set eyes were still scrutinizing the slip of paper. Was it not clear? He had set it all down exactly, and had headed it Billabillian, with two lines ruled under it and the date.

'Is the sum taken away rightly, sir?' he asked, into the continuing silence. A boat rowed by with squeaking oars, and its shadow passed over the ceiling.

'The subtraction is correct,' said the captain. 'It is all quite clear.' He seemed to notice the mulatto for the first time, and pointed silently to the door; the mulatto went out, giving Cornelius a strong, but incomprehensible look as he passed by him.

'Tell me, Mr. O'Leary,' said the captain in the same toneless, contained voice, 'how do you spell your names? Write them at the bottom here.'

He put the paper on the table, and Cornelius, confused and obscurely unhappy, wrote his name below the sum. Cornelius O'Leary.

'Thank you,' said the captain, sprinkling sand on the signature and folding the paper into the pocket of his black coat.

'May I go ashore when we have finished, sir?' asked Cornelius, smiling hesitantly, as he looked up into the captain's strange, withdrawn, inimical face.

'When next thou goes ashore,' whispered the captain, with a sudden cold ferocity, 'false thief, it will be –'

Popery knocked at the door, opened it. Behind him there was a man in a gorgeous sarong. The mulatto stood aside, and said, 'Billabillian.'

The Rendezvous

CLEARLY umbrellas must often blow inside-out (how many times has one not had to tack violently in the turbulence at a street corner, grasping the mast with both hands and just, but only just, succeeding in dipping the rim under the current?) yet all my life I had never seen one. There it lay, a smallish umbrella, neither particularly a man's nor a woman's, in the shining, wet-running street, well away from the tumultuous gutter. It was not an old abandoned thrown-away umbrella – everyone has seen *them* – but a fairly new one: you could tell at first glance that it was malformed in some way, but it was not until you saw the metal ribs sticking through the respectable bright cloth that you understood it had been blown inside-out and that its defeated owner had made an attempt at folding it again before realizing that there was no hope and laying it deliberately in that position, parallel with the street, in nobody's way, relinquishing it kindly, perhaps with a certain respect.

One's eye takes these things in at great speed (I was running at the time), and all the faster if there is any sense of crisis, any amorous excitement or impending catastrophe: afterwards one's mind has to plod along rationalizing the eye's instant answer, its explanation of the problematical wreck, the overturned car, the domestic scene in a lit window as the train runs by. The sense of crisis was there, as well as the other factors, for the town was on the edge of disaster. The heavy rains of the last three days had been followed that morning by a stupefying downpour: warm rain hurtling down in drops of far more than natural size and between these drops a fine mist of shattered water. The earth could take up no more and already the river was a great cambered churning ochre mass from bank to bank, tearing furiously at the bridge, and by the Prefecture the orderly canal had drowned its trim brick walls, while the municipal oleanders, their roots ten feet below, jerked their highest leaves, their tallest twigs, among the filth and rubbish on the uneven, breakneck surface. And apart from the general crisis I had my own as I ran splashing past this umbrella. The Paris express would leave (if it were still running) in eight minutes: the station was a quarter of an hour away, and there was not a taxi to be seen anywhere in this flooded town.

There is something odious, almost unclean, in picking at oneself, slapping labels on to emotions and behaviour – peering through your own keyhole and perhaps at the same time putting on a show for the voyeur. However, there is no doubt a discreditable side to this perpetual missing of trains: and the running, the sweat (and how I sweated under my mackintosh in that steaming heat) only makes it more discreditable still. The cast-iron alibi, even to one's own court of conscience (but I *ran*, I ran all the way to catch it), grows less convincing in the hundredth repetition, particularly when it carries on into dreams.

Sweating and soaked I saw the express pull out and gather momentum as I burst from my last-minute cab. The red lights on the back of the last carriage swung round the curve and vanished – oh familiar nightmare – and I sheltered in the station buffet with its coffee-urns, its silent, frightened waitresses, the thunder of falling rains, sirens, apocalyptic candles in the gloom (the electricity had failed), the deep roar of running water everywhere.

However, by the time the next train left, the slow train, feeling its way over the flooded plains where only the embankment stood above the water – the vineyards all drowned – I was almost dry: though it was impossible to say the same for my book, or for her letter, or for the bundle of notes, of money (a source of great satisfaction to me) that I had thrust into my pocket for this rendezvous and that had soaked up the water to a surprising if not to a dangerous extent. And by the time I was in Paris the whole sky was blue – not so much as a cloud, not even on the southern rim.

I had already missed my connection and the essence of the rendezvous, of course: there could be no Cossack hat at the far end of the platform – did she still wear that hat, or had worms fattened on the Persian lamb? – no tall head stretching taller still behind the ticket-collector, no pale-blue eyes looking cold and remote until they flashed into recognition. Should we have shaken hands, kissed? Stood lumpish, undecided, muttering 'How well you look – not changed in the very least', each waiting for the other to make the spontaneous unstudied gesture, to define the relationship? Should I have been able to control my voice? That had haunted me ever since I opened her letter.

So I had missed the essence of the rendezvous; and as for telephoning in London, hearing that mortal 'ringing tone' in an empty flat, counting thirteen, counting thirteen again before hanging up, I could do that just as well from Paris. But there was still a train to Dieppe I could catch if I hurried, and at that juncture it seemed to me I ought to go through all the required motions. In that phoney histrionic voice which comes booming out when in fact far deeper real emotions are there below, I said it was right that I should die by inches in a call-box at Victoria rather than in an archaic booth at Austerlitz – that it should in common respect for her cost me two new pence rather than ten new francs.

This time I reached the train by racing through the barrier and although two doors would not yield I wrenched the third open and leapt in as the whistles blew and red flags waved. An empty compartment, smelling of dust, with views of Bayeux, Caen, a grisly watering-place, and three graffiti: *Couple criminel, vomi par la cité, faiseurs d'orphelins*; *Je t'aime, Nicole*; and *Vive moi*.

For the first quarter of an hour or so the railway from Paris to Dieppe perpetually crosses and re-crosses the river: you see it now on the one side and now on the other, and far off through the window a toy Eiffel Tower where you do not always expect it. It was while I was sitting in the carriage that I worked out this piece about the umbrella, its significance (shield, broken, carefully laid aside) and its obvious connection with missing trains; and when at about tea-time we stopped on a blank stretch of line I had little hesitation about getting out. Little hesitation, but still some: the sewing of my right-hand or should I say right-foot shoe, overtaxed by my paddling in it and by its stewing hours of heat in the waiting-room, had started to come undone. It was not so much that the sole had come frankly off, flapping downwards, as that the upper part had begun to rise; yet it seemed to me that by now the relative movement had stopped, and as I had always wanted to see this piece of river close to I opened the door and dropped on to the stones that make the permanent way: rough, pointed stones, flecked with oil and tar, of a kind to be seen nowhere else. It was an odd feeling to lay a hand on the lower edge of the tall train and to know that I was still in touch with it, that I could still become an integral part of it, and that if I chose not to do so it would move off, *exit left, gasping and heaving*, leaving nothing between this side of the line and the river but transparent air: at the bottom right-hand corner of the carriage, in gold on the brown background, stood the single word Purge.

The river was exactly as I had hoped it would be. There are so many places that can only be seen from a train – landscapes as absolute as the moon, railway-cuttings filled with cowslips, and grave-eyed badgers pacing there between them. Here was the broad Seine, full but not flood-full, rolling from brim to brim, and on my right, where Purge had been, the long spit of a tree-covered island coming to a point in the middle of the stream. A motor-barge pulling a string of lighters was thrusting up through the current towards the far side of the island, and on the near side a bright blue and red ship with the Belgian flag came floating down. It was a great wide view that I had, though not distress-ingly large – none of the dehumanizing expanse that you see from an aeroplane: perhaps two miles upstream to where the island merged into the general blur, and somewhat less to a curve that shut off the water in the other direction. Just before this curve I could make out a hard line that I believed to be a weir; and if I was right, then, oh joy, there would be five acres of detergent foam, and swans swimming in the Tide.

It was all that I could have wished. Warm, still, gentle,

luminous air; a mild, veiled sun; the light brighter in some places than in others – Seurat near to, Claude Lorraine farther off. Before I moved the bow-wave of the motor-barge had vanished behind the island and a woman had hung out a line of bright washing on one of those that it towed. Some other vessels had come into sight here and there and not very far from the bank I could now make out the necessary fisherman, his heavy green boat moored against a background of reeds: but although there might be all this light and movement the whole effect was that of a uniform silence. Nothing that moved moved abruptly; there was the gliding continuity of the water and the swimming of the boats, and what human motion there was was small and doll-like in the distance. The angler never stirred.

I found the old tow-path and began to walk downstream, with the very agreeable sensation of being wafted along, of being part of the general flow. Of course, the sides of the path were some-what overgrown, but a bare white track ran down the middle of it, and no doubt it would take me as far as Rouen if I let myself go with it long enough.

The hard line was indeed a weir, a weir that I knew well from the train, and it had its solid park of froth ending in a rounded point from which the current plucked islands and white ribbons, carrying them far down the river, out of sight; but no swans, except for a disappointing grey cygnet on the other side. This was an area I knew intimately well, from having gazed at it out of the windows of another world, but my knowledge was partial, based upon another sense of time and distance, and it did not extend to names. It did not extend to the great works with chim-neys and open ironwork towers beyond the stream, either (I must always have looked too fixedly at the weir); but I was not surprised to see it, for there were many such things, vast inhuman enterprises that seemed to work themselves, spread out arbi-trarily along this river. The drifting smell persuaded me that it was a chemical works; yet as far as I could see the world was unaffected by it. The chimneys bore their plumes of smoke, the unnatural reek came across the air; yet the river flowed and the trees stood up round and green, as though the two entities were entirely independent of one another. How different this will be, I said with a little skip, when I come to the burning fields.

But they were far away. First I had to follow the Seine round a noble bend that curved back on itself in a more than S, and this took me upwards of an hour: an S that the train annihilated by drawing a dollar stroke across it at eighty miles an hour. Dutch barges in the middle, with their flags; a very long low vessel with its body awash and a ridiculous wooden house perched up on one end – French; another Belgian, riding high with its screw churning white; yet not a sound did I hear until the very tail of the S, when a magpie flew from a bush on the left and trailed far out over the river, cackling as it went. Until then there might have been a deafness on the world.

Now for the first time plain agricultural land came down on the river on my side of it. Fields, divided by post and wire; leys; a fair amount of stubble, some of it already ploughed; neat heaps of dung; no people – just the fields and in one of them an empty cart. Another turn: meadows with lapwings calling over them, and along the river-bank (propped by piles, black baulks of timber, at this point where it was so deep) the tall dipping gallows of a row of fish-traps, archaic things like lateen masts, some with their baskets hoisted up, others dipping attentively. Beyond them lay an empty ferry-boat, moored to a wavering pier; and here a road came down to the river, a cart-track from a village or from the small collection of farms whose dark outbuildings I could make out behind a line of trees. Another mile, with an easy path under my feet; a few boats, and nothing else moving in the world except for one moorhen that jerked its neck among the reeds.

Now I was coming closer to my Sodom: already there were some sickly willows on the bank, by no means as sweet a green as those on the farther side, and a far greater profusion of the rank yellow weed called Stinking Willy. A train went by on the other bank, running at full stretch for Paris, and it gave me a pleasant feeling of being both here and there – a feeling slightly marred however by a lingering impression of guilt that I did not choose to identify at that moment; the association of trains and morose delectation, no doubt. The vegetation was thinning out;

even the harsher kinds of grass had a stunted, lightless, sullen look; the naked earth showed more and more, a damp, soured desert; and here at last was my burning field. A great long rectangle, perfectly neat, perfectly level; and it was all made up of a black, coke-like substance, lying there in unspeakable profusion and emitting trails of smoke, yellow rising fumaroles, small pink flames here and there, and sometimes, where the smoke was darkest, a dusky crimson glow. No wire round it, no fence. No warnings: apparently no road. I had always wanted to smell it, and now, since the movement of the air was against me, I eagerly climbed from the towpath to the first black crunching scoriae. I could not stalk about on it as I had promised myself, because my gaping shoe would let in some furious spark; but I did take a few triumphant paces, and immediately the heat rose up through my soles.

Bare earth with a sulphurous efflorescence came next, then sparse foul shrubs, twitch, and rose-bay willow-herb in seed. Gradually the trees improved – taller, more sprightly. Almost all traces of my burning field had gone by the time I came to these allotments late in the day, these oblongs of kitchen-garden huddled together, speckled with tool-sheds made of old shutters, railway sleepers and metal advertisements; a scene that could only be explained by the presence of some industrial village hidden behind the rising land.

And now there were figures in the landscape, a group of youths clustered strangely behind one of the little sheds. They were near enough for me to see the black leather jackets, the big shining buckles, the unmistakable hair, the thickness of the frontal bone, the deep unluminous skin, and the shot-gun that the tallest had in his hands. They broke up on seeing me, some running, all moving rapidly away from the bothie; then they slowed to an exaggeratedly casual film-cowboy stride, with many an evil look backwards. In the first moment the group – they had certainly been breaking into the shed – had lost much of its cohesion, but by the time they had passed through the remaining allotments they had regained it, and with it all their bold inhumanity. Their direction, as far as they had any direction, was down the river, and for some minutes we all walked slowly towards Rouen. Slowly, because that was their pace; and slowly, because I had no wish to catch them up.

The river was beginning one of its smooth splendid curves again, bearing away to the left, and this bend enclosed a vast half-moon of marshy land, intersected by palely shining ditches and a much larger reed-lined canal. 'I shall cut across the bend,' I said, 'for although there is nothing against stepping out and passing through the midst of them, I do not choose to do so.' All lies, all lies, of course; there was everything against walking through the midst of them, for we were not indifferent; a relationship had already been established, and its rays were darting to and fro – fear, dislike and contempt on my side, and malignance, revolt and bloody dissatisfaction on theirs.

It was a great mistake, a bleeding error: I had none of the local sureness of a man of those parts, one who knew his way among the ditches and whose knowledge would have given him an assured countenance even through the back of his head. I had hardly begun my uncertain blundering through the reeds before I turned from a spectator to a quarry.

There was no overt move for a little while and indeed the knowledge of the situation did not spread to all minds and to all levels of awareness without a considerable delay. Besides there was a gap in time, a parenthesis, in which they shot a magpie (they shot at everything that moved), winged it, and thrashed about after it as it ran, hopped and fluttered, sometimes, poor bird, skimming to a moment's safety in the reeds on the far side of a broad ditch.

But soon enough there I was, going faster and faster along my predetermined chord while one straggling line of youths hurried shouting along the towpath and another, more compact, launched out across the marsh on a course that would intercept mine unless I either ran or deviated to the left. I deviated, all right. My chord became a curve, and the curve sharpened sensibly as the gleam of gun-barrels in the fading light caught my eye. At some point, unseen by me, the sun must have sunk into a band of haze low over the trees beyond the river, and now the white light of the evening was shining from all the water in the bog. Steadily on, with the marsh-smell rising to my nose and the marsh-mud (viscous, dark) packing into the gap between the sole and upper of my shoe, working under the arch of my foot. On, on. What dreadful galvanic energy possessed those youths, what superabundant activity, unnecessary life!

In front of me stretched a surface far wider than I had expected: this was the canal that drained the middle of the bog; and it looked very deep. Some ditches I had leapt, without too great an air of flight (I thought) and some I had crossed on planks. But here was no bridge that I could make out, and if I were seen attempting to jump it – it might just be done – then there would be no disguising the situation. The leap would be an open acknowledgement that the thing had turned into a hunt and myself into a legitimate prey. Besides, I did not know which side of the canal they were: they might have crossed it by the bridge that must certainly exist at the far end, where the canal fell into the Seine. Staring round did me no good, for here I was among the reeds, and their feathery heads cut off my view. An irresolute step took me away to the left along the canal, and here, just past a low-spreading willow-tree, there rose up an enormous shape. Straight up into the air it rose and after a stab of pure terror I recognized the broad wings and shape and colour of a heron: at once the shape diminished to a natural size. The slow beating flight rose and turned into the evening breeze from the river, mounting languidly, as herons will.

Then came the double bang-bang of the gun and the heron slanted down in a long glide towards the river-bank. There was a confused shouting and bellowing of orders, raucous, ugly, near-hysterical, and then another shot. I made my way fast along the canal, keeping down among the reeds and the willows, and at length I paddled my way into a particularly dense clump of bulrushes that stood around a little subsidiary pond. Here I squatted on a tussock of that wiry grass which stands dry in the wettest places. There was the best part of the shell of some bird's egg under the tussock next to mine, and one could still see the bent-lined hollow in which it had been laid. 'Tranquillity,' I said;

and I noticed that the light was too dim to make out the colour of the shell. To some degree I was still unwilling fully to admit that I was hiding; but in reply to the commonplace observation 'these things just don't happen – you are upset, nervous, all on edge' my memory produced details of gratuitous acts of this very nature and repeated them over a long period. And when I heard movements and voices again in front of me – that is to say further along the canal than the point I had reached – my whole being at once acquiesced and compressed itself into a smaller space, eyes glaring, ears and nostrils stretched: no doubt it also emitted a quarry's smell. And I was surprised to find my hand creeping towards my wad of notes: I had not consciously thought of them since the train, so very long ago. There was the faintest wetness still to be detected in their heart.

'There! In there!' shouted a voice, and someone threw a clod of earth into the rushes and the water: but it was twenty or thirty yards away. Still, this full admission was very bitter, and beneath the humiliation I felt a surly glow begin go rise.

It might have grown into something very rough and careless in time or with a sudden emergency, but it had certainly not reached that point yet, and I lay as close as a hare. As far as I could tell they were scattered promiscuously over the marsh – some of them shouting a great way off – and they seemed to be skirmishing about in twos and threes. What I could not make out was where the gun might be.

Nor, when at last I came out of my hiding-place, could I make out which way round I was. West I could tell, for there was the remaining yellow glow; but the closer lie of the land escaped me – the canal no longer seemed to be running in the right direction, and the chess-board ditches (as far as they could be seen at all in this dying glimmer, faintly helped by a weak-backed moon) had been slewed round so that they no longer pointed out my way. There were a few voices still to be heard, mostly quite far off. They no longer had the fierce zeal of the earlier stage, but still I went on cautiously, working in what I thought was the direction of the river; and when I heard a cry of 'Look out! There he is!' I turned at once.

The frightened tone was cordial to me, so was the sight of shadowy figures fleeting away from me over the marsh; but still I edged off into cover, since they might be running straight to their friends.

Now there was a great deal of that foolish ululating oo-ooh that townspeople keep up so in the country: but quite commonplace now, none of that implacable passionate intensity that you hear when hounds hit off the line – silly human beings was all. And I supposed, as I sat on my heels in a hollow, that they had gathered again, at least into two bands; though there was some isolated whistling and bawling over to the left.

The weak moon had gathered spirit: it had put out the Pleiades and it shone on every watery stretch. A heavy dew was falling: wet piled upon wet.

'If only I had a piece of string,' I said, 'how much easier it would be.' My sole was now a true drooping sole. I had to raise my foot six inches higher than I should ordinarily have done, to prevent it from stubbing on the ground; and at every step I grasped with my toes – a useless, unnecessary, and (after a thousand repetitions) a very tiring action.

My direction was unsure – quite vague. I had thought of making my way back to those allotments and thence to my hypothetical village, but on reflexion I preferred the towpath, and it seemed to me that if I kept on a general westerly course I must come to it in the end. It must surely be over there; and yet here was a metalled road, a meaningless road, if ever I had seen one. What was my right course now? On the far side, beyond still another ditch, stood a sign-post. I could have sworn that even a newspaper would have been legible in this brilliant moon – at least the headlines – but when I walked across (the road-grit sharp under my ridiculous foot) I found that I could not make out a single word. By now I was not going to leap another ditch with my shoe in that shape merely to learn, perhaps, that I might not deposit ordure there, so I considered for a while; and seeing that the road seemed to slope a little to the right, I went down it: in a quarter of a mile it brought me to a raised bank, and as soon as I had walked over it there was the Seine, there were the lights of some great installation far over on the other side, and between this bank and that two boats crossing on the black water. They hooted gently to each other as they passed, and their washes crossed reciprocally, the ripples showing in the light. The river was flowing the way I had expected it to flow – how comforting – and where I stood the metalled road ended in a gravelly place with a small ferry, just large enough for a single car. And here was the towpath: I started along it – so much easier than the broken surface of the bog, and presently the whole ludicrous, painful incident, which had already diminished wonderfully, dwindled into a foolishness long past.

It did not revive even when my mind was jerked from its mild inward rambling by a sound that it told me was caused by a bullock churning about in a wet pasture, frightened by its own shadow. But it did revive in all its full strength, it did shock my heart to a momentary halt and wring my stomach tight again when I saw the youth bolt upright by the mast of a fish-trap. The moon was shining full upon him. Was he dim-sighted, half-witted, a nyctalope, to suppose himself invisible? Had he read in a book that if you stand quite still you cannot be seen?

Quite still he stood, and as I came closer I could see the moon shining blue upon his teeth – a black hole of mouth and then these teeth. In that light his face seemed drained, eyeless, and sweating cold, for what could be seen did also glisten.

My foot had made the smallest pause when I saw him, hardly measurable it was so small, because I knew that the entire situation was reversed, utterly reversed; and I came on with my awkward lame-duck gait.

'Have you a piece of string?' I said.

No answer. No movement. The line of barges that had been following me passed by and I saw him silhouetted against the navigation lights.

'Have you a piece of string?'

His eyes showed in the moonlight, a sudden gleam (had they been closed?), and in an abrupt harsh rush he said, 'Yes, a whole ball of string. A whole ball of string. Twine.'

'Why does he carry a whole ball of twine with him?' I wondered as I sat down. I said, 'What is the name of the next village?'

'Bougival,' he answered gently, very soft.

'Bougival,' I said, seeing the map quite clearly now. 'Ah, Bougival. Why, yes, of course, it must be Bougival, the place where lettuces are grown. I shall telephone from there.'

The Stag at Bay

EDWIN, as the long and briefless years trailed on, devoted himself more and more to lecturing and journalism. At the moment he was labouring over an article on marriage for a women's magazine – 'Let it be chatty and smart. And rather profound – *human*: you know what I mean? And you can be wistful if you like: old, battered, experienced. But not more than fifteen hundred words.'

The article was proving much more difficult than he had expected. It was not for lack of raw material – pinned to the wall in front of him was a list of smart things that had already been said about marriage – and it was not for lack of experience or thought. Marriage was a subject that he had thought about a great deal, deeply, and he had supposed that the profound part of the article would be the easiest: yet although he was in the right mood, costive and solemn, the words would not form themselves into an orderly and harmonious procession. They remained in his head, swirling in grand but indeterminate shapes; or if they had any concrete existence at all it was in the form of scrappy notes, odd words jotted down: *marriage iceberg – sunk – top quarrels – corruption in state.*

Not from lack of experience: he was married himself and at this time he felt more than usually married, for not only was he immersed in this article, but Julia had left him again, had gone back to her mother, and he was conscious of this all the time, if for no other reason than that the place was in such a mess. He never cleared it up on these occasions, partly on what he called principle and partly because it gave him such a moral advantage to be found in a slum, with every crock and pot unwashed and dishes piled on the floor, bed unmade, laundry sprawling abroad. He would not deliberately make a hole in his sock; but he would not prevent it, either. And yet he would not consciously welcome the hole; he would say tut-tut over it and inspect it with distaste: still less would he acknowledge that he piled the dishes in an unnecessarily picturesque confusion. His recognition of his moral advantage took place on some remote and not very savoury level of awareness: the piling of the dishes was traditional in the helpless male – any comic strip would bear that out, and besides there was the principle Man works not in House – and it was quite unconscious when it was quite fair: it was quite fair of course because Julia was in the wrong; therefore it was totally unconscious.

Marriage iceberg. Somewhere he had read that seven-eighths of an iceberg is always submerged and that it is only the remaining eighth that one sees; and this he meant to liken to marriage, the visible berg corresponding to the squabbles and superficial disharmony and the vast unseen majority serving as a figure for the profound unity and deep affection that must always subsist, etc. A church-going expression covered his face: he nodded gravely, and bending over his desk he began to write.

His pen stopped, started again, faltered and limped: he crossed out the whole paragraph and began afresh. He must make it quite plain about the underneath of the iceberg being really there.

Slow, slow. The cat, which standing at the door had asked three times to go out, now paced deliberately into his bedroom.

It was a slow article to write. Julia had slammed the door behind her just after the smart pieces had all been collected and as the first words were being written, 'We all know Mr Punch's advice about marriage . . .' Yet the first section, the chatty part, had scarcely been completed before she had given Edwin grounds for divorce, and she was not by habit a flibbertigibbet, a fly-by-night, an itching palmer; neither loose nor fast. Her motives had been mixed: sizzling vexation of spirit, a conviction that nothing mattered; but also curiosity. She wanted to know, to really know, what adultery was like.

The article was still bogged down in the second, or human, part when, pursuing her research with an ardour that could no longer be attributed to revenge or a spirit of inquiry, she increased his grounds to a most liberal extent – to expansive and park-like grounds in which the horned beasts could be seen wandering at large.

At the beginning of the profound section she was in bed with horrible old Anthony Limberham, her cousin, to whose busy prayer she had yielded at three o'clock on Tuesday afternoon. She was quite accustomed by now to his faintly incestuous sheets – to their moral significance, that is – but not to the flagrant luxury of their hem-stitching, nor to the sinful depth of the carpet that met her feet when she got up. The unashamed magnificence of Anthony's flat, his delighted pursuit of the sins of the flesh, the huge and beautiful meals (no shopping, cooking, washing-up) they both ate so greedily, the flowers, the scent, the lovely clothes, all these refreshed her soul like rain after drought. She sloughed the anxiously contriving housewife, dropped ten years from her appearance, and responded to his cheerful obscenity with an assured impudence that no longer shocked her inner mind. Her eyes shone; she looked pink, virginal and inviting; her hair curled naturally; in all her life she had never felt so well.

Her sense of fun, much discouraged by life with Edwin and the hundred best books on the seventh floor of a cold-water walk-up, came suddenly to life again, and Anthony, scarlet in the face and wheezing, watered it with gin. She was going to the dogs – such agreeable dogs.

In the morning the tide of washing-up reached Edwin's desk itself, and at eleven a little congealed bacon-fat obscured his views on the state. These views had got into the article because they seemed to him to follow naturally after the piece about icebergs: he had expressed them forcibly, at some length, and with particular feeling today. He found them satisfactory and comforting even now, although the bacon-fat had reduced them to a kind of aphoristic précis: '. . . corruption in state, however bad, always occurs over basis of working integrity – unseen, unheard, taken for granted. – Crime not crime if normal; and once it becomes normal, unthinkable dissolution of the state.'

Scraping some of the grease off with the paper-knife he commended himself for not being angry. He thought of ringing up
his mother-in-law's house and telling Julia that she was for-
given: he thought of clearing everything away completely. But
he sickened at the prospect of the actual effort; and then it
really would be too Quixotic to throw away so much advantage. '
Magnanimity had its limits: and after all he had not been . . .

What exactly had he meant to forgive her for? His memory,
usually so very precise in such matters, could not supply the
grievance at once, and even after bungling about among the files
for some time it could come up with nothing better than general
disrespect, inattention, or answering back. There was no heinous
crime, like the unmended drawers of the last great row. The
prefect-Edwin was inclined to mercy; fright and the possibility
of dismay were beginning to creep through the levels of consciousness and he was growing less absolute. But there was such a
great deal of washing-up.

'Or we have a very fine oryx, sir,' said the shopman.

They looked thoughtfully at the noble, leaping symmetry of
the polished horns. 'No,' said Anthony, after a moment, 'What
I really want is a stag, and, to be precise, a royal with at least
twelve points.'

'Don't be pedantic, Anthony,' murmured Julia, with a blush.
She turned away and gazed under the arm of a polar-bear at the
hurrying traffic. '. . . a long way before you find a royal, sir. We
used to see them often in the old King's time, but now I'm afraid
you'll have to go a long way . . .' the shopman said, bowing them
out.

A long way, a long way, but they found it at last in the limbo
of an auctioneer's back room.

'A very fine 'ed, if I may say so,' said the warehouseman,
hurr-ing on the stag's eye and shining it with his handkerchief:
it gleamed, brilliant among the dust and cobwebs that veiled the
long muzzle, as bright and expectant as a natural in a bus. 'A
very fine 'ed, sir,' repeated the warehouseman, polishing the
other eye, 'And I dare say it was his pride in his days of life.'

He stood aside to watch Anthony, who had borrowed a clothes-brush, and who was busily grooming the stag with it, going shshsh-shshsh like an ostler. The preposterous old satyr, purple as he bent to polish the antler, winking at Julia through the tangle of tines, made the warehouseman nervous and talkative. 'A very fine 'ed and worth every penny of two, twelve, six which I couldn't take a penny less – the horn alone is worth twice the sum named for the manufacture of fancy goods – penknife handles, sir, carving forks. And when ground is used for the cure of certain female ailments as no doubt your good lady knows, sir: I am a married man myself, ahem. Oh sir, you may say "Oh, it is a very old article." Why, yes, sir, it *is* an old article and who denies it? But a horned stag is a very old article by nature. In its nature, sir, a stag is an old article.'

'Yes, yes,' said Edwin to the telephone, looking dutiful and attentive into the distemper three inches from his nose. 'Yes, Lady Dogge. Yes: yes. I'm very sorry, Lady Dogge; but it's finished now, Lady Dogge. Oh, please don't say that, Lady Dogge. No, Lady Dogge. Yes, Lady Dogge. Good-bye, Lady Dogge.'

'The bitch,' he said, but not very loud. He sat down quickly to his desk and read through the manuscript. 'It will do,' he said, without conviction, and crammed it into an envelope.

He hurried down the shallow flights of stairs, iron-bound cement in a chocolate-painted well that clanged and echoed, down to the wan hall with its lavatory tiles. The porter came out of his booth and watched him down the last four flights.

'Good afternoon,' he said to the porter, as he put the envelope into the slit. 'Is there any post?'

'Where's Mrs?' said the porter, staring up the stairs.

'She's away at the moment.'

'Oh. Visiting, isn't it?'

The porter was also the deputy hangman for the south-east region and the tenants had to humour his independence.

'Yes,' said Edwin. 'Has the postman been?'

'No,' he replied, putting his hand over his coat-pocket. 'No, I don't think. But there is a parcel for you. Mrs is leaving it this morning.'

'Then why did you ask where she was?'

'Oh I did not, Mr; and it is a big old parcel,' said the porter, suddenly changing his tone to one of close affection and laying his hand on Edwin's sleeve as if to test the quality of the cloth, 'I can have the string, isn't it?'

The porter had already unwrapped the greater part of the stag, and Edwin finished the unpacking there in the booth: then grasping the polished shield upon which the head was mounted he began his upward journey. At the third flight he had to change his hold, for the shield was too slippery and the head too heavy in front; but taking the creature round the neck he balanced the weight better, and although it was momentarily disagreeable to put his face against the old rough hairiness he soon grew accustomed to it and after a flight or two he did not mind at all. They went up, cheek by jowl, very well balanced, and with the same noble antlers shading them like an open-work umbrella; and as he climbed – far happier than when he had gone down – Edwin reflected upon this token of his wife's esteem, this mute forerunner of her prompt return.

'I had almost begun to think –' he confided to the stag. And 'It will be very useful,' he said to himself as he opened the door, 'and although it is far too large and spreading for the lobby, I will fix it solidly to my bedroom wall after I have done the washing-up, and I will hang my clothes on it at night.'

Samphire

SHEER, SHEER, the white cliff rising, straight up from the sea, so high that the riding waves were nothing but ripples on a huge calm. Up there, unless you leaned over, you did not see them break, but for all the distance the thunder of the water came loud. The wind, too, tearing in from the sea, rushing from a clear, high sky, brought the salt tang of the spray on to their lips.

They were two, standing up there on the very edge of the cliff: they had left the levelled path and come down to the break itself and the man was crouched, leaning over as far as he dared.

'It *is* a clump of samphire, Molly,' he said; then louder, half turning, 'Molly, it *is* samphire. I *said* it was a samphire, didn't I?' He had a high, rather unmasculine voice, and he emphasized his words.

His wife did not reply, although she had heard him the first time. The round of her chin was trembling like a child's before it cries: there was something in her throat so strong that she could not have spoken if it had been for her life.

She stepped a little closer, feeling cautiously for a firm foothold, and she was right on him and she caught the smell of his hairy tweed jacket. He straightened so suddenly that he brushed against her. 'Take care,' he cried, 'I almost trod on you. Yes, it *was* samphire. I said so as soon as I saw it from down there. Have a look.'

She could not answer, so she knelt and crawled to the edge. Heights terrified her, always had. She could not close her eyes; that only made it worse. She stared unseeing, while the brilliant air and the sea and the noise of the sea assaulted her terrified mind and she clung insanely to the thin grass. Three times he

123

pointed it out, and the third time she heard him so as to be able to understand his words. '. . . fleshy leaves. You see the fleshy leaves? They used them for pickles. Samphire pickles!' He laughed, excited by the wind, and put his hand on her shoulder. Even then she writhed away, covering it by getting up and returning to the path.

He followed her. 'You noted the *fleshy leaves*, didn't you, Molly? They allow the plant to store its nourishment. Like a cactus. Our *native* cactus. I *said* it was samphire at once, didn't I, although I have never actually seen it before. We could almost get it with a stick.'

He was pleased with her for having looked over, and said that she was coming along very well: she remembered – didn't she? – how he had had to persuade her and persuade her to come up even the smallest cliffs at first, how he had even to be a little firm. And now there she was going up the highest of them all, as bold as brass; and it was quite a dangerous cliff too, he said, with a keen glance out to sea, jutting his chin; but there she was as bold as brass looking over the top of it. He had been quite right insisting, hadn't he? It was worth it when you were there, wasn't it? Between these questions he waited for a reply, a 'yes' or a hum of agreement. If he had not insisted she would always have stayed down there on the beach, wouldn't she? Like a lazy puss. He said, wagging his finger to show that he was not quite in earnest, that she should always listen to her Lacey (this was a pet name that he had coined for himself). Lacey was her lord and master, wasn't he? Love, honour and obey?

He put his arm round her when they came to a sheltered turn of the path and began to fondle her, whispering in his secret night-voice, Tss-tss-tss, but he dropped her at once when some coast guards appeared.

As they passed he said, 'Good-day, men,' and wanted to stop to ask them what they were doing but they walked quickly on.

In the morning she said she would like to see the samphire again. He was very pleased and told the hotel-keeper that she was becoming quite the little botanist. He had already told him and the nice couple from Letchworth (they were called Jones and had a greedy daughter: he was an influential solicitor, and Molly would be a clever girl to be nice to them), he had already told them about the samphire, and he had said how he had recognized it at once from lower down, where the path turned, although he had only seen specimens in a hortus siccus and illustrations in books.

On the way he stopped at the tobacconist on the promenade to buy a stick. He was in high spirits. He told the man at once that he did not smoke, and made a joke about the shop being a house of ill-*fume*; but the tobacconist did not understand. He looked at the sticks that were in the shop but he did not find one for his money and they went out. At the next tobacconist, by the pier, he made the same joke to the man there. She stood near the door, not looking at anything. In the end he paid the marked price for an ash walking stick with a crook, though at first he had proposed a shilling less: he told the man that they were not ordinary summer people, because they were going to have a villa there.

Walking along past the pier towards the cliff path, he put the stick on his shoulder with a comical gesture, and when they came to the car park where a great many people were coming down to the beach with picnics and pneumatic rubber toys he sang, *We are the boys that nothing can tire: we are the boys that gather samphire.* When a man who was staying in the same hotel passed near them, he called out that they were going to see if they could get a bunch of jolly good samphire that they had seen on the cliff yesterday. The man nodded.

It was a long way to the highest cliff, and he fell silent for a little while. When they began to climb he said that he would never go out without a stick again; it was a fine, honest thing, an ashplant, and a great help. Didn't she think it was a great help? Had she noticed how he had chosen the best one in the shop, and really it was very cheap; though perhaps they had better go without tea tomorrow to make it up. She remembered, didn't she, what they had agreed after their discussion about an exact allowance for every day? He was walking a few feet ahead of her, so that each time he had to turn his head for her answer.

On the top it was blowing harder than the day before, and for the last hundred yards he kept silent, or at least she did not hear him say anything.

At the turn of the path he cried, 'It is still there. Oh jolly good. It is still there, Molly,' and he pointed out how he had first seen the samphire, and repeated, shouting over the wind, that he had been sure of it at once.

For a moment she looked at him curiously while he stared over and up where the plant grew on the face of the cliff, the wind ruffling the thin, fluffy hair that covered his baldness, and a keen expression on his face; and for a moment she wondered whether it was perhaps possible that he saw beauty there. But the moment was past and the voice took up again its unceasing dumb cry: Go on, oh, go on, for Christ's sake go on, go on, go on, oh go *on*.

They were there. He had made her look over. 'Note the fleshy leaves,' he had said; and he had said something about samphire pickle! and how the people at the hotel would stare when they brought it back. That was just before he began to crouch over, turned from her so that his voice was lost.

He was leaning right over. It was quite true when he said that he had no fear of heights: once he had astonished the workmen on the steeple of her uncle's church by walking among the scaffolding and planks with all the aplomb of a steeplejack. He was reaching down with his left arm, his right leg doubled under him and his right arm extended on the grass: his other leg was stretched out along the break of the cliff.

Once again there was the strong grip in her throat; her stomach was rigid and she could not keep her lip from trembling. She could hardly see, but as he began to get up her eyes focused. She was already there, close on him – she had never gone back to the path this time. God give me strength: but as she pushed him she felt her arms weak like jelly.

Instantly his face turned; absurd, baby-face surprise and a

shout unworded. The extreme of horror on it, too. He had been
half up when she thrust at him, with his knee off the ground, the
stick hand over and the other clear of the grass. He rose, swaying
out. For a second the wind bore up his body and the stick
scrabbled furiously for a purchase on the cliff. There where the
samphire grew, a little above, it found a hard ledge, gripped.
Motionless in equilibrium for one timeless space – a cinema
stopped in action – then his right hand gripped the soil, tore,
tore the grass and he was up, from the edge, crouched, gasping
huge sobbing draughts of air on the path.

He was screaming at her in an agonized falsetto interrupted
by painful gasps, searching for air and life. 'You *pushed* me, Molly
you – *pushed* me. You – *pushed* me.'

She stood silent, looking down and the voice rushed over her.
You *pushed* – you *pushed* me – Molly. She found she could swallow
again, and the hammering in her throat was less. By now his
voice had dropped an octave: he had been speaking without a
pause but for his gasping – the gasping had stopped now, and
he was sitting there normally. '. . . not well; a spasm. Wasn't it,
Molly?' he was saying; and she heard him say 'accident'
sometimes.

Still she stood, stone-still and grey and later he was saying
'. . . *possibly* live together? How can we *possibly* look at one
another? After this?' And sometime after it seemed to her that
he had been saying something about their having taken their
room for the month . . . accident was the word, and spasm, and
not well – fainting? It was, wasn't it, Molly? There was an
unheard note in his voice.

She turned and began to walk down the path. He followed at
once. By her side he was, and his face turned to hers, peering
into her face, closed face. His visage, his whole face, everything,
had fallen to pieces: she looked at it momentarily – a very old
terribly frightened comforting-itself small child. He had fallen off
a cliff all right.

He touched her arm, still speaking, pleading. 'It *was* that,
wasn't it, Molly? You didn't push me, Molly. It was an
accident . . .'

She turned her dying face to the ground, and there were her feet marching on the path; one, the other: one, the other; down, down, down.

The Clockmender

SUDDENLY he was awake. His waking had the abrupt complete-
ness of an electric light, entirely off one second and entirely on
the next. This was no warm transition from a confused doze to
a partial consciousness of the world, an awareness that would
begin with the pillow, the position of his relaxed body under the
bedclothes, and that would work slowly outwards to a comfortable realization of the world, with himself in it, each piece falling
naturally into its accustomed place. No. This was an abrupt
and full awakening from a profound sleep; and the world that
presented itself was naked, instantly concrete, sharply defined
and entire.

He knew at once that there was no hope whatever of drifting
off again, and he realized with horror that the grey light in the
room could not have been there much above an hour. He looked
over the edge of his bed at the pair of chronometers on the low
table: on each severe dial the steel hands showed five twenty-five.
Some disturbance, some chance noise had cheated him of three
hours of sleep.

It was a tragedy. He would have to get up very soon, for in a
short time the insistent restlessness of his body would make bed
intolerable and he would be forced into waste of another day,
another cruelly lengthened day.

Three hours more to serve. It was a tragedy: and it was so
unfair. He had spun out the evening until well past ten o'clock,
and he had won the right to sleep until eight or even nine. He
had gone on polishing the new-cut pallets of the Knibb clock
until they were almost beyond perfection, burnishing the faces
with a slip of agate – four thousand lengthways strokes to each
of the four angles. Two hours and thirteen minutes, timing each

stroke by the beat of a half-seconds pendulum. That had earned him his rest, surely.

But no. Here he was at half-past five, irrevocably awake and committed to the day. Something tapped on the window and scraped across the glass: that must have been it, he thought, looking round; the long thin branch from the wistaria: it should have been pruned years ago, when it was a stray twig; but now it had grown long enough to reach the windowpane as the cold wind of the dawn dragged it against the side of the house.

He had planted that wistaria himself when first he had the place. In those days he had been up with the first light – he had been up *before* the first light – for he had often switched on the lamp as he dressed. He had dressed in his gardening clothes at once, to lose no time.

He had dressed then: he had willingly gone through the process of putting on all those garments, selecting, buttoning, tying, turning right-side out, doing-up; every day he had accepted the series of motions that would have to be reversed at night. At that time he had been able to accept the drill of left arm – right arm, left leg – right leg, left foot – right foot, and its perpetual repetition. And the prospect of it had never kept him daunted in his bed: he remembered his eager getting up – springing up – in spite of his warm sleepiness, from a bed where he had gone to sleep still working out the details of the garden. Of the kitchen garden, mostly, for although he had a brave show of flowers it was the parallelograms of the kitchen garden that fascinated him – the drilled rows of the potatoes and the cabbages – and he would lie fighting against sleep while he carried out the mental arithmetic designed to show the total yield of his thirty-five rows of main-crop potatoes, if each plant yielded an average of three and a quarter pounds.

He remembered that now, as a fact: but he could no longer comprehend the once-vital urgency that had made it a fact; he could not feel that there was anything at all in common between the young man who had so enthusiastically worked out the cropping-plan for a seven-year rotation; who had, as the winter days grew short, dug the last double trenches by the light of a hurricane lamp to be doubly ready for the longed-for spring. Nothing in common between the man who had dug and cherished the garden and the one who now had not even visited the lower plot, the head-high jungle of nettles and fool's parsley, for months and months. Yet there was a physical continuity: the body was the same. And it was the same bed in which he lay. The wistaria, too, was a speaking witness. He had planted it, a straggling whipple, over the buried carcass of an ass, and now its trunk was like a grey python on the wall and its untended branches rapped against his bedroom windowpane.

One day, perhaps, he would go down through the tangle of roses to the kitchen garden and see whether among the rank growth below the apple-trees he could find the remains of his hives. It would be interesting to know if any of the colonies had survived. Once, nearly three years ago it must be now, he had seen a swarm clustered like an uncoloured shining bunch of grapes on the handle of a forgotten spade. They might have been from his own bees.

He would go down. But at the thought of actually doing it, of fixing a time for doing it, of dressing in order to do it, so great a physical repulsion seized him that to escape he turned his head further down into his pillow and fixed his eyes on the glass window in the side of the chronometer case.

The cylindrical hairspring contracted, swelled, contracted, the pulsation of a metal heart: he could not see the slow, even swing of the balance-wheel, but behind the links of the fusee, taut between the helix and the drum, he caught the recurrent flash of the scape-wheel pinion: the soft gleam of brass in the grey light was like the ever-returning wink of a lighthouse, impersonal, utterly reliable, continuing an indefinite series that drew out towards infinity; and in time the beautiful monotony steadied his mind. Now he could think more evenly of the prospects of the lengthened day.

They were horrible. But they were not so horrible as thinking of the garden and of all those other things that had once filled his life. Some of them he had cut out deliberately: he had amputated them when each in turn had threatened to grow into an exclusive obsession. Seeing his friends, for example; and his exact system of economy – that had been one of the hardest, but he had succeeded in the end, and now his rows of account books, with every item of expenditure balanced against each incoming penny, had remained unopened these many years. It had been so delightful to calculate the market cost of the garden produce: the bees had had their ledger too: and it had been such a keen triumph to deny himself for the reward of carrying over a surplus from one month to the next. But now he spent as he chose, not even taking a note of it; and in the second drawer of his desk the dividend vouchers piled up, still uncounted; and somewhere there was a clip of uncashed cheques.

This amputation had been successful, but it had required a dreadful effort: other things had fallen away of themselves. He had deliberately shut his door to callers, but he had never of set purpose opposed himself to books or music. Yet the one was as successful as the other, and it would now mean as much for-bidden and indeed impossible effort to open the piano and play as to open the door and engage in conversation with a casual visitor.

They had shredded away, all these things – all positive action, all doing, had retreated obediently to the other side of what was tolerable. When he got up now, he would slip on his dressing-gown. More than that would be – he wrenched away from the thought.

What do fleas do when they are not biting? he wondered. Or dogs, when they are not fighting, eating or being taken for a walk – house dogs? They must fall back into the stagnant pool of time. What a universal cruelty, repeated throughout an infinity of members, to be suspended in the fantastically deliberate flow of time, with no possible escape but the even greater horror of the farther limit, where there was no time at all. For very small creatures perhaps it would be worse: a day might be a year for them, by reason of their size.

Oh the days and the unending hours, he thought, turning his head from side to side. Yet all the time one's body lived eagerly in the flow: hair and nails – every night his unwanted beard thrust up another hundredth of an inch; and continuously, without a second's pause, his skin renewed itself, thrust on by innumerable subtle needless combinations of blind vitality.

Why should the clocks alone have stayed? There seemed to be no reason for their permanence, but in the next room, among the desert of unopened books, there was his workbench, clean, sharp-angled and precise with its rows of tools, broaches, dies and taps, throws, pliers of different shapes and sizes, all ranged so exactly that by now he could pick up each separate tool without taking his eyes from his work. This perfect arrangement called for years and years of use, but then of course he had begun years and years ago. To begin with the old grandfather in the hall could not be made to go: the watchmaker in the village was ill, so he had tinkered with it himself. A common thirty-hour movement, no more, but the simple mechanism, the wonderfully clear train of cause and effect, fascinated him and when he eventually mastered it, when the clock was ticking comfortably, he felt the strangest triumph. He bought books on clocks and even began to collect them in a small way: with the pleasure they brought him came the reproaches of his conscience – it was excessive and disproportionate to spend twelve hours a day for a week in wrestling inexpertly (he was inexpert then) with the escapement of a repeating verge – but in this case, and in this case alone, the reproach died of itself. The proposition that clocks should go was unanswerable. It was of absolute importance that they should go, should measure time exactly, and he concentrated all his powers to the task. He also bought more clocks.

'Well,' Dr Provis said, almost the last time he ever came to the house, 'I suppose it is a harmless way of killing time.' The remark was approving in substance but it was delivered with a kind of sneer: resenting this, he countered with a shrug of his shoulders and a half turn of his body. 'Ha, ha,' he replied. 'I think there is a difference, Provis, between *killing* time and *measuring* it.'

And then again, the full significance apart, this was an activity in which he could control all the factors: for clocks, rightly adjusted, would go; they had none of the intolerably frustrating imponderables of living things, yet for him they were alive enough. They exactly suited him; and his somewhat inhuman persistence suited them.

But in the last eighteen months the area of his pleasure had contracted. By now he had a very high degree of skill; he could cut a pair of pallets for any escapement the old clockmakers had ever made, and in case of need he could even produce a new scape wheel. But a new scape wheel was now a few hours' work: once it had been the toil of weeks, and once he had felt a tingling elation as the new wheel first revolved, ticked, and swung the doubtful pendulum. And by now he had an example of every variant; there was no new principle to be explored, and by the rules of his conscience he could not clutter up his house with clocks that would essentially be no more than duplicates of those he had already. Nor, now that he had the highest degree of manual ability, could he interfere with a clock that was going perfectly. Once, with no more than a half-imagined hint of irregularity, he had felt justified in stripping a clock and searching over every part of it, perfecting as he went; but he could not do so now. It must not be blind activity, doing for the sake of doing: it had to have the dignity of an end in view. That was a discipline which he must never, never break, or the whole thing would fall into an incoherent mockery.

He could do it all now, verge pallets, deadbeat pallets, ordinary anchor pallets . . . abruptly he remembered his evening's work. To make a long night's sleep more sure he had stayed up to finish the pallets of the small Knibb clock. He had finished the work entirely: he should have kept it for today. Without it the grey hours stretched away in an endless plain without anything at all to break the horrifying blank.

He lay there with the utter vacancy before him, and if no relief had come he might have screamed at last. But at a few minutes to six the arm lifted from the locking plate of the Graham bracket clock; the detent wheel spun three-quarters of a turn; the hoop wheel moved the distance of two pinion leaves; the clock was ready to strike six. It was immediately followed by the others. His practised ear heard the cocking of the clocks, and a springing hope made his thin heart beat.

There was no hope from the Knibb clock: that would be going accurately, with no shadow of a doubt. It was perfectly in beat and he had regulated its pendulum to the last hairs-breadth: he knew that clock. But it seemed to him that in his sleep he had heard the Tompion drop a stroke, as if the locking plate were worn: it had given trouble seven years before. Unless it were a dream it would be the Tompion, and it would probably have happened at three – he heard them through his sleep, he knew. And if that were so it would now strike five, not six. Five strokes instead of six: it would be an escape, a reprieve for one more day at least.

He listened intently, breathing shallow not to make a noise. The hands of the two chronometers crept in perfect unison towards the point of six. In the next room an assembly of long-case clocks, bracket clocks, wall clocks and table clocks stood poised to bell out the time. Only the equation clocks and the big regulator would not say anything: they had no bells. The others, the converted Cromwellian lantern clock, the early Fromanteel, the Tompion, the Graham deadbeat, the Mudge, the Quare, the Harrison, had all raised their striking trains. They stood there in no order, here and there about the book-lined room: he cared nothing for the beauty of their cases and some rested on rough trial benches, stripped of their hoods and covered from the dust with glass bell jars. Their ticking filled the room with a strange, depressingly urgent confusion of sound as they flicked the present by. Brass and iron insects, horrifying in their nakedness and numbers, perpetually eating time.

He waited, and as the moment drew nearer and nearer he clenched his fists under the bedclothes.

The first clock dropped and whirred; the pin gathered the tail of the hammer and bore down upon it. The first stroke rang out pure, but the second was lost in the clangour of the other clocks, whirring, striking faster or slower, all bawling out that it was six, pinning the moment down.

Straining his head up from his pillow he followed the deep, smooth tone of the Tompion through the competing din. At the fourth stroke his expression changed, and at the fifth his face lost its humanity. Now there was the racing pause between the fifth stroke of that one bell and the sound of the sixth, if it should ever come. The pause lengthened at last beyond the possibility of another stroke – it had missed for sure; but until the last of the clocks had finished, the Graham with its melancholy toll, his face did not change. Only then, when the last sound had died to a humming in the bell, did he allow his strained-up head to move. It sank down, and his eyelids fluttered over his eyes; but in another minute he was up, his fingers twitching with activity. He threw the dressing-gown over his shoulders and shuffled quickly to the door: and as he opened it he lowered his head to conceal the pale smile on his face.

The Chian Wine

WHEN FIRST HE CAME TO Saint-Felíu the middle and indeed
the dark ages still hung about the streets, while the beach was
classical antiquity itself. The village was so heavily fortified, with
two castles, five towers and a massive surrounding wall – so
heavily fortified against the Spaniards, the Algerine corsairs and
the inhuman people from the neighbouring province that there
was little room for the three thousand inhabitants. In the course
of centuries they had crammed their houses into narrow winding
lanes, so close that their roofs, viewed from the nearby hills,
resembled a swarm of bees, with never an open place to be seen.

Hanging from his window over one of these deep lanes in the
hope of air – he had been ordered to the Mediterranean for the
air – Alphard saw a world he had imagined long past and gone:
in those days mules paced by; women with loads poised on their
heads – heads that turned slowly, with infinite grace, to watch
the town-crier as he beat his drum and announced death or the
arrival of goat-cheese in the market-place. Tumblers appeared,
a family of dumb acrobats; they spread a dusty mat on the
cobbles and tumbled there in the street, turning somersaults and
contorting their lithe dusty bodies until it seemed they must come
apart, while their dumb, thin-faced children looked up with open
hands to the windows, catching the sparse shower of little coins:
and at All Hallows a Basque brought his dancing bear – they
slept together, by arrangement, in the cellar of Alphard's house.
The life of the village went on in the street. At noon the men lit
fires of vine-cuttings outside their doors, and the smell of grilling
fish wafted up; family quarrels also came out into the open, and
once he saw a stone-faced woman bring a chair and sit outside
a door all day and half the night until her husband should come

out. Every morning the women carried pots of filth mixed with ashes to the edge of the sea; every morning they and their daughters went to the pump recessed into the opposite house for water; every evening the grandmothers came back from the hills loaded with an immense faggot, held by a band across their foreheads. Every evening the ass that belonged to Alphard's landlord picked its way through the people, through the innumerable dogs and cats, and walked up the ladder-like stairs, followed some minutes later by its master, a man with a fair-sized vineyard and a market-garden, and one of the few who did not go out with the fishing-boats. The fishermen all had vineyards too in the terraced hills behind; and as peasants they lived by the rhythm of the sun for half the year, rising before dawn and sleeping in the heat of the day; in the due seasons they worked, sprayed, sulphured and pruned their vines, and every autumn, when the grapes came home in narrow carts or in eared tubs slung to the saddles of hump-backed mules – brass-studded, old crimson saddles – the streets ran purple and the smell of fermenting wine hung over the town. But as fishermen they lived by the moon, rising according to its motions and gathering in the darkness at the gate that gave on to the open strand. Sometimes they came back at moon-set, sometimes not until the bell was ringing for high mass, but more usually at dawn; and when, as it often happened, the cock upstairs made sleep impossible, Alphard would go down to watch them.

It was here on the beach that the ancient world showed purest: with his back to the town he could forget the two or three thousand intervening years. The sea was timeless, of course; and apart from the baroque church on his left the shore-line too was quite unchanged. The long, brilliantly-painted, high-prowed boats with pagan symbols on their bows might have been launched for the siege of Troy: the men who sailed them, rounding the jetty under their archaic lateen sails or sweeping in when the breeze failed them, might have been bringing back the Golden Fleece. In fact they usually brought anchovies; and when the catch was heavy they would heave to there at the edge of the sea, picking the silver fish out of their nets, tossing them into baskets. They would then carry the baskets up the beach – a line of men in red Phrygian caps and washed-blue drawers staggering abreast through the shingle with these gleaming fish between them, while their house-cats came running out, tails erect, each to its own basket. One day, when he was watching, a fisherman handed him a small amphora: after the south-east gales they often came up in the nets, tearing the delicate mesh, and usually the men broke them on the gunwale to make sure they would sink for good; but this was a neat little jar; it had done no harm; and Joseph thought Monsieur Alphard might like to have it, the seal being still intact.

It was indeed: beneath the incrustations of the sea the wax stated that Aristolochus of Chios had made this wine; and beneath the seal the wine, or at least a liquid of some sort, could be heard and felt. 'I shall try it some day,' said Alphard, setting it on a tripod from the hearth. 'Wine of the nth Olympiad! I shall try it one day, when I have good news.'

Now ten and twenty years had passed, a generation and more, and the wine still stood among the books, its seal unbroken. Alphard himself looked much the same, though his hair was greyer still, his sight was dim, his taste for music and for reading had almost gone, and even his longing for salvation; and his long solitary walks had shrunk to an occasional stroll along the jetty: his heart was quite shrivelled with habitual woe and its conse-quent selfishness; but he still cared for his everlasting bird and for the mice that came for its seed. He still looked with automatic eagerness for a letter in the morning, although by now he would not have known what to do with it if it had come; he still divided his morning, after early mass and the post, between *Le Monde* and the *Gazette de Lausanne*, lunched at home with his bird on a piece of cheese, dined at the Café du Commerce, and then sat for an hour or two over his coffee on the terrace, watching the passers-by and the sea beyond. He had become inured to the tragedy of growing old; his jets of rebellion had faded, and he knew that presently he too must die – he could hear the crier's voice announcing it before the goat's cheese and the eels. Yet still for the children of the village Monsieur Alphard in his dark and shabby suit was as unchanging and as little noticed as the clock-tower.

But Saint-Felíu had changed, changed almost out of recognition. Pert white houses had sprung up outside the walls, with red-brick well-heads over nothing, gnomes, plastic storks; drains carried the filth into the viscid sea, now spoilt at last; water ran in every house; bottled gas or electricity had replaced the faggot-bearers; the braying of the conch was no longer heard, announcing a haul of mackerel, to be given to anyone who chose to bring a dish; what was left of the fishing-fleet ran on diesel-oil, distributed by a scarlet pump in the sea-gate itself; and the well-clothed younger generation no longer spoke the ancient tongue. At the autumn fair of the patron saint raucous microphones had replaced the human voice; the bear, the magpie that picked your fortune from the cards, the sword-swallower, the performing fleas, the fire-eater, were no longer to be seen, nor the pig-faced woman; and the hand-cranked roundabout had given way to an enormous whirling mass of supersonic planes. Hotels abounded – the Café du Commerce was now the fifty-roomed Commanderie du Soleil – and in high summer the villagers wandered like strangers among the tourist hordes: out of an obscure sense of shame the men had laid aside their red caps and broad sashes and the women their white lace coiffes. The ass and the poultry had long since vanished from Alphard's house. After a marriage the sheets no longer hung from the window: no ribald voice called up 'How much for a pint of pigeon's blood?'

'Yet still,' he said to Halévy as they sat there after dinner, 'the spirit of the place is quite unaltered. This is not the Spanish coast, whose soul has gone, quite gone. Whatever you may say, these people have kept their integrity: this is a true, an eternal microcosm . . .'

'When I used to come here as a boy,' said Halévy, 'Louise made the best fish soup known to man – pounded lobster-claws, a sea-devil's liver, the garlicked bread singing from the pan. Now she has hired a fellow with a tall white cap, and the soup comes out of a packet: I detected the criminal industrial crumbs, uncooked, this very evening. And this is not even the tourist-season. There is no excuse. No: it breaks my heart to contradict you, but these people have lost their sense of beauty. The doctored wine alone, and what they buy from me, must convince you of that. Here too the past has died: two thousand years of tradition have died! There is no bridge between the jet-age and the past.'

'Monsieur le Curé,' cried Alphard, rising from his chair and bowing to the cassocked priest, 'good evening to you. There,' he said to Halévy, 'there is your bridge – one of your bridges. The Church has not changed.'

Halévy smiled, raising his shoulders and spreading his hands; but he only said, 'He seems an excellent man, to be sure; it does me good to see him.'

Alphard felt the strength of Halévy's tactfulness and the naivety of his own remark in the present circumstances, and he cried, 'Not changed essentially, not here, I mean. The vernacular is so close to Latin any way that it makes little difference. The natural piety of the village is the same as it always was. Take my grocer Fifine, for example: she has sugar blessed on Saint Blaise's day, and whenever you have a sore throat she gives you half a dozen lumps – *gives* them, I say. Because to sell a blessed object would be gross impiety. There is your true mediaeval spirit, vigorously alive in the midst of electric refrigerators. Or take our curious vespers this day week, in which they have used the vernacular ever since the night of time.' He paused, recollecting that the traditional proceedings at Saint-Felíu on Good Friday were far too truly mediaeval to describe to Halévy. He was an Avignon Jew who had recently opened a small gallery outside the sea-gate, not far from the church, where he exhibited a few young painters and bought antiques for his brother's shop in Paris. He was old and fat and he had a mane of white hair; he meant to retire to Saint-Felíu, with the gallery for fun. Hitherto he had known the village only in the summer.

'What is so curious about your vespers?' he asked.

'Or take our bull-fight at Assumption,' said Alphard, feigning not to hear. 'There is continuity for you . . . and apart from anything else, these people are still at the mercy of the sea for one half of their living and of the sun for the other half: they dare not presume, or go whoring after other gods. They must keep the ancient ways, so long as the ancient ways keep them. But speaking of continuity, I should like to show you my jar of Chian wine one day. The seal is unbroken – a seal pressed at least two thousand years ago! We might even try it.'

Halévy did not follow the sequence of these observations – how could he? – but he saw that Alphard wished to change the subject, and he said that he should be very happy to see and even, if he were allowed, to try the Chian wine. 'I shall be back before Easter, to get the place ready for the tourists. First I have to go to Gosol, where a man tells me his cousin has a Romanesque Virgin he might sell. I doubt the story very much. A true twelfth-century Virgin is scarcely to be hoped for today – all that were portable have already been sold. But I shall go: I love those strong, pitiless faces, even when they are fakes.'

Good Friday's dawn could not be seen for the clouds coming up from the south: a hot brooding day with a great many flies about. They even came into the cool depths of the church where Alphard was listening to a foolish young Dominican rattling away – an involved, enthusiastic sermon about ecumenism. The friar was in favour of it, but that was all his hearers could make out, since the reasoning was tenuous in the first place and the preacher had lost even that thread early on. The greater part of the congregation sat quietly as the excited, electrically amplified voice went on and on, booming from loudspeakers hung in the aisles. The acoustics were poor, but even if the Dominican had been content with the voice God gave him most of the older women would not have understood his French. They stared before them in a mild, holy stupor, watching the candles flicker or the choirboys scratching themselves as they read their comics: they did not seem to mind the flies, either. Alphard wondered at their patience. He himself had outlived his desires or had seen them dwindle into mere velleities – nothing mattered very much – but he had not outlived testiness, and as he brushed away a cluster of heavy, sluggish flies he muttered 'frying in Hell . . . frying in Hell.' He had had the greatest respect and affection for John XXIII as a man, but as a pope he thought him utterly disastrous – the results of his actions were utterly disastrous. Temerity, wild zeal, enthusiasm . . . Could it really be true that he was a freemason, a Communist?

The tedious friar came down from the pulpit at last, but he contrived to give the mass a new-fangled twist at the very end: if Alphard understood him right he asked for the congregation's blessing.

'At least one will know what to expect this afternoon,' he said indignantly, dipping his hand into the dried-up stoup. 'That will be a comfort.' Their old priest would be taking the traditional vespers, as he always did: a dear man, untouched by modernism – nothing histrionic there – no innovations to be feared. The moment he passed the door heat enveloped him completely; it was as though he had walked into a physical substance, for now the sirocco had set in. The flies were thicker still, hatching in multitudes from some hidden filth; and looking up to the ominous sky he saw that the mountains behind the town had that particular livid glow that often came before a storm.

'I hope it will not spoil the children's day,' he said. Not that he liked children: and most of the present crop, born since the village had grown so much richer from the tourists, were rough, aggressive, ill-mannered. They despised their illiterate parents; and their worshipping illiterate parents gave them far too much money. Far too much to the adolescent boys especially, who shrieked about the village streets on mopeds. Not that the girls were much better: a bold, gum-chewing, confident set. It seemed an unhappy generation for all its wealth; old and hard so very young. But still he hoped their day would not be spoiled. It was a particular ceremony, essentially for them; and it linked them with a very distant past – to the Crusades, in all probability. Many of them were dressed up for it already. He saw Fifine, leading her niece and her hulking great nephew by the hand. The children (if the hairy Albert could be called a child) walked stiffly, their arms away from their fine new clothes, and the free hand of each held an enormous rattle, of the kind that whirls

about its stem. Both looked over-excited, and there was a glow
of anticipation on their aunt's Visigothic face as she steered them
through the throng.

A few yards farther on the shutters of the gallery were up,
but to his surprise Alphard saw Halévy in the door, sweeping
vigorously. He was bare to the waist and sweat ran through the
grizzled mat on his bosom: he was wearing a beaded skull-cap,
however, presumably against the dust. Averting his eyes from
the mat, Alphard said, 'Are you back already?'

Halévy said that in fact he was – that he had found no
Madonna – four hundred miles in pursuit of a myth – and that
he was profoundly discouraged.

'Come and try my Chian wine this evening,' said Alphard.
'Come at half past six.'

'I should be very happy,' said Halévy. 'Thank you. Such a
privilege.' They talked about the weather – Halévy said the
mountains made him think of El Greco – and while they were
talking a horseplaying band of youths and boys, throwing sand
and stones at one another, lurched into them. 'Jean-Paul, what
are you about? Dédé, say you are sorry to the gentleman,' cried
Alphard.

No apology, no reply: only a 'tough guy' look.

'Ill-mannered brutes,' he said. 'Really, I am ashamed for the
village. I beg your pardon.'

'They all seem over-excited today,' said Halévy. 'All the children. What are those rattles they are carrying, and why the
saucepans?' But before Alphard could reply, he went on, 'Oh, I
have a horrible piece of news for you. The municipality has
forbidden sardines to be grilled in the street: it seems the tourists
do not like the smell.'

'They may forbid until they grow black in the face,' cried
Alphard, flushing. 'The past will have its rights. The past will
rise up and have its rights.'

Alphard was not used to receiving guests, and after his lunch
and his siesta he spent a considerable time setting his room in
order, brushing the table, cleaning two glasses, moving chairs,

angering the bird. Outside it was even hotter, dustier, and more oppressive. He was late for vespers and he slipped into a side-chapel: the ceremony was perfectly familiar to him now, although it had seemed so strange twenty years ago, and he 'found his place' as it were, without hesitation. The remaining psalms and antiphons followed their universal course and then the ancient local variation began, in the vernacular – the Magnificat and its antiphon, followed by the curé's address. Alphard understood the language pretty well, and as the address never varied year by year he followed it with ease: yet it was not really a very interesting address, except on historical grounds, being an allegory showing the relationship between the Church and the unbelievers under the outward likeness of the conduct of the lion towards the ass, taken straight from a mediaeval bestiary; and as the curé's triple r's and explosive participles rolled round the church Alphard's attention wandered. Sometimes his eyes strayed over the shrouded form of Saint Eulalie, following the ecstatic baroque swirl beneath the sheet; sometimes he looked at the instruments of the Passion, the lance, the sponge, the cruel pincers, hanging unveiled beyond the saint; and sometimes he gazed at the packed congregation. On most days their conduct left a great deal to be desired; awe and even common respect were wanting, and the people, above all the children, usually whispered, giggled and stared about. But now, in spite of the heat, the flies, their new clothes, and the temptation of their rattles, whistles, saucepans and drums, they were exemplary; every year they delighted in the piece about the lion, and this year their interest was even greater. Leaning forward in their seats they listened with the keenest attention to the unvarying description of the beast: 'His head is the head of a king and he has a terrible neck and a mane and his chest is vast and square: he holds his great tail high above the ground. His flattened legs come down to his huge feet, which are divided, with long hooked claws . . . the ass alone resists him, braying there in the wilderness.'

The curé never used the microphone, and his fine deep voice filled the church, each word as distinct as a stone. The description was done and now the allegory was to be unfolded and made plain: here he might well have lost his grasp upon his hearers as he went on, right through the list; but they knew the climax was coming, and they never stirred. '. . . and the tail of the lion is justice, divine justice high over us. The lion's leg is flattened, and here we see the coming of the Passion: the shape of his foot is God's own sign that the world is to be held by the clenched fist. The sharp crooked claws are vengeance against the Jews; and the ass, who is the evil ass but the Jews? With the terrible face of a lion He will appear to the Jews when He judges them, for they damned themselves . . .'

Now the tension was growing to its height. Alphard had heard this twenty times and more, but he too leaned forward on his chair.

'For they damned themselves: the Jews betrayed their king.' In the momentary pause all the children drew in their breath: every mouth was open, every tongue shaped to form the sound of D; and the moment the priest cried 'Death to the Jews!' they all burst out 'Death to the Jews!' an enormous shrilling, instantly drowned by the even greater din of rattles, whistles, saucepans, drums as they rushed in a body from the church, leaving the adults to listen to the collect, read in a mild and unemphatic routine voice.

To recover from the shattering din and to avoid the racing bands of children as they howled and whistled in the streets, blind with excitement, Alphard usually walked on the jetty for half an hour; but today he went straight back along the beach towards his house. The sirocco had dropped: a brooding calm.

There was indeed something unusual about the general hubbub: less of the high small-child piping and more of the crack-voiced adolescent bawl, with here and there a woman's shriek and the bass roaring of a man. But Alphard's mind was far away until he reached the diesel-pump. Here there was a dense crowd, an impenetrable swarm – every youth and child in Saint-Felíu – and something was terribly amiss. The fun had turned oh so sour: the smell of a bull-fight or worse. In the heat and the dust and the shouting he tried to push through: somewhere in the middle of that tight mob outside Halévy's gallery there was a rhythmic crash; and striving, thrusting his way through the smaller children on the fringe he saw half a dozen great boys swinging a baulk of wood, a launching stretcher from the beach, swinging it end-on against the door – a battering-ram. All round the edge there were women screaming, grasping at their own children: astonished men and dogs came running. Alphard shouted 'Jean-Baptiste, Jojo, put it down – stop, stop at once,' but as he tottered there, children underfoot, children pulling at his legs, the door gave way and there was Halévy, terribly pale, his white hair streaming, with an antique, bell-mouthed gun in his hands. A high triumphant roar, the shriek of rattles, a shower of stones, and he fired. Alphard went down. Had he been hit? No. But the swarm of children struggling over him three-deep kept him in the dust and by the time he struggled to his feet it had happened. The jet of diesel-oil played straight into the shop: Alphard stood there, bumped into, unsteady, tossed from side to side, amazed, tears running down his face, shouting 'Stop, stop, stop,' and the flames shot up, straight into the windless air, mounting high, high under the black and swirling smoke, an enormous fire.

The men were there, hitting, kicking, turning off the pump. Alphard turned away and he came face to face with a small beaming round-faced child who had not yet understood the change, a child that danced still, marvelling at the fire, waving her rattle and chanting 'Death, death to the Jews.'

The Virtuous Peleg

EVERY YEAR a great concourse of people come to the place they call Kevin's tomb in the mountains and they pray him to intercede for them, for although he is not a saint upon the calendar – he is not that Kevin, but another – he is much revered in those parts which is no doubt a great solace to him as he burns for ever in the extreme torment aggravated as it is by every device and artifice known to the fiend of hell. The pilgrims suppose him to be well placed to intercede for them, in which they are right, by far the most of them being false lechers, damned in every inch.

Kevin was a young man when he first lived in the beehive cells that stand around Deara. He had no inclination to the warfare which was the occupation of his sept, nor to work, and equally none to women; he was as soft as a cat and sober in his discourse and he slept inordinately, which made him fat despite the diet of Deara. In the first years of his life with the holy monks he was unable to avoid a small share of the work, but when his young cousin Peleg was allowed to join him this was no longer the case, which was a consolation to Kevin.

Peleg had little enough inclination in his nature to work, but he revered his cousin, who had an awful and persuasive way, and had been held up to Peleg as a man perfect all the days of his life, and daily young Peleg forced his nature and conquered this aversion and cleaned the cell and tilled the apron of garden and carried stones from the common field. The carrying of them, even the huge square ones, was easy enough for Peleg, being the length and breadth of an ox as he was, and that of the larger kind.

They did not hold Peleg in much estimation at Deara, for he

had no learning and if they had known he was incapable of his letters even, Peleg would have been put out of the beehive cells and they would have made him go back to watching his father's herd of swine, a meagre herd that was watched already by his nine brothers.

Peleg was humble in his mind and freely acknowledged his deficiencies; he studied meekness and told over his letters by day and by night, but they ran by like water or the mist and he had no hold upon them, which made him low in his spirits: his mind would also turn of itself to young women, especially to the three daughters of Turlough who were so kind and loving to him; and whenever his mind did this he would leap up and plunge into the deep pool to his neck and tell over his letters. Kevin told him each time how wicked he was, and the monks would offer to scourge him at any time, by day or by night, whenever he felt himself invaded by the flesh or the Devil.

It was at about this time that news came to Deara of Brothen's wonderful voyage to the Picts, how he went on a millstone that happened to be on the shore, and he sleeping most of the way and without oar, rudder or sail, and how he had baptized seven Pictish kings in one day, eleven dukes with their families, with many other nobles and four large fields of ordinary people.

The news edified the monks of Deara, as well it might; but it seemed to Peleg that he noted a certain restraint, almost a sourness like that you may see on the face of the second man when he says how well the first has run. Peleg too felt that the honour of Deara was in some way lowered by this success from the north, and daily after he had returned thanks for the spread of the faith he prayed that some one of the holy men of Deara might be moved to take to the sea, to be wafted by ghostly hands to the pagan coast, there to meet a bloody martyrdom with unflinching delight or to convert fourteen kings with the numerous family of each while the sun should stand in admiration and the day grow long enough for the numbers of the common to pass the end of counting. He prayed especially that the reverend Kevin might be the chosen vessel: he prayed with fervour and his four bones were flayed and his blood soaked into the stone.

Days passed, and the monks of Deara looked at one another sideways and anxious, but none went near the strand.

Peleg watched Kevin for signs of a trance or an exaltation perhaps, but Kevin still moved slowly and slept the day long in his cell, waking to eat or to go through the motions of worship. The only hopeful sign at all was his increasing absent-mindedness; for day after day now he would forget that the stir-about was for two and he would eat it all, as well as the nuts.

Many days Peleg fasted and that apart from the usual fasts of Deara which were known in all the Christian world: it was for his soul's health, as he found one evening, it being Friday and his birthday. There was an angel sitting on the heap of stones by the side of the common field that Peleg was picking for ever.

'Now, Peleg,' said the angel. 'God and Mary to you.'

'God and Mary to you and Patrick, sir,' replied Peleg, with good manners all over his ugly face.

'I have two messages for you, Peleg,' said the angel, and he stuck a moment in his speech, and Peleg could see that the messages had flown out of his memory and it was a question whether he could get them back or no.

'I have two messages for you, Peleg,' he repeated, slowly and leaning upon the importance of his words.

'I am much obliged for your kindness, your reverence,' said Peleg. 'It must have been the weary road, the day being close and thunder coming.' It was a little at random that he was talking, to save the angel from embarrassment.

'Now I will tell you what it is, Peleg,' said the angel, getting up off the heap of stones. 'Should you like to try a couple of falls with me? You was always the one for wrestling, I think.'

'If it would not be too forward in me, sir, I should welcome it of all things,' said Peleg. 'To try a couple of falls with your honour would give me all the pleasure in life.'

The angel stretched his arms and stamped his feet; he was a cheerful angel, the sort St Paul warned women about, and Peleg thought he had taken drink upon the way.

'I shall dust your jacket, mind,' said the angel, and he was right, for in five minutes he had put Peleg down on the flat of his back three times with a bang that made the dust fly up.

'Now sit down upon the stone, joy,' said the angel, 'for you are pale in the face, I see, and I will tell you the two messages. The first is, "Heaven helps those as help themselves," and the second is, "There are those who seem more than they appear to others or themselves notwithstanding the appearance of some as they would appear in the first place; or the contrary."'

Peleg thanked the angel many times over, and asked might he hear the blessed words again.

'Why, no, Peleg,' replied the angel slowly, getting himself ready to go. 'I doubt it would be exactly right for me to repeat them, being the way it is. But they will certainly echo again, and bear the most elegant fruit.'

So Peleg walked with the angel to the edge of the field, where the path came in, and said, 'If your reverence chooses to take the road, the path that crosses the bog by those willows is the best, and the second house on the way is Seamus's, where is the best refreshment and easy bedding, with butcher's meat every day of the week almost.'

'I know it,' said the angel. 'I was there on my way.' And he said as he went, 'Health and glory and salvation to you, Peleg,' and Peleg replied, 'A hundred thousand thanks to you, your reverence, and glory and health and happiness for ever to you.'

The messages did indeed re-echo in Peleg's mind, they churned about until the inside of his head was full of night, and there was no sense in it. He went wandering over the bog in a daze until it was dark, and then he went vacantly into his cell where Kevin was asleep, and lay down on the hard floor.

He could not remember going to sleep, but he woke up very suddenly in the dead hour of the night, his mind a blaze of illumination: there was a little sickly moon but enough to see by and he looked closely at Kevin who was in the very depth of stupor and his mouth open. Peleg eased up his chin gently to improve his appearance, and gently, like a woman, gathered him up in his clothing as he lay there and carried him out of the cell. As he had often done, he struck the lintel with his bowed shoulders and bore off a handsbreadth of skin, but the pain did not discommode him nor the prodigious vast weight of his cousin and his bulk overflowing.

The dew was thick on the grass and his footsteps showed clear, running straight to the strand. There were boats there, and three millstones of different sizes, but millstones were for the beneficed clergy, abbots, bishops and deans, and Peleg put Kevin into a little neat curach. The sleeping Kevin groaned and settled himself and Peleg sat on a thwart while the tide swept them out and away on the far, broad ocean.

For hours and hours Peleg sat there in a holy calm, contemplating the beauty of the calm sea, for it was like a small pond in its calmness and there was the long path of the moon behind them. The air was warm and sweet like hay to smell and the curach slipped through the quiet water, creaking a little and the water making a little slipping noise under it.

Dawn came up with the glory of heaven and still Kevin slept. Peleg longed to wake him so that they could be speaking of the voyage; sometimes he moved with more noise than he needed, and sometimes he coughed, but it was not until just before tierce that Kevin moved. The fat man gaped stupidly at Peleg, with his mouth dragged open, and when Peleg bade him rejoice because they were on the sea moving fast with the push of unseen hands towards the heathen shore he made no reply. He stared wildly round the pale bowl of the sky, green and grey where it met the sea all round and no land, no land at all; unending waters stretching away and away to the edge of the world and the sun glittering on them. He moaned aloud as he sat there crouched, and Peleg told him of his angel and about the glory of their approaching mission. Kevin made no answer, but when Peleg said he thought they might sing a loud prayer, he leapt up and stood balancing in the curach as it rocked and screamed curses at Peleg with the worst words in the world so that Peleg wondered how he had ever come to know them: and Peleg grew weary of hearing Kevin staining his soul and he rocked the boat the way Kevin was not expecting it so he fell in over the edge and swam in the sea among the fishes of the deep, and monsters came into his mind as well as the fear of drowning. So Kevin was in a great taking and nearly dead from his various fears and the furious amount of salt water he had taken in while shouting under the sea and breathing there too, and he spoke civilly to his cousin Peleg to have him into the curach again, which Peleg did, though with difficulty.

Now Kevin lay in the bottom of the curach weeping with cold and so frightened that he had not the look of a white pudding, far less a man, and Peleg sat on the tail end of the boat thinking, while he trailed his hand in the water.

A little spirit came back into Kevin as the sun dried him and he asked had Peleg brought any food, but Peleg had not brought any food; then he said they ought to go back because he had no licence from his superior to be converting heathens and because there was a book in his cell of great power and efficacity and he did not know how he could turn them from their heathenish ways without its help, and if Peleg would turn back now he would get the book and the licence from his superior as well as some relics and they would start again in a more respectable vessel than a common curach stinking of old fish the way it did, and dangerous with its thin, leaky sides.

'There is no sail, reverend Kevin, nor oars, nor a rudder to turn with: furthermore, we are impelled by unseen hands.'

So Kevin lay down again in the bottom of the boat and groaned until the sun went down into the sea behind them and night spread over the waters and still the curach slipped on with the push of unseen hands.

In the morning the sun was in front of them again and at their side was a grey island rising high out of the sea: Peleg awoke from a kind sleep and there by the side of the curach was a seal watching for him to wake. He blessed the good seal, which was his custom, and the seal brought him a fish to his hand.

The island was full of sea-birds, white, black and pied, as full as a hive of bees, and their screaming awoke Kevin, who said they were fiends and cursed them. He wished to go on to the island to escape the sea and would have swum, for they passed very near, but he saw the seals as thick as a fair and he was afraid. 'They are fiends,' he said. 'The sea is full of fiends.'

The island sank into the sea behind them, but before it was quite down they saw land ahead stretching far to the either hand. Presently Peleg could discern the mouth of a broad river, and the curach went up into it, over the bar with no more than three inches of water covering it at this state of the tide, but that so godly quiet that they slipped over with no danger, and now Peleg saw on his left hand a sandy waste and on his right hand a rich, fruitful country, green and red where the soil showed.

Kevin's heart and courage had grown since they had crossed the bar, and he was talking when the curach grounded gently in the sand of the right-hand shore. The jar threw him flat on his face, so Peleg picked him out of the boat and put him on the dry sand, where he sank down in a heap, gasping. Peleg looked and he saw the neat curach turned about already and running easily through the water, which had waves now, though small. He watched it going on the broad waters and he felt a small quell in his heart, but only for a moment, he being maintained by the zeal of his mission.

They went up the shore, Kevin blaming Peleg very bitterly for letting the curach go, and into a green wood, where Peleg lit a fire, having returned thanks, and he cooked the fish, which was a mullet; and the heathen of those parts surrounded them in the bushes.

The first they knew of the heathen was a terrible howling and an ululating that would have daunted the heart of an emperor, it was so near and the men unseen. Then there was a shower of arrows and stones that tore the green leaves and the heathen rushed in upon them. They were painted orange and they carried long, bare knives and it was the way they had to flay all strangers on their coast. Peleg and Kevin without drawing breath for one peaceable word sprang, leapt and sped through the trees and beyond inland with all the agility in the world, running so fast they passed the startled deer, and the heathen ran after them to have their hides, but their heathenish cries and howling delayed them, whereas Peleg and Kevin ran without a word, seeing they needed their breath and could not be sparing it in hallooing and bawling aloud.

It was a wonder to see the fat man run with his face and belly quivering and shaking like the bag of a cow, but soon he faltered and cried out to Peleg, who took him by the hand and they raced over the strange country with flying strides and the heathen drawn out behind them, howling angrily in the distance, angrier as the distance grew.

For hours and hours they ran until they came to heathery land, high and rolling, with standing meres and bogs and they could see clear miles behind them with nobody following. It was a harsh and desolate country, and its brooks ran dark between black, steep banks. White mist curled in the lower parts and already with the coming of the night the mist was rising to cover the whole country.

On the top of a craggy piece they lay in a cave, a great deep cave that went back and back, and Peleg's mind troubled him because he had avoided his martyrdom and because he had uttered no peaceable or godly word to the heathen. Kevin wept from exhaustion and lasting terror and the pain of his feet as well as for the memory of the grey mullet uneaten by the woodland fire: he uttered a few watery prayers and slept in his moaning. But Peleg remained waking, working in his mind, and when the devils of the waste-land came they found him awake.

The sight of so many fiends at once appalled Peleg beyond the power of speech, and Kevin turned the colour of lead, with never a word in his mouth, though it opened and closed. The devils sat about the cave, quite easy, and lit it up with the effulgence of their persons.

The captain of the devils, a grand spotted one, spoke in a loud commanding voice to Peleg and said: 'Now, Peleg, we don't want but two words with you, just renounce the Trinity at once, if you please, and we'll cry quits.'

But Peleg said never a word, and he made no answer again when the captain of the devils said, 'It is only a form, you know; there is nothing to it, at all.' So the devil grew angry and sent for a rack and a portable furnace and when they had put down the rack, together with a variety of instruments like iron flails and saws which the messengers brought of their own motion, with a ringing clash on the floor and had set up the furnace the way the cave stank of brimstone the captain nodded to Peleg and said, 'We'll sort you directly, my man.' Then he turned sharp on Kevin and gave him the same order and he said, 'Kevin, stand up at once and renounce the Trinity out of hand,' and he stamped fire.

Kevin stood up at once, but Peleg cried to him to have courage. The devil nodded to a great hairy thing of uncertain shape that had been standing behind Peleg's neck all this time, breathing on him, and it struck him down and gagged him. He lay and heard Kevin renounce the Trinity and everything else he could lay his mind to, and indeed Kevin blasphemed until even the devils stretched their eyes and looked behind them.

'It's all very well,' said the oldest hob-devil to the Captain secretly behind his hand like a man at a fair, 'but we shan't have his soul for certain like this: he must be damned of his own will, you know.'

The Captain said, 'Sure, you're right, my dear, but if he's got a soul at all there would be hardly any taste in it, or flavour, as you might say. We'll not spend anything on getting it, so. However, try an ordinary temptation or two by all means, if you're so inclined.'

Then they turned to Peleg and threatened him like blackguards, but Peleg said, 'You old blackguards, the back of my hand to you all.'

Then they had him to the rack, but it was too small by half for one of his length, and even when they had it wound right up it hardly stretched him above an inch. So they started on him with their flails, but they had small confidence in them, seeing that Peleg's father had always beaten his sons whenever they did wrong with a holy rage far beyond the emulation of devils, and Peleg had often done wrong in his young days – nearly every day, indeed. When they were tired and had spoilt three of their flails they stopped and took Peleg into an inner cave. There they made him sleep and let him rest while they considered of what they should do. He woke up to find the three daughters of Turlough in the cave, they who had been so kind and loving to him before he went to Deara after holiness, and a voice said in his ear that he could have whichever he chose as a reward for his fortitude. But the devil himself could not have told the confusion in Peleg's heart at the sight of the three together, by reason of the passages he had had with each separately, and Peleg blushed fiery red and hid his face. The she-devils who personated the daughters of Turlough thought themselves scorned and they stepped out of the cave with bitter anger and said they had no business with geldings, nor with unnatural men, they said.

This put the devils out of countenance, for they saw they were improving Peleg's chance of salvation hour by hour, and this was poison and death to their minds. When they had tempted him with meat and drink and fire and water as well as with gold and silver and the promise of land with no success, they said he must be more holy than he looked, and the great scholar of the world, no doubt.

'There is only one way with these scholars,' said the Captain and he called for a pen. For seventy-three days they kept Peleg by while the Captain worked fourteen and fifteen hours a day and his claws grew long and curved for want of the wear of exercise and fiends ran hither and yon with sheets of paper at every hour on the heather of the waste-land. At the end the Captain had two books written, the one of elegant poems so lewd that they would have been a danger to St Anthony, and the other, in fine elm boards with silver clasps, a book of homilies so eloquent that they would have struck Chrysostom dumb, and they poisoned through and through with the creeping poison of a heresy so persuasive that no ecclesiastic much under the degree of a saint could have withstood it.

They put them by Peleg while he slept and they penned him up with them and a good, clear light and a reading desk and no other kind of diversion at all until his beard grew to the middle of his chest and they judged he had had time to damn himself. But Peleg had only opened the books once apiece to see were there capitals painted on gold with every variety of colour and beasts interlacing, but there were not, the Captain having no turn that way, and he had closed them without taking more thought, for his strength was not in reading and indeed he could not exactly recall above half a dozen of the letters themselves at this distance from Deara. He had spent his time in mortification and prayer and learning the meekness that he lacked, and particularly in praying for his cousin Kevin, which had done his own soul so much good that it was now practically white and in better shape than it had been since he was first capable of sin.

It was on a Friday that the Captain sent two devils to the inner cave to fetch Peleg, and when they opened the door they understood how it was with him and they turned grey and stood there abashed. Now Peleg had had plenty of time to collect himself and to consider what he would do and he was accustomed to the sight of fiends, however plain. He came at them briskly and struck their heads together for the glory of God so hard that they gave out a sound like a mallet on wood and no other but lay there like sacks. And he stepped over them and came to the outer cave where the Captain of the devils was waiting and the Captain saw how it was with him and stood up, grey in his colour and shrinking. Peleg struck him down for the glory of the Trinity and bent him back so that his horns, which were his pride and joy, locked in the long curl of his hoofs, and Peleg bowled him in a hoop out of the cave and down the slope to a bottomless mere, where he lies still, mopping and mowing for ever in a powerful rage and heating the waters of the mere so that neither fish nor frog can live there, far less breed, whereas before it was the great place for the snigging of eels.

Then he took his cousin Kevin from the corner of the cave and asked had any of the other devils a word in their mouths, but they standing mumchance and looking meaner than any book can say he gave them all a great devastating curse and walked out into the light of the day.

He walked with his head in the air for seven miles, glorying in the verdant world and the blue of the sky and longing for some honest meat, and Kevin followed him with the meanness of hell showing in his face. Then Peleg remembered his humility and made Kevin go in front, and they came to the edge of a chasm. This chasm was a furlong across and far deeper and it

barred their way, and as Peleg stood there on the edge considering it and marvelling at its black depth and the wafting fog in it
Kevin thought of the thirty bags of gold and the life-long idleness
and safety for ever that the oldest hob-devil had promised him
by the holiest oath if he would do Peleg a mischief, and he
considered too how that he was already damned for sure, and,
trembling all over, he crept behind Peleg and with a desperate
moan he hurled his weight on Peleg's back and Peleg fell with
his two hands outstretched grasping the air.

Before Peleg had fallen a yard the fiends of hell were upon
Kevin and they snatched him away to their own place, he screaming like a stuck pig about their oath and they laughing white-hot
tongues of fire.

And the angel at the bottom of the chasm peered up through
the shifting fog and altered his feet, and as he caught Peleg he
said, 'There, easy now, Peleg.' And he put him down and looked
kindly in his face and said, 'Sit down upon the flat rock, Peleg,
for you are pale in the face, I find.' 'God put a flower on you,
joy,' said Peleg, and thanked him with all the civility at his
command and many elegant turns of speech.

The angel let him breathe awhile and said, 'Stand up now,
Peleg, for I have a message for you. It is you must go down to
the sea again, to the heathen of the pagan shore, and there are
fourteen kings of the pagan shore to whom you must preach the
faith, for now there is virtue in you. That is the message: and
now we shall take a glass or two together, for I have a bottle
conveniently near at hand, and it appears that I will not see you
again until I stand with my trumpet to sound you in over the
mossy walls of Paradise.'

A Passage of the Frontier

THE THREAT from the north grew stronger, and the stateless persons and undesirables began to move towards the Mediterranean and the southern frontiers. Then suddenly, overnight, the full danger was there, immediately at hand: blind tanks roared down the motorways, endless lines of trucks full of infantrymen, guns, the political police; and far ahead of them all parachutists were setting up roadblocks, directing the military traffic, requisitioning houses, carrying out the first arrests. All trains were stopped, all main roads, bridges, tunnels closed.

Now plans that needed more than a few hours for their execution were abandoned; now the nearest road was the only road; and before dawn on Friday a hired car put Martin down at the end of a charcoal-burner's track on the high slope of the Coma du Loup.

They would have preferred to get him out of the country by way of Switzerland, but that was impossible now: all frontiers were closed to those with no legal identity. Encantats was the only solution, a small Pyrenean smuggling centre inland from Andorra, even higher and more remote. It possessed no motor-road into France, but as even the mule-track was guarded they had him set down in the Coma du Loup with a drawing of the smugglers' path and a carrier-bag of food; and Jacob lent him a hard-weather coat. The driver also had an envelope of paper money, to be handed over at the last moment; but he did not see fit to hand it over – he turned his car, throwing up loose earth, bark and scraps of charcoal on the blackened ground. Martin made stiff, inadequate gestures to guide him – stiff because he was still cramped by the long night's headlong flight. The driver took no notice until the car was round; then he put his huge face out of the window, and through the smoke and steam he shouted, 'You follow the river. The ford is the boundary. Cross and follow the right-hand stream. You can't miss it.'

'Thank you very much,' said Martin. 'Good-bye.'

'The stream on the right,' said the driver, holding up his left hand. 'I've never been there myself, but you can't miss it.' He gave Martin a cold nod, crashed the gear home and jerked off down the track. The car was gone in a moment, but for some time it could still be heard, winding down through the trees in the darkness. Martin did not move until the sudden chatter of a jay startled him into motion, breaking a spell that might have lasted until the rising of the sun. He picked up his paper bag and began to climb through the trees.

This was near the top of the forest: he had passed up through the last half-mile of beeches, and now on the higher slope it was all pines, scaley pines standing steep from the mountainside. On his right hand the broad stream ran fast and deep, fall and pool, fall and pool all the way, and the brown water racing between high banks of rock.

At the beginning, under the beeches, there had been a clear path, indeed several paths; but up here the pine-needles did not hold the track. There were great heaps made by ants with wandering lines among them that might have been made by any number of beasts; but nothing like a distinct trail. The slope increased, and soon he was gasping; and as the day grew warmer, so green clouds of pollen began to drift through the forest, an enormous vegetable act of love. He came to a rocky shoulder where the trees grew sparse – no canopy to shut him in – and far over he saw the opposing mountain-flank, smoking green as though the whole forest were on fire.

In another hour he reached a level stretch of the river, a place where he could reach the water and wash and drink at last. Drying, he sat on a grey boulder and picked raspberries. They grew all along among the rounded boulders, now that the trees were thinner, together with columbines and yellow lilies. Out there in the stream, where a fallen trunk had made an island, stood another lily, a tall purple spotted one whose petals curved back to touch its stem; and lying among the leaves at its foot, a blue crumpled packet that had held cigarettes. Nearer, in the gin-clear water, a rusting sardine-tin. 'Might this be the ford?' he said, and looked more attentively at the banks. Yes, certainly this was a place where one could cross, perhaps the first he had seen between the deep-cut banks; and certainly people had been crossing here for years and years, since the steep rock on the far bank was worn into steps. And farther up another stream joined this, as both the drawing and the driver had said.

So this was the frontier itself. He stepped into the water, unbelievably cold, and stood for a while with a foot on either side of the middle-line: then he waded over, to another country.

It feels much the same, however, he said, looking back to the bank he had left. The same trees over there, the same wild falls of rock, furred over with dry grey lichen; and a very small bird continually flitted to and fro across the water, busily from tree to tree, minding him no more than if he had been a cow.

Where it ran along the difficult course of the right-hand stream, the path was clear again; and often whole stretches of the bare mother-rock were trodden out into a smoothness that showed the grain and inner colour of the schist; but sometimes the steady upward sweep of the mountain was broken by broad level steps where the river soaked promiscuously among the bushes and the swampy earth, the coarse hummocks of grass and sour brown pools; here, and even more in the frequent steep gulleys, the path would divide, wander and dwindle into unmeaning ribbons. Yet time and again when he seemed to have lost it for ever his hand would reach out for a branch whose bark was already worn to the wood, or as he leapt a small ravine his foot would land in a place worn deep by other men. The path always reappeared, and it led him high, high towards the last thinning-out of the trees; now they stood wide apart, each one lower, with its under-branches touching the now frosty ground, and each looking older by far. The whole character of the forest had changed; the trees no longer hemmed him in, but stood casually, with junipers between them and even broad glades of low pink-flowering rho-dodendrons or open grass, studded with unopened gentians.

Then came one last belt of ancient twisted moss-clad pines, hardly more than bushes, and abruptly he was out of the trees altogether: they were ruled off as though by a line, and the sky, no longer patches of light above the branches, spread wide over-head. An enormous sky; vivid and brilliant beyond anything he had imagined: these hours of climbing had kept his head down, and now the immensity of this vast bowl overwhelmed him.

Another five hundred feet over the bare grass and he sat down to gaze round the world. His heart was pounding and his breath came short – visible breath that lingered in the unmoving, frigid air – and for some time his gasping body would scarcely let him comprehend what he saw: it was as though he were contemplating a brilliant but entirely foreign universe. Yet in time it resumed an intelligible form: there was his dark forest, sweeping down in wave after wave to the dim lower clouds; and beyond the great valley to the north rose answering mountains with rounded tops. Somewhere in the hidden land between them must be the last remote village and the road. It was an enormous landscape, on a scale that quite abolished hours or miles, but this was not the half of it – behind him the high mountain cut off the rest of the world. To his right as he turned there were two soaring peaks, joined by a ragged curtain-wall; they were very dark on this northward side, and the snow that lay in their deep gulleys showed with a deathly light; they had screes and beds of shale hanging on their steep sides or running down to the chaotic rocks below, and the screes were cold and grey, severely inanimate. But on his left the solitary peak had caught the sun. Every detail of its warm brown and ochre cliffs was clear, and in this brilliant clarity it might have been no more than an hour away, but for the golden cloud that floated between him and the nearest spur. Between these mountains, and due south of him, there appeared the upward edge of a wilderness of rock that threw up uncounted peaks; their grey northern sides were powdered with snow, and deep snow lay here and there in streaks. These raised, distant peaks were all he could see of the waste beyond. 'The necessary pass will be clear, no doubt,' he said, 'once I can survey the whole.'

The cold seeped into him from below; the air bit his ears and nose; and when at last he felt for the map his hands were numb. The single mountain was certainly Malamort, and it was beyond it, on the sunward side, that he must go, through a gap between the mountain and the chaos to the south: he could see no gap, but his drawing showed the path, a line winding up to the shoulder of Malamort. The gap must be there, and it must be exactly to the south-east, hidden by some nearer crest. With a sudden eager desire to know what was on the other side of the limiting ridge, to find the pass, to be moving in this silent enormous world, he started up the slope, a smooth alp dotted with pale boulders like gigantic sheep.

It was a rounded slope whose skyline mounted pace by pace with him, false crests in an interminable series, and it was steep; yet he hurried up it, sometimes chuckling, sometimes singing loud; and where the slope was less he ran in bounds, waving his arms and singing louder still. The grass thinned and the bare earth showed more as he gained height, gritty earth among pale grass, dirty and crushed from the snow that had left it a few days ago. Now and then he slipped and fell; but he fell easy on the wet sloping ground; it did not affect his elation nor his speed and in time he gained the true ridge at last, with its long wave of standing snow. Here he fell silent: now he was standing in the sun, astride of a vaster world by far, because the last two thousand feet had brought up mountains on every hand, and he was above them all, above everything except Malamort; and clean round the horizon these mountains rose and fell, a brown infinity. The great valley on the north was gone, obliterated by the miracle of breeding cloud, rounded white masses rising below him into the middle air, forming slow whirlpools and momentary towers. Once the whole gleaming ocean parted from top to bottom, and he saw a heightened fragment of the common world – thread-like roads, the railway-line, a winding river, the huddle of a town with smoke, the minute patchwork of fields. But with the closing of the clouds and their continual mounting there was nothing on that side but the great ranges as they stretched away, illimitable against the lower sky, rising from the rising sea of white: but on this side, the new, southern, sunlit side, no clouds; nothing but a desert of broken rock, brilliantly lit yet dark and even black in places, with sheets of snow and many lakes, black-rimmed, shining water in the hollows; screes everywhere, and rarely a touch of green. The wilderness filled all the middle distance, and beyond it the saw-edged ranges ran on and on: the mountains of Aragon, no doubt, and perhaps those of Navarre.

The snow under his feet was crusted, granular and hard; it was pocked with old rain and powdered with a dust of earth, but beneath the crust it was the purest white. Its taste was thin – insubstantial – yet it left a burning in his mouth.

Virgin snow: there seemed a want of piety in walking upon its unbroken smoothness; and never was there such a world for piety – it might have been created yesterday. Others had not felt the same, however. Twenty yards away to the left footmarks crossed it at its lowest point. What is more, they continued beyond the present limit of the snow; and these compressed footprints were still unmelted; they ran on, a series of white dots pointing straight to a cleft under the sheer rock-face of Malamort, a slit perhaps an hour away, hardly to be seen at all in the blaze of the sun without their help. For this necessary pass, this Portal Nera, lay in the deep shadow among black, impassable rocks.

Once he was across and fairly on the southern slope, the sun warmed him through and through, comforting him to the bone. The gentians were open here, stars and trumpets, fields of them, and the air was like good news: he said, I could go on for ever.

He walked with long, reaching strides, on and on: yet the sun climbed and the pass barely moved. The air was stirring now, and a black vulture rose in spirals on a thermal current until it was no bigger than a lark: the bowl of the sky turned an even intenser blue. This was perfect walking, these miles of level or slightly downward path, almost like a slow gentle flight or even levitation after the grind of the ascent: slowly the pass changed shape, and to his left the peak soared higher still, growing until it filled the eastern quarter of the sky.

For long stretches he watched the alternate reappearance of his feet and the even flow of the ground beneath. Once he looked up at the clatter of a band of chamois crossing a scree a mile away to the west, and once he followed the flight of a large white butterfly with red eye-spots on its wings; but upon the whole he kept his head down, in a floating dream.

The third time he looked up he was in the very entrance of the pass, and he saw a man in a grey cloth cap, a surly red-eyed man with his legs wrapped in coarse brown paper from knee to ankle: he was sitting on a dark boulder in the shadow of the cliff, beside a shapeless load, or burden. He asked Martin had he the right time?

'I am afraid I have not,' said Martin, 'but it is early yet, I am sure.' He sat down and watched the man as he knotted two broken ends in the sacking of his load.

'Whore of Babylon,' said the man, forcing the knots tight; and he muttered continually as he turned the bundle over and over to verify the fastenings. 'What is your name?' he asked.

'Martin Kaftan.'

'Where do you come from?'

'France.'

'Where are you going? Are you alone? Do you know anyone in Encantats?'

Martin answered these questions, and after a pause the man, pretending to inspect his burden still, drew out a knife. He feigned to cut the loose end of a string and said, 'You know nothing about the mountain. Look at your shoes. I dare say you have a good many pairs of leather shoes in your house,' he added, with a cunning leer. Martin looked at his shoes: their soles were shining from the grass; they were indeed quite unsuitable. 'Come,' said the man, 'let me scratch them with my knife.'

With the shoes in front of him he did not scratch them yet, but pushed up his sleeve and began to shave the hair on his forearm. The hairs skipped under the edge, leaving a bare, mown tract of skin. 'Sharp,' he said. 'That's what I call sharp.' He was looking uglier now, with white spittle between his lips, his eyes were squinting with excitement, and the defect in his speech grew more pronounced. He said, 'You are afraid to be on the mountain alone with all that money and your fine coat. Let me feel your coat. What have you got to eat?'

Martin laughed, leaning back against the rock. He said, 'How would I be afraid on the mountain, my dear? And no one can rob me on this journey, because I was robbed before I began. The coat is not mine, and I left all my food at the top of the forest, by mistake: a chicken, bread, and a bottle of wine. What is your name, pray?'

'Joan,' said the man, vaguely. He seemed to be coming out of his fit, and although he said 'No,' when Martin asked him whether he had anything to eat either, after a little while he brought out a flat black loaf and two onions and unslung the greasy leather bottle he wore on his shoulder. He scratched a cross on the loaf, cut off a piece and gave it to Martin with one of the onions; and when Martin held out his hand for the knife to slice the onion he passed it without reflection. He also passed the wine.

Munching fast he told Martin how good he was: uniquely good: took no advantage of the situation as any other man might, nay *would*, for the laws of God were not observed and God Himself had never reached these parts. 'There was the izard-hunter from Politg – they cut his throat in this very pass before he could say hail Mary and Espollabalitris ate his balls.'

'What are izards?'

'Izards are what you make chamois-skin out of: where were you brought up, God forbid? But I should never have eaten any Christian's balls. I am too good,' he said with his eyes closed tight, and he pressed Martin to eat more, to drink as much as he could. 'Drink, man, drink. I do not reckon the cost,' he said, squirting the jet into Martin's mouth.

'You are very kind,' said Martin, when the skin was empty. 'I hope you will find my chicken, in time, and the bottle. They are in a paper carrier-bag, on a rock where the trees begin.'

'Never mind, never mind if the bears have had them. I can go all day and night without refreshment, to help a poor man. I do good, but I never mention it. There are hundreds and thousands down there' – jerking his head backwards – 'who owe everything to me: but I say nothing.' Shading his mouth he whispered, 'There are evil tongues down there,' and nodding vehemently he set to scratching the shoes, raising diagonal weals on their soles with the point of his knife.

'Thank you very much,' said Martin, making to put them on.

'No, no. Let me,' cried Joan, cramming them on to Martin's feet and lacing them with terrible force. He grew excited again when he described the course of the path as it led on to the Cami Real, the great mule-track, confused in his description, obscurely angry and contentious; his ugliness was increasing fast, but when Martin said he supposed the burden must weigh a great deal Joan turned off directly to tell what he could carry, compared with common men. And indeed when Martin lifted it, meaning to help it on, the weight was staggering. Joan thrust him aside, swung it up with one hand, looped it on with a sordid web and stood displaying himself with angry satisfaction. 'Watch me,' he cried, setting off at a furious pace up the hill. His voice came fainter: 'You have never seen anything like it. But this is nothing to what I can do, Mother of God.'

'Thank you for telling me the way,' Martin called after him; but Joan ran on and on, without another word.

For two hours more the path ran sweetly round the shoulder of Malamort, dipping to a lake: other paths had joined it, coming from valleys to the east, but they were obviously less important; and in any event this lake was marked upon his drawing; it had been named by Joan. All that he had to do now was to walk left-handed round its shore, climb by the stream the other side, reach the high snowy ridge beyond, find the westward pass above two small lakes, and so drop to the road.

The great hollow, a ring two miles across, was surrounded by cliffs on three sides; they had beds of shale at their feet, and in three places they were broken by streams coming from the higher ridge. Three streams, and one of them a waterfall; yet clearly the first was his. It was much larger; it was directly on the other side of the lake; and there had been no mention of his crossing water.

The fourth side was filled by a marsh, covered with cotton-grass, and among the boulders on its edge grew a low, fern-like plant in great profusion; the last year's growth, brown, dry in the sun, and fragrant, made the softest resting-place. He sat down and gazed at the water, his whole body relaxing at once, limp, boneless and pliable: the lake had no banks, in the ordinary sense – there were just these falls of rock, and then, without transition, water. It had no vegetation in it or round it: no clouds passed overhead, no birds. No breeze touched its surface. It seemed that there was no life here, only sky, rock and silence; but presently he saw rings spreading, and later he heard the splash of a rising trout. There were other sounds too: stone avalanches rumbling in the distance; the thunder of rock falling from the cliffs, several times repeated, and startling at first. He watched the rings form, spread and intersect; he dozed, awoke, dozed again, and fell fast asleep in his bed of fern.

It was a nearer rock-fall and the cold that roused him. The sun had left the water, the whole bottom of the ring, and now it lit only the upper half of the eastern cliff: already the air down here was sharp. There was no time to be lost, and quickly putting on his shoes he hurried round the lake. He climbed fast up along the bed of the first stream, but the shadow climbed faster still: before he had reached the ridge the lower sky was violet, and the arch of the day was closing towards the west. He had seen nothing like a path for the last hour, but now the snow was coming closer, and surely he would find it there.

Indeed, there it was, a track slanting westwards across the snow, almost exactly where his anxious theory had placed it. But alas, when he came to it there was clearly something wrong – too slender, far too neat – and when he bent in the fading light he saw the mark of cloven hoofs. This was the path, and no doubt the habitual path, of a numerous band of chamois. Certainly it was: ten minutes later he rounded a bluff with the breeze in his face and came full upon them. The group exploded, racing away, leaping skip-skip-skip down and across an impossible rock-face, so that he was in dread for their legs and necks.

However, they were gone, safely gone, before he could even count them, and his anxiety returned to himself; the twilight was mounting fast to these regions, and the only hint of real path that he could see led upwards, still higher, to no pass that he could discern among the massive peaks ahead.

'Yet it may very well drop again suddenly,' he said. 'It may very well show me the pass in half an hour; and as soon as I am on the road I shall find a shepherd's hut. Joan spoke of one where the road leaves the forest, and two not far from the chapel.'

On. Higher and higher, winding where the rocks would let him rather than where a fading sense of direction urged him to go on. He often fell now, once losing his hold on a scree and sliding down a hundred feet with stones falling all around and beyond him. Eventually, with his breath gone, his strength going, and a deep cut in his side, he found himself creeping in the near darkness along a snowy ledge with a sheer face on his right hand and a precipice on his left.

The snow had melted away from the rock-face, where the sun had warmed it, leaving a passage wide enough to stand in – wider in places – and then, on the outward side of the ledge, a firm white mass as high as a counter. He leant on this counter, surveying the night as it rose from the east – Mars blazing already, even the small stars pricking out, but never a hint of the moon – and the dark shapes of the mountains looming against the sky. 'I am far, far too high,' he said. 'But I cannot go any farther. Snow is said to conserve the warmth: I shall try to find a wider place, and there I shall lie.'

Fifty yards along the ledge turned sharply: he was observing, 'And if it does not, then I shall run up and down until the day,' when he heard a snort, a muffled, hurrying sound ahead. At the same moment he caught a goatish smell, and his feet were treading in dung. 'So this is where the chamois sleep,' he said. 'How wise.'

It was the most sheltered place that could be wished at this great height: beneath the counter there was no wind at all; some warmth still emanated from the cliff, and the smell soon passed unnoticed. His body was so tired that the rock seemed soft at first, and he lay there in a half-doze, watching the stars as they swept over the narrow trench above.

A long, long night, however, with an increasing cold that reached to his heart at last. By two o'clock it seemed to have been going on for ever. But at least he was beyond hunger, and his thirst he could satisfy from the snow. When the stars were paling he fell into a tormented sleep, cramped and uneasy, but so deep that the sun was as high as the Malamort before it woke him.

'It is over,' he said, shading his eyes from the glare and unscrewing himself from the tight ball in which he had lain. 'It is over at last.' He got on to his knees, then to his feet, and as he slowly straightened so the pure revivifying sunlight darted straight into his upper half: his blood began to flow, the tension and shivering died away as the heat pierced deeper and deeper; his teeth no longer chattered. He took off his soaking bloodstained filthy coat and stood back against the warm rock with his arms spread wide and his eyes closed. All around him there was the drip of melting snow.

Now his shirt was dry and even his frozen spine was supple; he leant his elbows on the counter and looked out. Below him, cloud. Nothing but that white sea of impenetrable cloud, rising to within five hundred feet of his ledge. Mountains thrusting through it – to his left the familiar praying hands of Malamort – and a perfect sky above. He said, 'They will lift in time,' and his eye caught a white-splashed shelf of rock below, within spitting distance below. Three bearded vultures stood upon it, the parents and their huge blowzy child, sluggishly preening themselves and waiting for the day to warm. His gaze made them uneasy, and presently one cocked its head upwards, shuffled to the edge and launched itself silently into the void. The others followed, and for a moment he saw six great sharp-winged forms gliding over the clouds, the birds and their close-following shadows.

'I have slept with vultures too, I find,' he observed; and wedging its sleeves into a horizontal crack he spread his coat to dry.

There was no attempting to move except upwards, which was absurd; so during the hours in which the cloud slowly boiled and rolled in upon itself below, sometimes sending off long streamers

but never breaking, he also dried his trousers and his handkerchief, luxuriating in the heat as they hung.

Gradually the unseen waterfall to his right increased in sound
and volume as the sun unlocked the higher snow and ice; and
when at last the cloud began its definitive rise, the jet came into
sight, a single arch of water shooting out from a broken cliff and
plunging into the whiteness, now only a hundred feet below.

Tenuous vapours were drifting overhead: all the sharp defi-
nition of the cloud was gone. The sun dimmed, and a moment
later it was no more than a white ball in the enveloping fog. He
put on his good dry clothes, grateful for their warmth, and
relapsed into timeless waiting.

Would the cloud continue to rise? Or would it hang about the
mountain-tops all day, all night, perhaps for weeks on end? A
small shining beetle climbed laboriously about the pellet-shaped
droppings and the compacted masses of izards' dung. Several
times it fell on its back, waving its legs, and each time he set
it on its feet; but it seemed to possess no sense of purpose or
direction.

The cloud lifted. It took a great while to do so, but it lifted,
and the last stage was as dramatic as the raising of a curtain. A
hint of thinning, and then suddenly it was overhead, completely
overhead, revealing the lower world, whole, clear and plain.

There, immediately below him, was the forest. There, on the
flank of a valley, was the road, rising to a saddle to the west.
There was the river. And there, on the grassy slopes above the
forest, he could see minute shapes that must be grazing cattle.
Poring over this landscape spread below him he made out three
shepherd's huts, all far away, the nearest being close to the upper
limit of the trees, between the forest and the road, on the far side
of the river. From one blue smoke was rising; and each had a
strange brown square in front of it, like a field.

There too were the small lakes, far away to the east; and there
to be sure he saw the path, so well trodden by the herds down
there that it might have been a road. He had not gone so far
wrong: the general direction had been right. Only he was three
thousand feet too high. And his precipice fell half that distance

without a break. How to get down it? Along the ledge in the hope of its joining that far shoulder? Back the way he had come, trusting to find a way along its foot? There were not so many hours of daylight left, with the tall mountains cutting off the sun so soon, and the best way he must find, or he was lost in sight of home.

Backwards, forwards, sideways, up and down, climbing, sliding, sometimes falling, it was not until the evening sky flushed red that he was down to the two small lakes, fetching them at last by a long tack that lost him an hour and more. 'But once I am round this pool,' he said, forcing his exhausted body through a bog, 'I am certainly on the one true path: then if I do not fall again I may very well get there by night. And surely I shall not fall upon the road itself?'

Five minutes later he missed his leap on a shifting rock; but the fall sent him sprawling on to the undoubted path, and now it was only a question of clearing his head, gathering himself together, choosing the right direction, and going on and on for some hours. 'Providing the shepherd is at home,' he said.

Past the lakes, on, and a long haul, to the first of the trees, strangely familiar with their hanging moss in the deepening twilight; down through the trees to the river and the ford. The swift icy current, knee-deep and more; the slippery stones in the darkness. He said, 'Shall I ever make this last half-mile?' as he paused long on the farther bank, searching for strength to stand up again. There was only a plain meadow between him and the light of the open door, but now the cruel frost came dropping from the sky and he was as weary as a dying man.

Ahead of him stood the herd, packed into the trampled square in front of the hut – mares with their mule foals, cows, heifers, beasts, some sheep, two goats, two pigs, with a mist of soft breath rising from them all – a guardian dog at each corner, huge woolly dogs with steel-spiked brass collars. They had heard and smelt him coming since before he crossed the river, but they said nothing: only one young subsidiary dog slunk close behind his legs and gibbered its teeth uneasily; and he walked very slowly past them towards the door.

It was open to let out some of the smoke, and it showed a glowing stone-built room. There were two fires blazing inside, one on the hearth, another, a small and clear fire of juniper, burning on a stone shelf beside the bench; and this bench, this broad wooden platform against the back wall, filled the entire width of the hut. The shepherd lay there on a deep pile of sheep-skins, and he was reading in a book. One arm held it to the light, and the other lay round the lamb that slept against his side. A very old bitch and some cats filled the rest of the bed.

The very old bitch grunted as Martin appeared in the door, and the shepherd turned his eager smiling face towards him. 'Have you come?' he said, closing the book, disengaging the lamb, and beginning to rise. 'And have you come at last? You are the Christ? I have been waiting and waiting for you.'

'No, my dear,' said Martin, leaning against the jamb. 'I am not the Christ.'

'Are you not?' said the shepherd, touching his arm. His face clouded painfully; but he said, 'Lie down on the warm bed, while I milk a cow.' He looked searchingly into Martin's face again and said, 'And are you indeed not the Christ? Yet the dogs never spoke; and this is the time. No? Well,' – smiling once more – 'then I shall not have to kill the lamb.'

The Voluntary Patient

'WHAT IS that noise?'

'Which noise?'

'Like a dog howling. There it is again.'

'Oh, that. It is only Mr Philips. He is upstairs this afternoon,' she said with a satisfied smile. 'We have been a little troublesome, and we shan't come down until we are in a better mood. "You can't do this to me," he said, "I am here on a voluntary basis, you understand, and can leave whenever I choose, upon giving proper notice."'

They both laughed, and the second woman, still tittering, said, 'Always the same old tale. But which is Mr Philips? The one who looks out of the window?'

'No. Isn't he a scream? No, this is the one with the fiddle I told you about. You haven't seen him yet – he is at the back.'

'Well, why doesn't he play his fiddle?'

'He has quite given it over, and spends all his time writing. I said to him the other day, "Mr Philips," I said, "why don't you give us a tune?" No answer. Just scribble scribble scribble, as if his life depended on it.'

They both laughed again, and the second woman said, 'You get all the funny ones.'

'Not that he's as funny as some, but he does get some funny ideas. "Make the punishment fit the crime" is his latest.' She hummed a bar and they both sang.

'La di da di da di da
Make the punishment fit the crime.'

'How do you mean, though?' asked the visitor.

'Well, he says all this psychosomatic stuff – you know what I mean?'

'Of course I do.'

'Don't be offended, love. He says it is all part of the same thing, and you bring it on yourself.' The visitor grinned and nodded, and the tall, black-haired woman went on, 'It's all part of the same thing, he says. Oh, we get it by the hour sometimes, and then he writes it all down.'

'You do have more fun than we do,' said the visitor crossly. 'On the accidie side they are a dull, mumchance, pompous lot, all puffed up with their own importance.'

'Oh, I don't know,' said the other in a modest tone. 'Here,' she added, leaning sideways and picking up a closely written sheet, 'this will tell you all about it. It will make you howl.'

The visitor, a woman with sparse sandy hair and a dead-white transparent skin, flushed so that the redness could be seen mounting above the rounded protuberance of her forehead and far into her scalp. She took it greedily, but she said at once, 'This is not the beginning.'

'It doesn't matter: it's all the same.'

'". . . and as no two crimes are exactly the same,"' she read aloud, '"so every punishment is unlike every other punishment. When a man wakes in the night and finds his head filled with remorse and bitter, old regret, if he chose he could reflect that no other man in the world would be suffering precisely that remorse nor exactly that regret: it might be quite as vain and sterile and long-lived, but it would not be wounding him with the same sharp terms. Of course, he would not choose to do so, for he would be too busy dodging about inside his mind, trying to escape – unless, that is, he were occupied with feeling the wound to see how much it still hurt and trying to persuade himself that there was virtue in mere remorse." He, he, he,' went the sandy woman; but putting her glass on the paper she said with an affected prim indifference, 'He writes very neat.'

'I don't know that that's the best piece,' said the other, peering at the writing upside down. 'There was a good one I meant to show you the day before yesterday.'

'From Mr Philips?'

'No, the pale fellow.'

'He's another funny one, isn't he?' she said abstractedly, as her eyes ran down the paragraph below the round of the glass's foot.

' "So in sinning you create your own punishment," ' she read. ' "In the act of the particular and unique sin the compensating punishment is born: it is inevitably born, and it always exactly counterbalances its cause." '

'Does he ever put any address?' she asked, breaking off.

'No: he's one of our new boys. They haven't let on yet.'

'Has he told you what his trouble is?'

'No. But you would have screamed the other day: they were asking him about his eyes and I couldn't help hearing. Osborne says, "And what about this shadow in the left-hand field of vision, Mr Philips?" And he says, "Oh, it's nothing much." So Osborne says, "But it is still there, I collect?" And he says, "I'm afraid so. Do you attach any importance to it?" – trying to put him off, you know. Then Osborne hums and haws about sciasis for a bit, tips old Prince the wink, and leaves them together. Old Prince, of course, begins to lay on the soothing syrup right away – dear, kind old man, butter wouldn't melt in his mouth.'

Both the women laughed, slapping their thighs and rocking to and fro. The dark one controlled herself first and said, 'A drop more, love?'

'I don't mind if I do,' she said, holding her fingers to the glass. 'Ta.'

At this moment the black-haired woman was called out of the room and the visitor, dangling her tongue into her gin, but not sipping it, read on over the rim of her glass.

' "It is not the observer who must be asked, but the sufferer. To the observer it must appear that there are many identical crimes, which may or may not have identical punishments. If we take the ordinary crimes, lying and theft, it can be said that in every case the criminal is punished by being a liar (for obviously it is not the punishment of being disbelieved that counts –

that is no more than a haphazard retribution for lack of skill) or by being a thief, by inhabiting the mind and body of a thief: but that is a merely superficial view. Take as an example the commonest criminal of them all, the selfish, disagreeable man: this sufferer, heavy under the self-inflicted punishment of an ever-lasting evil temper fixed into his body by his indulgence in unpleasantness, can point out a thousand significant differences in his punishment as compared with the next man's; the weight of his sour life presses on innumerable points of sensitivity that no other man can have. It is the same with the ordinary hysterias, neuroses, and psychosomatic diseases. Yet it is true that in this range we do have an apparent similarity: the enormous differ-ences, the differences that instantly convince the most casual observer, come from huge and monstrous crimes. It is these that cause the monstrous births upon the other side. I think of the horrible thing at the bottom of the Last Judgment at Albi: that must have been created, automatically created, by one appalling crime alone. That crime may have been called by the same name as other crimes (Judas' sin is nominally shared by the latest petty traitor) but obviously it was as unique as its result. This thing at Albi could never possibly have served to counterweight two crimes: it was made by one alone. Bosch and Breughel, too; they show the harmony and equipoise . . .""

Her eyes skipped down the lines until a capital began again. '"It comes to this: each of these acts adds another to those things that live in Hell – *creates* it. It creates a new fiend."' A pleased smile spread slowly across her face: she nodded her head, staring intently at the blank wall in front of her.

'What was it?' she asked, as the door opened again.

'Oh, nothing. Only the brimstone going out. But as I was saying, old Prince sits himself down and goes on and on in his quiet, soapy voice – gets very confidential and friendly.'

'He is a proper card, old Prince.'

'Yes. He likes to see how far he can make them go. If only he can get them to go down on their knees and blubber the whole thing out while he does you know what behind them, it sets him up for a fortnight. Sometimes he borrows Ambrose's outfit, but the pure jam is when he can firk it out of them voluntary, sobbing in mother-bull's bosom. Anyhow, this time he gets our gentleman on to his hobby-horse about this psychosomatic business and rewards and punishments and so on; then after a bit he breaks off and says, "But this figure that you think you see, Mr Philips, it has no certain form?"

'"No!" he says, as quick as that. Then he hesitates and says, "No. No. It is only dark. Always behind me, as I told you; and when I turn it goes."

'"It always goes? Vanishes?"

'"Yes."

'"Always?"

'"Yes. Well, that is to say . . ." He hesitates, and old Prince looks grave and sympathetic, very interested and kind. ". . . that is to say, almost always. But once I turned too quick and I thought I saw it then."

'"Was it – forgive me if I seem indelicate – was it a dreadful thing?"

'"I hardly know what to say," says Philips, pretending to blow his nose and dropping his handkerchief. "Not really, perhaps. Not in itself. I thought it was the shadow of a barn – the sharp line and the corner."

'"Just that? No more than that?"

'"The shadow of a barn. The side going up so sheer and the angle of the roof."

'Old Prince leans back in his chair, looks at his watch, and coughs. "Shadows, my dear sir," he says, rather impatient but covering it up, you see . . .'

'He's a cunning one, old Prince.'

'". . . shadows," he says. "We all know how a horse will shy. We all know, too, how our bodies can deceive us, and especially our eyes. An unwise indulgence, a late supper, and we are apt to dream at night and to have our faculties disturbed the next day. Singing in the ears, spots floating in the air. They tell me it is the liver." And he looks at his watch again. But our Mr P. is getting very agitated, gripping the arms of his chair so that the whole floor trembles.

PATRICK O'BRIAN

'"Don't go," he cries – as if old Prince had any intention of
going – "I should like to . . ." He bogs down there; but after a
minute he says, "I had an interesting talk with Father Ambrose
the other day."

'"Oh indeed?" says Prince, very solemn. "Well, I am sure it
must have done you good. My dear colleague has a brilliant
understanding: I only wish he could be here more often. But
they keep him so very busy, you know."

'"Your colleague? But I thought you were . . ."

'"Why, yes. Father Ambrose is my colleague. In my humble
way I fulfil a dual function here. I am very proud of my connection with him: he is a wonderful person, and I have learned a
great deal from him. I am sure he must have done you good?"

'"Yes, yes," he says, "Father Ambrose was very kind – wonderfully patient – most considerate."

'"May I ask what you talked about?"

'"It was mostly the same subject that we have just been discussing. But he is so sympathetic that I ventured to put it on a
personal plane."

'"I see. I see. You told him everything?"

'"Yes."

'"Everything?"

'"Yes."

'"So of course he was able to reassure you completely?"

'"It was not a regular confession, you understand," says Mr
P., still holding off.

'"No. I quite understand. But, however, he was able to
reassure you."

'"Yes."

'I thought that was the end, but after a while old Prince leans
forward and says, "My dear Philips – I hope you do not mind
me calling you that – my dear Philips, I am afraid that you may
have some unexpected reserve. Unfortunately Father Ambrose
will not be back for some considerable time, but if I can be of
any service to you, I am entirely at your disposition."

'"It was *after* my talk with him that I turned and saw it
clearly," blurts out Mr Philips.

'"Dear me," cries Prince, and I knew he was so near a fit of the giggles that I nearly went off myself, although I was alone in the corridor. But he goes on very grave and earnest. "Dear me, you must have found that very disturbing."

'"I can't bear it. I can't bear it," he says.

'"Now, now, my dear Philips; let us be calm. Calm. I am here to help you: you know that, don't you? Let us look at it this way: as it happened after you had had your, your 'talk' shall we say, with Father Ambrose, there cannot possibly be any connection between this and your former – what term shall we employ? – your former visions. For as I understand it you told Father Ambrose *everything*? The account was quite complete?"

'"Yes. But perhaps it was not valid."

'"If it was complete it was certainly valid. There were no omissions?"

'"Oh no. Certainly not – no voluntary omission at all."

'"Perhaps some little suppression almost unnoticed at the time, which has occurred to you since?"

'"I don't think so. No. But I can't bear it – I can't. It is getting so much worse."

'Prince calms him down a little and then says, "Perhaps if we were to run over the main points of your conversation with Father Ambrose you might find it helpful, and it is possible that you might bring something fresh into your memory, something that you unconsciously kept in the background before. As I am sure you have noticed, our memories are extraordinarily unreliable, and they have a strange capacity for hiding things that we do not wish to remember. Yes, I am sure that that would be our best course: but may I beg you to be frank? I am sure that you will realize that complete frankness is of the first importance."

'"You are very kind. But I am afraid of trespassing on your good nature. I kept Father Ambrose here for hours."

'"Not at all, not at all. Now I think – yes, I am sure of it. I think you would be more at your ease if you were to kneel here, facing the window. I shall be able to hear you perfectly well. Remember, you cannot be too minutely detailed."

'So Philips gets down on the floor and puts his face against the cushion of the chair old Prince has been sitting in and old Prince stands behind him in the middle of the room, bending up and down on his knees and going like *that* with his hands.'

'He, he, he.'

'But instead of beginning, he jumps up again and says, "Do you feel that my theory of punishment is sound, Mr Prince?"'

'"Eh?" says old Prince, rather put out and giving him a dirty look under his eyebrows. He hadn't expected that, and nor had I; but he recovers himself and says, "A very interesting theory, Mr Philips, very interesting indeed. But these are terribly difficult questions and I am sure that our best course is to do as I suggested. Shall we begin at the beginning?"'

'Of course, he wants to get him down on his knees again, and for a moment he does go down. But then he bobs up again and stands there wringing his hands as good as a play. "I can't bear it," he keeps saying, "I can't bear it."'

'"There now, my dear Philips, let us collect ourselves. Let us be calm. I will be just here behind you, and I will listen without interruption, I assure you. And we must bear in mind the absolute necessity for complete frankness, must we not?"'

'Old Prince is looking very ugly, but Philips is half turned to the window and doesn't see a thing: he keeps moaning "I can't bear it. I can't. I can't."'

'Prince sees that it is no good going on with that line, so he hands him back into his chair, waits until he has come off the boil, and then, after a little while, he says in a thoughtful voice, "The shadow of an upright wall, and the angle of the roof. Now let us reflect. What, by your theory, could have called that into being?"'

'"It is not only the line and corner now. I didn't tell you. I didn't like to say," he gasps.'

'"There is something else?" murmurs old Prince, to help him on.'

'Philips whispers something, but what it was I could not catch: the next thing is old Prince saying, "Perhaps you could give me a general idea, eh?"'

'But "I can't name it," he says, jerking his head over his shoulder.'

'"Just some hint –?" says old Prince, for our man is very near the point now, and old Prince is all hot and excited. But it won't do: he has pressed him just an inch too far and at that point our man sticks. He can't bring it out, and it's no use, although Prince soothes him and soft-soaps him for half an hour and more. You would have screamed. If you had been there I would never have been able to hold out.'

'Was he cross?'

'He was livid, my dear. He got out of the room all right in the end, still the dear old gentleman; but he gave me such a look as he shoved by.'

'He doesn't like to fail. But he'll have him next time.'

'Oh yes, he'll have him next time. But he likes it first go off, and this was rather a special one.'

'I wish I had seen it.' She paused for a while before adding, 'You have all the funny ones.'

'We've been lucky recently. There's another comic in the upper wing who –'

'What was that noise?'

'Which noise?'

'Like a dog howling.'

They both listened. The inhuman cry swelled to an enormous volume and after an instant's silence a furious trampling shook the ceiling of the room.

A slight frown creased the forehead of the black-haired woman, and she stood up, very tall and solid over the rickety table. 'The students?' she said. She stood considering for a moment with her lips pursed, while the hellish din continued overhead. 'Yes, the young devils must be teasing him. Old Prince said he might give them leave.'

A moment later she said, 'They've left him now.' She turned to a cupboard, took an instrument out for herself and handed another to the visitor.

'We'll go up too, shall we?' she said.

'Oh *yes*,' cried the other, jumping full of glee, 'and we'll make him say who created *us*.'

And laughing they hurled themselves out of the room and raced up the stairs, screaming with laughter that flew before them to the door of Mr Philips' private room.

The Long Day Running

THE FIRST SONG Lemuel Kirk ever learnt was John Peel; he loved everything about it; he knew all the words, and he often made the palm-trees tremble with his view halloo. He had longed to go out with a fell-pack from his earliest days; and now that he was settled in Wales he had the opportunity of fulfilling this ambition – indeed, of surpassing it, for the country inland was made up not of fells but of mountains.

His predecessor at the hospital, a Welshman with a wide acquaintance in the surrounding counties, gave him an introduction to the master of a famous old pack that hunted them, and in the autumn a postcard came to tell Dr Kirk that hounds would meet at Hafod Uchaf on Thursday, at half past nine.

The dogs were a mixed body – fell-hounds, Welsh hounds, a beautiful English bitch from the Pytchley, and almost as many terriers as foxhounds: small terriers of different colours, most of them whiskered and hairy, all coupled with heavy chains. The Master was followed by a personal dog, an old cross-bred black retriever that farted every few minutes and that took no notice of anyone. The Master himself was a spare, remote man with a hawk nose, a curling moustache and a piercing blue eye: his horn could be seen under his Burberry and he carried a long-lashed crop slung over his shoulder. Something had occurred to vex him, which disturbed the rest of the field; but he greeted Kirk kindly, and hoped that they would be able to show him some sport. Gerallt Williams, the huntsman, had brought his son to the hospital for a course of treatment, and Kirk already knew him. And there was a weather-beaten woman whom he recognized as one of the magistrates who had fined him for a motoring

185

offence in the summer. The rest of the field he had never seen, to his knowledge: some local farmers and artisans; a tall soldier called Major Boyd, some other 'educated' men; a schoolmaster with a hard-faced virgin at his side. They were all dressed in strong, shabby clothes; they all wore boots; they all carried sticks. Kirk felt too new altogether, except for his boots – they at least had seen service during his long walks in August and September.

Little did Kirk know about hunting, and the apparent competence of the others disturbed him. Following at all seemed to him to imply a moral duty to keep up, to go through thick and thin, and to be in at the kill. He could not possibly expect to distinguish himself in any way, still less to be given a brush; but he did hope to avoid disgrace. He was the only black man in those parts; and apart from that these people seemed to him stand-offish – it would be painful to expose himself in front of them. Yet perhaps this was no more than a question of language: many of the patients from the hill farms and villages needed a Welsh-speaking nurse to interpret for them when it came to the finer points; and in his farther walks he had noticed how people avoided conversation, not to display their imperfect English.

At this point the farmers were all speaking Welsh – the word *llwynog* kept recurring; the Master spoke Welsh or English indifferently when he spoke at all. 'For Christ's sake let's cut the cackle, Dwch anwyl,' he said, pulling a watch from his waistcoat. 'If he don't choose to meet my bloody hounds prompt, let him go and – himself.'

They moved off, the huntsman; the lean pale pack, smelling strong of hound; the Master and his familiar spirit, farting as it went; the shabby field.

As they came into the high valley, the fox slipped up over the edge of it and away. He went with no hurry, picking the easy path through rocks and shadows, and if it had not been for two sheep that started violently, making the shale rattle on the mountainside, he would never have been seen. A big dog-fox, long-legged and uncommonly dark: he paused on the skyline, on the edge of the steep slope, and looked down before he vanished.

There were half a dozen of them there at the far end of the lake and more strung out along its barren shore, all staring up at him: the hounds were farther on, where a fall came down to the water at the head of the valley. It made no difference to the fox that he had been seen, because the dogs were already working along his drag among the black rocks; but it pleased the followers – Kirk's heart leapt with delight.

This was Cwm Llyn Du, a great bowl of a valley like a crater with a quarter of its wall broken away at the lower end; it had high steep sides, so sheer that on the two arms before the break the grass could only just get a footing, while the top end was savage, bare and sterile.

The pack was on the true line, with Bashful and Melody out in front; and its meandering path showed exactly the way the fox had gone up some hours before. This was a fair scenting day up here, and suddenly as they came to the place where he had been lying, Melody bawled out with passionate conviction, then four or five more all together, and they were away with a splendid wild crash of music, all close together with no doubt or hesitation, sweeping away in a tight white line, noses down, running fast.

Kirk stood entranced for a moment, but already the followers were toiling up to that far-away crest, taking different lines, all of them steep the moment they left the water. Out to the right there was the long-legged huntsman with four of the terriers. Running along the flat Kirk came up behind him; but Gerallt went so fast with his long legs and his ceaseless springing stride that Kirk could stay with him only by putting all his closest attention to it, taking advantage of every easy step, watching the huntsman's feet in front and above, concentrating all the time. The least stumble jerked the breath out of him, losing distance; sometimes he was on all fours; often he seized the grass with his nearer hand to help him along, always too far behind to relax his concentration for a moment. He saw almost nothing of the hounds as they hunted up and along the side and over the rim at the very nick in the rock where the fox had stood, but all the time there was that lovely remote barbarous din to keep him tearing along like a boy. He meant to keep with Gerallt if he possibly could, both as an expert fox-hunter and as his only acquaintance – the Master was too awful a figure by far – and already there was a tacit understanding between them: most of the followers hunted in pairs.

Kirk saw the top of the ridge coming at last, and he fairly ran up the last stretch. Gerallt was already there, gazing down at the great sweep of country the other side.

Below them stretched a tumult of rounded hills, a heaving ocean of rock frozen and set aeons ago. From high above, from this Craig Llyn Du where they stood, the roundness was strikingly apparent, although from below nothing of it could be seen. The lower hills sloped down to the shining face of Llyn Cidwm far in the distance – Llyn Cidwm he knew – and beyond the water the mountains rose dimly, merging into the general grey of a dull overcast sky, cold, with rain threatening and the worse threat of low cloud: already the bare head of Moel y Gigfran had wisps passing over it.

Most of the other followers were on the ridge. The woman magistrate's hair straggled somewhat, but on the whole they all looked surprisingly composed. 'They must have hearts like steam-engines,' reflected Kirk, privately feeling his own.

There was no sign of the hounds. Once the distant clamour of the sheepdogs of Rhaiadr Mawr made all heads turn, and once a movement of sheep far below half deceived them: then the Master spoke briefly to Gerallt and they began to move down towards a jutting crag that would command the ground directly beneath them – a wide tract that was invisible from the ridge of Llyn Du. From here they saw a man far below, a small dark figure pointing away towards the lake with repeated emphatic jerks of his stick.

'He's gone for Moel y Gigfran,' said Gerallt, in a voice between statement and question: the Master nodded, and they turned northward, keeping along a high broad undulating ridge with outcropping pillars of granite. Presently the followers were scattered over a furlong or two, with Gerallt and Kirk somewhat ahead, taking the higher ground. They were not going so fast now by any means, and Gerallt told Kirk about a noson lawen where he had sung penillion all last night to Maire Votty's harp. 'Up until three I was, and home by the light of the moon, four miles over the old mountain.' He sang one or two of the penillion, and a stanza from *Timotheus cried*. Kirk had loosened up now; his second wind had come, and as he swung along over the close turf he felt a great well-being – he could go on for ever – he would be in at the kill! They went up and down, up and down, but there was nothing steep, and Gerallt was not pressing himself.

Now there was a distinct cry of hounds before them, and every face lightened: it was clear they were in the right road. Then from a knoll Gerallt saw them and pointed them out, a line of long white dots, like sheep, but moving fast and continuously. The wind was increasing now, blowing from behind them, snatching the noise of the hounds from their ears; but when the wind slackened, or when they were under a lee, they could hear it plain – clearly the hounds were quite near their fox, pushing him along handsomely.

At a given point the Master came to a halt, with the followers ranged at various distances from him; and they all gazed up at the massive side of the Moel y Gigfran. It seemed a terribly long way off to Kirk, and he could hardly distinguish the hounds at all by the time they ran over the ridge, over the back of the bald mountain, away from the lake. There was some talk about the line the fox would take – a flood of place-names, for every rock, pass, pool or bothie had its name – and presently Gerallt started away again, bearing left-handed: the Master and most of the others stayed in the shelter of the crag, a few more in a dell below, and Kirk hesitated, unwilling to attach himself to the huntsman too obviously – to appear to cling. A few minutes later the tall soldier, followed by the schoolmaster and the virgin, struck directly up towards the top of the mountain, while another group went away diagonally for the ridge. Gerallt was already a small active form, moving through the heather in the middle distance. The Master sat down and lighted his pipe. Kirk stood irresolutely a little longer and then dropped down from the crag in the same direction as Gerallt.

Soon he was out of sight of all the rest, both before and behind.

To his right he had the high irregular side of the mountain and to his left the valley, with the road far below and the lake: he was going along a rough, boulder-strewn plain, a great step or terrace half-way up the side of the Moel.

Presently it seemed to him that he had been on his own a long while, with nothing but the wind and the emptiness around him – too long, and he was increasingly afraid that he would never be with the hounds again. It was a world given over to the raven: a pair of them passed high over it, communicating through three miles of air, steadily croaking one to the other. He might have been alone in it – no sign of men at all – for although he caught distant glimpses of the road it was so remote that it belonged to another planet entirely, another life. The ground, which had been reasonably plain in the distance, now proved to be full of bogs, some standing in defiance of nature on the slope, and with rocky clefts that needed care and circumspection – pitiably slow. It called for a great deal of effort too, and in time it warmed him finely in spite of the searching wind: he was wiping sweat from his face when he saw Gerallt far up on his right, much higher than he had expected and farther away than he had supposed possible. It was heartening to see him at all however, and Kirk turned directly up the main slope. The lie of the land was now such that the valley, the sweeping great valley Nant Cidwm, was shut out of his view, and only the rising hulk of the mountain with the racing drifts of cloud on it remained to show him the way.

The stimulus of the sight of Gerallt died after he had gone another cruel hard mile, and on the top of a viewpoint that showed him nothing but a thousand acres of desolation and the dislocated skeleton of a sheep he stopped to take breath and to consider. There were so many ways they could have gone without his seeing them, and the likelihood of his being still in the right direction was very small. For the last long stretch he had been working round the side of Moel y Gigfran, climbing and turning among rocky gullies, going where he could rather than where he would, and now he was by no means sure which way round he was. The mountain seemed to rise in both directions, and he

stood there in a state of tired despondency, undecided and
wet-foot, with disappointment welling up.

He stood long enough for the cold to get at him, so that he
was glad to be moving again. But he went heavily now, with no
spirit, and his sad mind had already returned to the prosaic road
so far below and how he should reach it and the paper-work that
would be waiting for him at the weary end when he came round
a shoulder of the mountain and saw the hounds and the followers
not two hundred yards ahead.

They were grouped among a tumbled mass of boulders in a
sloping waste of shale – the backside of the Moel – and the
hounds were lying here and there upon the rocks, licking their
paws or staring vacantly. Kirk's face creased with instant joy: his
heart beat double-time. He walked up, looking as unconcerned as
he could manage.

This was the Ddear Felin, an ancient fox and badger strong-
hold; and in the middle of the boulders he could see the bowed
back of the Master, head and shoulders down a cleft between
two yellow rocks. Gerallt's head was also down the hole, his body
arched over the Master's: they were listening intently. Major
Boyd sat by the earth, holding a tight mob of terriers: an empty
couple showed that some of them had already been put to. One
thin black-and-tan bitch barked unceasingly and every now and
then all the others would join in, screaming and bawling. When
they were not pulling, reared on their hind legs, they sat trembling all over, whining shrill. Boyd's temper had improved with
his walk; he told Kirk that they had run their fox in, that Bellman
had marked him true for quite half an hour, and that it would
be the Devil's own job to bolt him. He suggested that Kirk should
post himself on that tall rock down there to view him away, if
the terriers could make him budge.

The boulder was rough and harsh – a pleasure to creep up
after all the treacherous wet slate of the other side – and from
its flat top Kirk surveyed the whole of the earth, a mass of loose
rock ten yards across and running twenty down the slope; some
of the boulders that formed it were as big as a cart, but most were
smaller; and many of these had obviously been moved before –

they showed raw yellow underneath. Above the earth shale ran up clear for three or four hundred feet: below, the slope was less, and there was some grass and heather among the rocks. On the far side from Kirk, the way he had come, there was the shoulder of the mountain, and it broke the full force of the wind: behind him still more shale stretched away, its lower edge ending in much the same kind of grass, heather and bog, scattered with boulders fallen from the high crags of the Moel y Gigfran. Above the shale nothing but bare rock, vague in the thickening cloud.

Other followers were posted here and there on vantage-points, and Kirk saw with satisfaction that there were not so many now as there had been. In the lee of a crag the women were mending a torn skirt with safety-pins. Clearly it was his duty to watch the broken ground below him, a gully whose nearer end was hidden from the rest, and for the first quarter of an hour he stared eagerly, rarely taking his eyes off to see what they were doing at the earth. Then his nearest neighbour began to eat his lunch – a turkey's leg with crusty bread. The sight brought an instant, painful salivation, a grind in his stomach, and Kirk realized that he was shockingly hungry. Cautiously he dragged his sandwiches from an inner pocket, still keeping his eye on the gully; but what with the business of separating the wet conglomerate and of keeping insistent hounds from eating the pieces before he could get them to his mouth – gently insistent hounds, but tall and pervasive – his very close attention dwindled. He engulfed the food, a wretched pittance, mostly bread with cake-crumbs ground into it from his repeated falls; and by the time it was gone all the warmth he had generated on his way up had left him. Now the wind was a continual enemy; no crouching or huddling would escape it, and soon it pierced even into his pro-tected middle parts. His eyes watered as he stared at the gully; his hands, reaching for his pipe, were too numb to do more than fumble impotently at the buttons; his neck and shoulders were rigid with shivering. He looked enviously at Gerallt and the Master, now shifting masses of rock, scarlet with exertion. They had changed terriers – the magistrate had charge of the disgraced muddy couple – but still the little dogs were not doing very much:

all cry and no wool. A Jack Russell kept skipping about on the top, searching and searching for a new entry – she thought nothing of the place where the others were, four or five of them who kept up a muffled bawling and scuffling deep underground. Kirk watched her with an apathetic stare: he had never been so cold in his life.

The present seemed always with him, and this vile wind. The man on the far side seemed to be suffering even more, cupping his frozen ears with an unconscious look of pure misery.

The Jack Russell was screaming away, bouncing over the rocks with desperate energy, yelping at every bound: nothing of this pierced Kirk's numbed mind for two beats of time, then everything was movement – hounds streaming down and round the far shoulder, the men all standing, bolt upright and motionless, the Master shouting to the highest of them all, incomprehensible words in the wind – and he realized that the fox had stolen away, had crept an unbelievable distance from the earth before breaking, and although he had passed close by two or three hounds only the terrier had seen him.

One of the farmers was already racing up the crag at the corner of the shale: at the top he paused and pointed, with a shout flung back over his shoulder. A moment later the hounds swung right-handed, all giving tongue, and they came back into view. Kirk stared ahead of them, searching the heather for the fox. To his intense surprise he found himself hoping that the fox was well ahead – that it should at least have a fair run for its life. Indeed, that it should get away.

The whole pack crossed on the flat ground three hundred yards below, and behind them the white terrier, yelling still. The whole pack in deadly earnest: there was not a hound but spoke, and the music echoed from the Moel behind and a ragged cliff in front, echoed and reverberated, though torn by the wind. Its beauty had a devilish, pitiless quality, thought Kirk; yet when the hounds checked at a bog over to the right and fell almost silent, his excitement faded; and when almost immediately afterwards they hit off the line again with a splendid crash, he felt a wild exultation.

It looked as though the fox were making for a small earth farther along at the bottom of the shale, but they were pressing him too hard and he ran on past it, on and round. They were running so fast that they were out of sight in a few minutes; and presently they were out of hearing too, the wind being foul.

The followers waited to see whether he would turn left-handed again into the high broken country behind the Moel, and Kirk took the chance to peer into the earth. He could see nothing but tumbled rock with here and there a brown shrivel of small fern or a handful of crude harsh red earth. It seemed quite impossible that a fox should have got away so far without having been seen.

There were still two terriers down, and Gerallt stayed to bring them out. Major Boyd started up the shale in a sloping line for the ridge: another group went along the bottom in the direction the fox had taken. The Master watched them go, then turned back the way Kirk had come: as he left he spoke to Gerallt – a word over his shoulder, torn away by the wind. Gerallt understood it, however, and laughed.

When they were alone Gerallt asked Kirk to hold the remaining terriers, and bent to the earth. Without looking up he said, 'So you came along then, Doctor?'

'That's right,' said Kirk.

The terriers were wedging one another far down under the rocks; they could be heard quarrelling, and nothing Gerallt could do would bring them up. Eventually he and Kirk and the other dogs walked away from the earth together: two minutes later the terriers came out, matted and entirely changed in colour.

They set out after the Master, and now Kirk was glad that Gerallt was going fast; in a little while warmth flooded through him, reanimating all but his hands and ears, and he could enjoy being alive once more. They were going directly away from the obvious line, but it was clear that if the fox carried right round the top of the Moel this course would bring them out charmingly.

Once they were round the shoulder they caught the full force of the wind, colder now by far, and the first handful of rain came driving flat along it. Kirk and Gerallt turned up their collars at almost the same moment: it was not much of a protection, to be sure, but they treasured that two inches of dry neck.

It was a long while before they saw the Master again. He was walking rapidly up a distant slope, away from them and below, strangely foreshortened. He and they were going in almost exactly the same direction. 'Surely,' thought Kirk, 'this is a good sign.' For now to him *good* once more meant being with the hounds, hunting the fox and eventually killing him.

Ever since they had come round into the wind and they had been travelling diagonally towards the Cidwm valley: hard going all the way, and Kirk had to put so much physical and spiritual energy into keeping up with the huntsman that he had little time to inspect his own attitude towards the fox, towards the fox's fate. Once on an even slope he made an observation about 'wanting to have his cake and eat it'; and another time, when Gerallt was untangling the terriers, he recalled the same ambivalence at a bull-fight – his pleasure when the goaded bull hurled a torero into the crowd: but no more than that.

The mountainside stretched away behind them, and now they were looking down again into Nant Cidwm, with the lake almost behind them. They must be in the next county by now, thought Kirk, glancing at his watch. It had stopped, however; stopped hours or miles ago, some unremembered fall having sprung its works.

The Master was sitting under the lee of a rock with his black dog, watching his hounds work along a dry ravine. The scent was poor down there, the day growing so precious cold, but they were working it out cleverly, all close together, with their noses down and their bottoms wriggling eagerly. After a while the Master said that young Lucifer was shaping well – he might be quite a good dog yet. They carried the line right across, and at the far edge of the ravine they started running again, a hound with a deep mouth speaking all the time. Still they bore away right-handed, and it seemed that the fox was running a true ring, a great elliptical path with the Moel at its centre, irregular in places but always tending back to its beginning.

They walked now on the inside of this ring, keeping the hounds in view for a good while. Since they were on the higher ground, they could see the hunting of the pack to perfection, and Kirk was so taken up with doing this and with remaining upright that by the time the hounds ran clean away he no longer had the least notion of where he was – from this high table-land he could see not a single familiar shape: north and south were buried in the clouds.

Some time after the pack had disappeared the three men sat down on a knoll: now and then they heard the dogs, and some-times, from the movement of sheep, they could tell where they were. Kirk could not make out why they sat there, why they did not go on after the hounds; but he was happy to sit, and what strength his mind still possessed was taken up with thoughts of food.

A quarter of an hour later they were going along at a great pace, pushing in a straight determined line across the country: the reasons for this move were utterly obscure – Kirk thought he must have dozed momentarily in spite of the cold, because he had suddenly started up to the sound of urgent Welsh, and then immediately afterwards they had set off. 'Without sleep, there is no waking,' he said, nodding to himself. 'That's logic.'

Time passed, and his hunger with it. From time to time as they traversed this stony wilderness they paused to listen, and it seemed to Kirk that they were anxious now. At last, far ahead, they heard a hound, a single deep bell-like voice. They stopped to make certain, for the wind had often made a noise like baying as it eddied in the higher crags; and indeed there it was, clear and certain, directly forward.

'It's marking in the Ceunant he is,' said Gerallt: or rather he put out the words as a suggestion. The Master waited a moment longer and then nodded. They went on faster still and presently four or five hounds met them, young hounds, capering idly about. The pack had run their fox to earth; they had grown tired of waiting and they were scattering abroad. Unless the marking hound stayed where he was, the fox was lost.

Gerallt called them in and ran forward, bounding like an

enormous hare and bawling 'Yo mark her then, Countess. Yo mark her then, Ranter. Ooick, Ranter, yo mark to him, boy.'

Some of the hounds that had broken back began hunting away to the right on a frivolous line and now the Master's voice joined in as he lifted them off it. 'Aah, you bloody rebels. Lucifer, Lucifer, you bloody sod. God damn and blast that bloody Lucifer.'

Kirk heard the twanging of the horn as he toiled up the slope, and all at once there he was on the edge of the Ceunant, an abrupt, unexpected cleft, a narrow gorge, a shale and grass slope running down to jagged rocks and a white stream far below: it wanted only a few more vertical degrees to be a precipice. Gerallt was already far down its face, scrambling and sliding at a breakneck rate, still roaring like a bull. He was making for an outcrop of grey rock that jutted from the slope, with three good hounds below it, marking still – Ringwood, Countess and Ranter.

Half consciously Kirk noticed the care with which the hound in front of him launched itself over the edge: nothing much, but a horribly significant little check that made him feel sick as he too went over. It was worse than he had thought, the farthest limit of what two feet could manage; but his stick, his nailed boots and two or three providential rocks kept him from plummeting headlong to the distant stream, and with a last wild rush he reached the outcrop. Here, with the flat top firm under his feet, he found that his body was trembling all over – that the height had made him so dizzy he could hardly stand.

The Master was there immediately after him; without a pause he passed his terriers to Kirk and slipped down to join Gerallt below. A double note of the horn brought the stragglers racing in from the far side, and now the terriers were put to. The earth was a long cleft in the base of the rock, a cleft that ran up until it became a hair-like crack. The terriers below were madly excited; they set up the wildest bawling, and before he was aware the little brutes that Kirk was holding hurled themselves at the edge and very nearly had him over. He braced himself against their pull, squatting on the rock, and he yelled at them; but they took no notice of his voice, nor of his stick, though he rapped them hard.

From this position he could see nothing: he did not mind that at all however – the near prospect of being plucked over that edge had quite daunted him. The sheer twenty feet and the plunging slope below had woken all his latent vertigo: his stomach heaved: the landscape turned.

Presently he heard Gerallt's voice calling him. The terriers, who had grown resigned, instantly redoubled their fury, heaving him towards the break. He thumped them brutally and edged to a place from which he could see the huntsman.

'Would you come down here just a minute, Doctor?' he asked.

'May I let the terriers go?'

'Oh no indeed. You must not let the terriers go, Doctor bach.'

It was a hellish experience. Where the rock met the shale was the only way down, and it was vertical – only a few widely-spaced and uncertain stones to give any footing at all. Without the right use of his hands and with the terriers liable to hurl him off his balance at any moment, it seemed impossible. However, this time his low, savage, earnest cursing impressed the dogs: he dangling them ruthlessly by their collars, dragged them over rock; and, gravity and good luck helping, it was done. He came into the comparative safety of the slope under the outcrop: Gerallt handed him those terriers that were not already underground and recommended his going back to the top, as the best place for watching for the fox to bolt. Kirk faced the return with a kind of desperation; in fact it was far easier than the descent. The terriers pulled eagerly, and he clawed up after them.

With all these dogs milling about it was hard to find a firm place to sit: but with brutal dragooning he did clear a good recess, a recess with a grip for his heels, some way back from the hideous edge; and there he sat. He could not tell what was happening below without peering over – an impossibility until this vertigo could be mastered – so there he stayed, feeling his bruises, reflecting upon giddiness and its unreasonable panic, and staring vacantly at the terriers until the Master's voice called for more by name. Kirk did not know any of their names, but he slipped those who seemed most eager to go. He seemed to have done right, for there was no sound of reproach, and some minutes later the Master called for another couple, adding 'That Tory had a grip on him now'. Kirk was left with the two quietest: old bald-faced bitches with few teeth between them, who had been brought only because it broke their hearts to be left.

He felt the dizziness recede, and the illogical dread; and to test the effect of height again he stood up. He had taken two paces towards the edge when he saw the fox on the shale twenty yards below the earth, running hard and fast in a bunched-up long-legged gallop, its tail held up in a curve.

Instantly he bawled 'Gone away', and there again was the Jack Russell with another terrier by her, flying over the rocks. But every hound had been idling on the far side, and although they were laid on with might and main they were slow away, and with intense relief Kirk saw the fox racing between the boulders right down towards the stream before they began to run on his line.

This time the terriers were all out directly, all but one, and they did not wait for him. The fox had run straight up the Ceunant for a quarter of a mile, then up the side where it was very bare and rocky, and so over the ridge behind. They talked a little as they followed – the atmosphere was different, now that there were only the three of them left – and the Master said that until this last minute he had supposed they had changed foxes, had put up a fresh fox by Llys Dafydd; but now he saw that it was the same. Gerallt said that Countess had marked very well, and the Master agreed – she was a nice little bitch.

The wind met them again at the top of the ridge with even greater force: they saw hounds on the other side of the valley, working slowly up the far slope: far more slowly now.

'It's this damned cold wind spoiling the scent,' said the Master.

They went down, across the marshy bottom and up the other side. Up and up the other side: it seemed unending, and the muscles on the front of Kirk's thighs hurt so much that he thought they must refuse their duty. He poled himself up with his stick, working out each step ahead: and there was the top, the strain gone as though he had dropped a heavy load. He paused a moment to look at his meaningless watch and breathe deep, staring round the grey, indeterminate landscape. The others were twenty yards ahead now, and he broke into a shambling run to catch up. Down the hill, then up another. How he wished they could stop, if only for a minute. To sit in the shelter of a rock long enough to smoke a small pipe out . . .

How interminably the upward slope climbed on! How he hated the steadily marching backs in front of him. Now a wall, a stone wall with a strand of old barbed wire on top of it; and the terriers had to be helped over. Kirk went last, and by the time he had leapt down, jarring every fibre of his being, the others were well beyond it, going fast. Again the stumbling run, the trip and fall, before he joined them.

Another wall – this mountainside was checkered with them, great unsteady dry-stone barriers – another slope. But at least this slope was down and for a few hundred yards it changed the strain, until the long fore-reaching jolt made a climb almost welcome again. Now the hounds were at a check in the wet dead ground at the bottom and the men paused to let them work. With Bellman and Ranter and the cleverer hounds leading they cast round and about on the far side, but it was some time before they could hit off the line again. Kirk was happy to see the others sit on stones as willingly as he did himself and show evident signs of fatigue: he had begun to think them immortal. As the ghost-like hounds wafted to and fro he felt a hint of strength coming back into his legs: he might, if pushed, manage to get up again. Now Ranter hit the line; Countess owned it too, and some other hounds; and although they were no longer speaking with that old passionate conviction, they ran straight, all together, and up the other side.

It was not until he was half-way up the next slope, climbing a wall again, that Kirk recognized the familiarity of the darkening countryside. They were mounting towards the Craig Llyn Du, going painfully up the way they had come down so very long ago. Here the scent was patchy; the hounds had to puzzle out the line almost yard by yard, and now they hardly spoke at all. Slowly they carried it up and up, right to the great curtain of rock; and as their white forms zigzagged up the steepest part

Kirk fell behind. His lungs and heart seemed to be bursting, and although he was climbing still it was only because of a check that he was able to come up with them. Up up and beyond to the edge of the bitterly cold lake from which the water fell so far to Llyn Du. Up here the ice was forming, and the crust tinkled underfoot.

From the high lake the hounds came back along the stream to the falls, and now it seemed that they had certainly lost their fox. It took them twenty minutes to work over the bare rock in the howling wind, but at last Countess, casting ahead as far as the heather, spoke on the true strong line – the fox must be failing, his scent growing fatally strong – and the others came to her. They ran fast down the length of the fall, checked for a short while at the bottom and then while the men sat and watched them they ran with a fine cry along the shores of Llyn Du and over the lower edge of the valley that enclosed the lake, down to the broken country out of sight.

They must be very near him, thought Kirk as they began to go down. Down, from rock to rock with here and there a patch of heather; they dropped fast, ten times faster than the weary road up, and when they reached the bottom Kirk reflected that he might as well have stayed below all the time. More usefully too, for then he could have gone along to see which way they had taken in the difficult country beyond: his heavy mind was obstinately fixed on the notion of the chase.

They splashed along – it was marshy here – and both the Master and Gerallt were listening – they were uneasy – the hounds had fallen mute too suddenly. Had they run into their fox? He was sure they had not.

The lake was far longer this time; there were waves on it and a yellow foam on the leeward shore. It took a long time to reach the place where the sloping ground began; and there they were met by several hounds coming slowly back, quite at a loss and dispirited. No sound of any marking, and indeed Ranter, the most steadfast hound in the pack, joined them a moment later, with Countess and Bellman. It was clear that the unceasing bitter wind had been too much at last – the failing scent would not lie;

and when they came to a little ravine with a path running through it the Master said, 'Well, I think I shall go home now, Doctor. Where did you leave your car?'

'At the end of the road,' said Kirk. He was standing with his back to the wind, facing one of the many sudden upthrusts of rock that lined the hillside: on the face of it, seven or eight feet up, were three ledges, two bare and one with heather growing. On the heather-covered ledge there lay the fox. Dead-beat, wet, matted, flattened. Kirk closed his mouth suddenly with an audible intake of breath: he peered furtively at the Master's tired, drawn face and turned away from the ledge in case it should be obvious where he was looking. The Master bent to his horn and blew a lovely note, long and true; then another: the fox did not stir.

At last they were moving down the path, the huntsman in front, then a long string of hounds with more joining them from either side, then a bunch of sober terriers, many of them carrying a leg, then the Master with his old black dog moving stiffly, then Kirk; they went down the rocky defile with their heads bowed against the wind, down to the long road home.

On the Bog

'IT IS TIME to be moving,' said Boyle.

'What? What?' cried Meagher, starting wildly out of his sleep – a cry of alarm.

Boyle made no reply, but flashed his lighter to look for the leg of the tall thigh-boots beside him; indeed there was no need for a reply, since the momentary gleam showed the whole scene at once, the interior of a reed-walled butt, guns, a game-bag, duck-boarded floor, the wooden bench. The flame also lit Boyle's handsome face, exaggerating its high arrogant nose and the morning beard; and in this brief flash Meagher's being fell back into its present context.

They had lain out on the bog all night, so that they could get out to the far end for the geese, for the dawn-flighting, well before daybreak and well before any keepers were moving.

Of course it had been Boyle's idea entirely. In Jammet's a man was prating about geese, great skeins of greylags brought down by the hard weather, and turning to Meagher Boyle said, 'How should you like to have a shot in the morning? I know a capital place, and you are the great wildfowler, I believe.'

Meagher was pleased, flattered with the notice and the prefer-ence – particularly the preference, because toad-eating Clancy was there, eager for any invitation that might be going; and although he had been up at a party all night before he said he would be very happy indeed – 'wildfowling is meat and drink to me'. They left at once, walked over the river to Boyle's place – Meagher was one of the few who had been there – and loaded gun-cases, cartridge-bags and tarpaulin into the car.

'It is the devil we have no dog,' said Boyle. 'Clancy spoke of a labrador.'

'Oh, that was only his froth and pride; he has never owned so much as a cat in all his life. I'll act as the dog,' said Meagher, laughing.

Boyle sent him for cartridges with a five-pound note and as soon as he came back they drove straight out of the town. A long drive, too fast for conversation with the hood off, fast along winding lanes and boreens, and Meagher was excited with the rushing air, pleased to be sitting there next to Boyle: then the stop in the lee of a turf-stack and the walk out, a great way across rough pasture as far as a dyke. 'We are not going in there, are we?' asked Meagher, reading a notice in the fading light. It was one of many posted all along the near bank forbidding trespassers, warning of mantraps, stating that dogs should be shot on sight.

'That is the general idea,' said Boyle. He felt for a plank in the rushes, laid it across, lifted the wire the far side, slipped through and stood waiting.

'I don't mind a bit of poaching,' said Meagher, 'but . . .' He could not find an acceptable way of putting 'but only when it is fairly safe', so he said no more. This was certainly far from safe: he did not know which county they were in even, but they had run along two miles of park wall with an enormous house inside it before stopping, and now they stood in flat open country without a bush or a hedge for miles. The notices were fresh and trim; this was obviously a strictly preserved estate.

'Never worry about them,' said Boyle. 'You are only an honorary dog; and in any case geese and duck are not game. They are ferae naturae – they have no animus revertendi.'

Meagher could hardly reply to that. He walked on over the tussocky forbidden ground, looking as unconscious and confident as he could. They had not gone a hundred yards before a single partridge got up in front of them, a little to the right. Boley's gun leapt to his shoulder; he fired, and the bird hit the ground so hard it bounced twice. He said, 'I beg pardon, Meagher. That was really your bird. Just pick it up, will you, there's a good fellow.'

Meagher picked it up, glancing round in every direction; and he picked up two rabbits and a snipe as well before they reached downright bog with redshanks in the cuttings and curlews crying high overhead. Looking ahead in the twilight he could see tall reeds, dense cover that would hide their nakedness; but between them and the reeds lay an intricate series of channels, many of them newly dredged. Boyle led the way through, walking casual and easy like a tenant for life and a man who knows his way well.

'You seem to know your way well,' said Meagher.

'I used to come here in the old duke's time,' said Boyle. And some time later, pushing through the innermost reeds, he said, 'The old boy always did himself proud. Just look at this butt, will you? Now that's what I call a truly ducal butt. Benches, duck-boarding. There will be straw in that barrel; but suppose you cut some rushes as well – here is a knife. I will keep an eye lifted in case the duck start to move.'

Meagher could have sworn he had not slept at all that night. Certainly with his prickling eyes and general weariness he felt he had not. The greater part of it (all but the last twenty minutes in fact) he had lain listening to Boyle snoring on his back, listening to the desolate call of marsh-birds he could not put a name to, weird shrieks and groanings, and to the stir of the reeds as ice formed on them. He was not very cold as he lay there in his nest of rushes and straw under a piece of tarpaulin, but he was wet from below and hungry, and as the hours wore by he smoked until he had no more in his packet. He was a heavy smoker, deeply addicted to cigarettes.

It was partly anger that kept him awake, anger and resentment. They had not been in the butt half an hour before the duck began flighting, mallard, wigeon, teal, pintail, great numbers of them, and Boyle set up a fusillade, a firework display, an artillery battle, that must have been heard five miles off at least in this deathly calm air. Every shot made Meagher wretched, and by the time the movement was over and he had searched out a good score of birds he was in such a state of nervous indignation that he almost cried out, 'You invite me to shoot and without a word of warning to expose me to this sort of thing – you have no consideration at all.'

The only words that actually passed were Boyle's. He said, 'I think it is over: in any case it is too dark to see. I cannot wait to get at the geese. Good night to you, now.' No jocular or commiserating reference to the few ineffectual half-hearted shots that Meagher had let off: tact, that was the lay, a tact so obvious that it was, if not a studied offence, then at least most unfriendly.

Their acquaintance ran back a considerable way, so far that Meagher could say of Boyle, 'We are old friends: I have known him for years,' but it had never really matured: there was too little in the way of candid interchange, too much reserve for that. Meagher admired Boyle's undeniable style, his offhand way with people, and his occasional lavish generosity; but he had few illusions; he knew that Boyle liked to have a companion – he had no girl, no permanent judy, preferring temporary drabs of the lowest kind – and as Meagher was generally available so he was the most frequently chosen. Then again he knew that although Boyle could talk freely about Stockhausen, Schwitters, Brecht, he was virtually illiterate: none of the things that interested Meagher concerned Boyle in the least: he would see the National Library, the Gallery and the Abbey go up in flames with cheerful indifference. Occasionally a wild, unpredictable gaiety would come over him and then he would lay aside his reserve, horsing around in Mother Daly's like a boy; but on the whole he was elusive – there was no coming close to him at all – and rather than friendship between them there was a kind of exasperated love on Meagher's side alone, a love not only for Boyle's thoroughbred grace, his elegance, his ability to cope with guns, rods, horses, waiters and girls, but also for his vulnerability. Boyle was a man who had to be on top: he had to excel in every field. Humiliation would destroy him – if a girl were to turn him down or if he were to scrape a bus as he shot his car one-handed through the whirlpool of College Green he would be undone. In some fields – in talk – Meagher could protect him; and to protect such a creature was a privilege, an infinite superiority. Boyle walked a perpetual tightrope, and although up until now he had never stumbled badly to Meagher's knowledge he was continually in danger of doing so, in danger deliberately created by himself. Blazing away as though he owned creation on preserved land stuffed with keepers: a perfect example.

As though he owned creation . . . he must own quite a share of it, however. How much nobody knew, but certainly more than most of their circle, certainly very much more than Meagher, who lived by expedients – small journalism, a little reviewing, the occasional grant. Once he had taken Meagher and a couple of dreadful little bus-stop tarts to a house behind Enniskerry, letting himself in with his key: half had been ruined so long ago that trees grew twenty feet out of it, but the rest was deeply comfortable, though dusty – carpets, huge leather chairs, mahogany – and the drive was kept up. He also had a tower in the County Clare, where he fished: but many of them claimed to have towers in the County Clare and what really impressed them was this visible car, the sight of him coming out of the Kildare Street Club, and his beautiful cigarette-case, made of gold. The car might be uninsured, the tower a myth, but the case was there all the time.

Money: that was the great trouble. When they went out, who picked up the restaurant bill? Who paid for the drinks, the petrol, the tickets? Usually Boyle was delicate, but he had a sadistic streak in him and sometimes he could make Meagher feel all the difference between a man with fifty pounds in his pocket and one with a packet of pawn-tickets done up with an elastic band. There were times when instead of offering a lift, a dinner-jacket, a loan, he would compel Meagher to make the direct request; once or twice he had casually borrowed one of Meagher's precious pounds and had forgotten to repay. Odd little meannesses too, such as disappearing for a moment and coming back with a freshly-lit cigarette. No doubt they arose from a dislike of being sponged on, of being manipulated; and fellows like Clancy were shameless at sponging.

Yet in spite of all this they laughed at many of the same things; they enjoyed the same films; they could be companionable enough; they had fun; and surely, said Meagher, fundamentally Boyle had a liking for him, and respected his parts.

The liking was not apparent on either side at this moment, however. Something seemed to have happened to their relationship during the night, as though Meagher's resentment and silent injurious expressions had conveyed themselves into the other's sleeping mind; or as though Boyle had reflected upon Meagher's 'I do not mind poaching but . . .' and had filled in the gap, or upon his ignominious performance with the gun (Meagher was a countryman only by theory). While for his part Meagher could not see why he made all this coil about a mere dilettante, a sciolist, a dabbler. 'I am far more intelligent than he is, far better educated,' he reflected, plucking straw and rushes from his clothes. 'He may have a bodily, an animal intelligence – he is good at killing things – but surely to God a man is above a brute. He has read nothing at all.'

Here Boyle finished buckling his thigh-boots and walked out of the butt, leaving the game-bag for Meagher to carry: in the reeds outside he lit a cigarette, and at the smell of the returning waft Meagher's stomach gave an avid craving heave. He remembered not only that his packet was empty but that he had had neither dinner nor tea. To be sure, Boyle had eaten nothing either; but Boyle was well padded, whereas Meagher, who lived by his wits, was painfully thin. The gap of a meal told on him at once.

'Perhaps that is why I am feeling so very brittle all over,' he thought. 'That and two sleepless nights. And I dare say I have a cold coming on – to lie out all night in the wet, what a notion! – a bad go of flu.'

He followed Boyle through the reeds: they walked without speaking to one another, as though there were an acknowledged breach. Through the reeds round the lake and out on the far side; and here, stretching infinitely far beyond them, was the landscape of a dream, perfectly silent, perfectly still; the whole bog, with every rush and clump of grass upon it, was white with hoar-frost, and it gleamed gently in a suffused shadowless light that came dropping from the frozen air together with minute crystals of ice: no visible source for the light, no stars, no moon, only this high luminous mist. A world before the creation. An enormous flatness with no details in it, for the impression of light was illusory and at any distance everything merged into uncertainty; there was no one object that could be seized and defined apart from the sea-wall away to their left, the single firm line in this universal vagueness, a line that ran curving away for ever.

Boyle was screwing himself up to see his watch, to make the hands show in the darkness of his bosom. 'Just hold my gun, will you?' he said. A beautiful short-barrelled hammerless ejector, lighter by far than the old-fashioned brown keeper's gun allotted to Meagher.

'Can you make out the time?' asked Meagher, and to his shame he heard a placating note in his voice.

Boyle did not answer directly. In a cold impersonal tone he said, 'Only two hours to go. We shall have to step out if – oh for Christ's sake don't hold your gun like that, you silly whore! Don't you know you must never point your gun at anything you don't mean to kill?'

Meagher was on the edge of crying out that it was not pointed, that it was not loaded; but the shocking brutality of the assault, quite outside their habitual intercourse, choked back his lies and he followed Boyle in silence.

Two hours, he had said. Surely they had been walking more than two hours? The night seemed a hundred years old. The sea-wall was unchanged, the one firm thread in a shifting interminable dream; it stretched before and behind, a broad ten-foot earthwork with sluices here and there and every few hundred yards a set of posts, startlingly upright in a world so flat, like black exclamation marks signalling danger: each one might be an armed keeper. The idea of running away from a keeper, of labouring over the bog with a gun pointing at his back, was horrible to Meagher: and who could tell what Boyle might do, in such an encounter out here at the far end of the world with no one to see? He was a deeply bloody man. 'A whore, a pillar of ignorance,' said Meagher.

But although the sea-wall was still the same it no longer ran through the same country: now they had primaeval saltings on their left hand and the deep mud of a tidal river, while on the right the sweet-water marsh shone and glittered with creeping water. A landscape even more inhuman, desolate and unearthly than before: vaster too, for now an increase in the light had brought the indeterminate sea into its farther rim. The falling aerial crystals had turned to penetrating wet, but so far this had not affected the whiteness of the ground. The frost still struck upwards.

The mud seemed deeper underfoot, however – it had long since filled Meagher's inadequate shoes; and certainly his sick hunger and abject craving for tobacco had grown immeasurably. He felt even more brittle and his lack of sleep had got into his red-rimmed bleared watering eyes, so that when he concentrated on a post it flickered and even waved its arms; his sense of smell and his hearing had become unnaturally sharp. He heard the whistle of a flight of duck before Boyle, as they passed high overhead. These must be the first birds of the dawn-flighting; so surely the day could not be very far off, and release from this nightmarish entertainment?

Certainly there was more light, even if it was only the rising of the moon; but at the next set of posts this did not prevent him from catching his leg in the barbed wire slung between them. He gave a strong kick to be free of it: the wire broke from the post and snarled right round his leg, the barbs running deep. It nearly had him down: he staggered on one foot, his loaded gun swinging in an arc, pointing now at Boyle's head, now at his loins as he walked steadily on. Meagher recovered his balance, laid down the gun, laid down the game-bag (it weighed forty pounds), and knelt to wrestle with the wire. Wet with drizzle and mud, his numbed hands merely fumbled, and in a sudden flare of anger and resentment he tore at the wire with all his force. It was no good. He was still held fast, ignominiously kneeling there with the mud soaking into his knees; and in a sudden collapse of spirit he crouched against the post, watching Boyle stride away. He knew Boyle was aware – it was a conscious back – and he knew Boyle would not turn unless he were called upon for help.

Meagher did nothing until he saw the small leap of a flame: Boyle had lit a cigarette and was waiting for him. Meagher forced his mind to be cold, followed the pattern of the barbs and disentangled them one by one, tearing the cloth as he did so. He picked up the bag and followed, limping: as he got under way so the glow of the cigarette moved on.

Long before he caught up, the cord of the bag was biting into his shoulder again and the weight of the gun was a torment: he was wet through and through; he was full of yellow rancour and spleen; but with something of the cunning of fever he said 'I shall keep up with him: even Boyle has not the face to smoke without offering me one if I am right by him – a guest, for all love!'

He could feel the paper cylinder between his two fingers and his thumb, the glowing end sheltered in his palm from the drizzle, the deep inhalation, the yielding of the tube at the very end, the red arc and the hiss as he threw it into the water.

Still the old night faded and little by little the marsh came to life – heart-broken cries as dim birds fleeted away; rails grunting and squealing in a reed-bed; far over the devilish yell of a vixen. 'Do come along,' said Boyle once or twice. 'We shall never get there in time.'

A little while after they had passed a patch of black quaking bog with a dead bullock in the middle, its peeling horns and part of its head showing above the mud, a brace of teal sprung from a flash of water to the right of the wall, rising fast, almost vertically. Boyle missed them right and left. He walked on, saying nothing, faster than ever; and Meagher could tell from the set of his back that he was bitterly crossed.

'Do come on,' he said again, and now the light was spreading fast from the east, showing the white carcass of a boat on the far bank of the river. 'All I ask is a couple of shots at the geese. Just one pitiful shot; and we shall not get even that at this pace.'

On, faster still: Meagher did not give a damn in hell for the geese or the prospect of shooting at them, but Boyle's failure had revived his spirits a little and he walked along with his resentment somewhat appeased. Yet at the same time the sense of unreality – this unearthly landscape, his own light-headed fatigue – grew on him: his mind wandered off to other places and times, to odd, disconnected fantasies of triumph, and when he returned to the present he found he had dropped behind. He also found that his anger was dead: weary tolerance had replaced indignation.

Boyle had left the sea-wall some way before the point where it turned right-handed, and he was making his way cautiously through the mud towards a plank that led to a dense screen of reeds. Meagher did notice a soft gabbling in the distance, but it meant nothing to him. He only saw that by going straight along the wall he would avoid the mud and come to the bridge as soon as Boyle, thus making up for lost time. He did not catch Boyle's backward signal – the flash of his hand he would have used to a dog – and he hurried along with a sudden quick softening and a resolution to ask Boyle openly for a cigarette, to accept the humiliation of doing so, to gratify him. This was to be an offering, a reconciliation, and he called out 'Boyle, I say, Boyle.' As he called he saw the furious gesture and ducked; but it was too late. There was a monstrous threshing of wings on the far side of the reeds and the geese, hundreds, even thousands of geese, lifted high out of range.

As if he were alone Boyle walked on through the screen, taking no precautions now, and he went along the edge of the turlough where the smell of geese lay heavy, looking at the droppings and feathers: after some time he emerged, much farther round the bend, and came back along the wall. Meagher ran to meet him: his apologies died in his throat at the look, not of intense dislike or anger nor even fury but of utter contempt. A frigid, objective, dismissing contempt like a blow, breaking even the most rudimentary social contract. And while Meagher was uttering the few words he could force out, Boyle's eyes wandered off, bored, uninterested: he reached for his case, opened it – it gleamed like a chalice inside – deliberately chose and lit a cigarette.

Beside them, lower than the wall itself, a huge pale-blue bird came gliding through the frozen air, shadowless over the white ground, never moving its wings: behind and a little higher came its mate, even larger, dark and forbidding. They turned their heads to look at the men but they never deviated from their course; and as they flew a silence spread over the marsh – duck and small birds had been stirring; now they were mute. Not a sound, not a movement. Meagher's sense of the world was so altered that he saw them with no surprise: in this universe huge pale sinister birds might very well pass within handsreach.

Boyle's gaze followed them, and then as he turned to go he glanced at Meagher again, noticed that he was still speaking, moved his mouth into a civil, well-bred rictus, and walked off.

Meagher walked along behind him: the distress of this look, so much more fundamental than the rough words at their setting-out, combined with the unreality of the scene, with the monstrous birds, the silence, the unbelievable final severing of their relationship and with his own state of physical wretchedness to shake him so that he hardly knew what he was at.

He walked on a mile, close at heel, the general pain separating into its various components. Rage predominated, and the extreme of humiliation – ultimate humiliation: the rage made him tremble; it knotted his throat and his stomach. The expression on his very pale face was strange to him, like a mask imposed from outside. Yet he still thought he was indulging in fantasy when he said 'But it is you are the fool, Boyle, to go out no one knows where with a man you humiliate: it is you are the fool to put a gun in his hands and turn your back on him and walk where he can push you down into the slime for ever, you whore.' And even when he had the brown gun up and quivering behind Boyle's head it still seemed only unreal show and mime, part of the abiding nightmare all round; but his finger curled on the trigger and squeezed as he cried 'Like that!' and the gun shot out an orange flame.

The unexpected bang and the recoil quite stunned him: it was not until the slow smoke cleared that he saw Boyle in the water, motionless now. Meagher slid down the wall and stood up to his knees, straddling the body and bowed as though to heave it out. Blood flowed from the shattered head, pouring and turning like smoke in the water, and through the eddies rose an enormous eel.

Silence returned: only the raucous panting of his animal

breath. Then from far away on the motionless air over the bog came a sound. He looked up – the sky had turned pale – but there was nothing above him. The sound grew stronger, a rhythmic singing beat, and turning his appalled staring face still higher he saw three swans. The first light of the sun touched them from below and they flashed pure against the blue, flying straight and fast from the north with their long necks stretched out before them. The rhythm changed a little, sighing and poignant: changed still more, and as they passed high overhead their wings sang in unison, bearing his spirit away and far, far away.

The Lemon

A MAN who lives alone grows strange: and I have been solitary now, how long? Some years at least.

It is the peace he has, the room to develop. Most people are bound to observances; the clock if they are employed, the routine of a life in all events; but a man alone can live to himself, lie three days abed, work through the night, sit motionless for hours, think in the way he likes. He grows unlike the others; for a man must think to grow, and thought is a slow process, a cumulative thing that grows: you must not check it. But meals, visitors, and hot and cold, set hours, do check it. They dissipate the cloud, the haze inside which your mind can turn. The solitary man grows strange; but it is the strangeness of an adult among children.

It must be the right kind of man, of course. It is not every man who can live by himself: two of the other painters here are mad. With old Dupont it is probably a question of senility, no more; but Laforge is mad directly. He goes by with a quick shuffle, just not breaking into a run, and there is such a look of concentrated unhappiness on his face that if it were not so annoying you would be desperately sorry for him – providing you thought there was still a 'him' alive behind that closed-in, wretched face. The people in the street turn after him and stare. They make the usual gesture, and although they have seen him for a long time now they watch him avidly to find him worse. Presently they will shut him up, no doubt.

In madness, I understand, there is nearly always this misery: not quite always, but certainly very often in the kind of solitary madness that I am thinking of. There is always – and this is the vital distinction – a loss of objectivity.

PATRICK O'BRIAN

They also lose (a consequence, I think) whatever sense of humour they ever had. And that I do possess, as strong as it was when I was a child, to whom so very many things are funny, even the sound of words. The last time I had dinner with the Lemaîtres, Marie said that someone or other had a sponge factory, and the words themselves were so absurd – not the meaning, the words intrinsically – that they made me laugh and laugh and laugh, although I did not want to. I did not want to hurt Marie (I do not know her well, nor yet Lemaître) and it was not an explicable joke, *fabrique d'éponges*. It depended on the *i*, long and high, and the round *ponges*, and the particular air of solemnity. But I could not stop, though I turned my eyes away from their ludicrous wondering faces, faintly displeased behind their polite smiles: I swallowed a mouthful of scalding soup, dropped my napkin: but it was no good, the tears came into my eyes, and when the *fou rire* gained the others and they began to giggle too, I burst out and gasped and gasped until I was nearly sick and could not breathe. We said *fabrique d'éponges* and howled: sometimes we could say no more than *fab* . . . It wrecked the dinner: but my God I laughed.

However, that is only a minor point: the essential is the insight, objectivity. I have watched a clock for hours, the wonderful peace of the pendulum's swing, and I have seen it swing left and right, left and pause, back across the nadir, rise and pause. And stop. Stop poised up on the right until I have let it go, to swing and tick, swing and tock. But all the time I have known just what it was, that my mind was spinning free and time was not. No loss of insight there.

And I have looked at my naked feet, bony and long on a chair before me, and I have seen the stigmata form, and from each crimson wound a rose.

Yes, I know that road: I am quite clear there. That is not what can do you any harm, nor make you unhappy. On the contrary, I should say, all things summed up, that I was a very happy man. I was less so when I still roved after women, when that hunger and excitement drove me out; when a dark warm evening came and I was restless, could not settle until I had defined my need. But that was long ago. I have had all the common girls here, and some others too; Thérèse and Rose, Conchita and that Denise who made me ill. The fair one – Marie-Claire? Denise again? I never could recall her name. But since the fire went out, I have been happy, in my way.

Yet so much hangs on what you mean by that. A calm euphoria, an isolation: that is what I mean. A burrowing in, deep, deep down until you reach a kind of peace glowing inside a haze.

Sometimes it will not work; something goes astray. This morning it was like that. I was reading, and between the paragraphs the associations piled up, so that I was thinking on two or three separate levels: that is normal enough; every man does it who talks, and at the same time thinks of what he is going to say next, and at the same time bears in mind that he must not stay more than five minutes because he has an appointment, and at the same time sees a creature flying and says in some inner compartment, 'That is a wasp: it might sting.' It is normal, and with practice it can be developed.

As I say, I was following out these associations, and that usually settles down to a line of wordless thought which goes on while I read and after I have stopped, reaching, in the end, my happiness far down.

But this morning, the associations grew and multiplied; they were obstructive, unmanageable, and I became confused. Generally they act as planes, planes that dissolve, one behind the other, like my painting: though that is an inaccuracy, because like the sheets of colour in my work, they are not *behind* one another – that is not the relation at all. They are *different* planes; but I will not dwell on this.

This time there were two other features, both quite familiar, but now they were out of place. The first was that the whole thing was a game, a pretence that I could stop at any minute. The whole thing, my sitting there, my being in that room, my existence indeed; that was a game. This feeling I have known for years and years, and sometimes I think it first arose from some dishonesty, from some insincerity and forcing of emotion.

When I was a very young fellow I played at being in love, saying the words, making the gestures, while my heart pumped blood hard through my veins and real tears blurred my vision; but all the time I had a faint (not always so faint) glimpse of myself from a viewpoint generally in a corner of the room and I would say something more or less satirical – my corner-self would say it internally. Later, a good deal later, when I finally abandoned figurative painting, I worried about the honesty of my work, and I believe the worry, the question at all, was a proof that somewhere I was cheated, worked myself into an attitude where the self standing in the corner could rightly smirk and say, 'Oh behold the new-born Braque.'

There was more to it than that; much more, but these partial causes are very remote now. The important thing is that at times the feeling is very strong (it hardly ever leaves me entirely) and then my surroundings seem so impalpable, such a hollow pretence, that it makes me if not unhappy, at least confused. Ordinarily it is not unpleasant, rather the reverse: one can pretend to be going for a walk, to be talking in a friendly, sociable manner, to be living very cheerfully – it simplifies daily life very much. No: what I have said might have been the cause was not the cause at all. The two pretences are quite distinct, different in nature. The first was dishonesty; the second is not – it is a feeling that the illusion is slipping away.

The second thing that spoiled my reading and its consequences was a sense of having been there before. The words had a vexing half-familiarity, though it was a new book: now and then a whole phrase would be entirely known and (what was more troubling) my own reflection on the known phrase would come out pat like a sentence learned by heart. I knew what I was going to read, what I was going to say on discovering that I knew it, and my own rejoinder to that second discovery: and so on, seven deep.

My own comfortable, favourable mist or haze was now a fog. I no longer felt that at the worst I had only to stop pretending, stop playing this private game, to stop existing. I was getting lost, losing control: and to reassert the discipline of my mind I deliberately read a page of the book. That did very little. I got up and washed my hands and face.

I was sorry now that my cat had gone: I had had an affection for that distant creature although I knew it was a descent into emotion; and now I was sorry that the cat was not in the studio. I would have opened it a tin of fish if it had been there, and doing that would have been valuable.

I looked at the painting that I had up on the easel and I began to work on it mechanically. Soon I had spoiled the canvas, and I let my hand draw criss-cross lines.

The base and cause of the wretched state of my mind, I found, was a sort of dream that I had had in the night. It was about my neighbours.

They were good neighbours, below, in front and on each side. They were often very kind to me – took in parcels, told me the news of the quarter when we met, and when my cat was still here they were kind to her, too; gave her milk. I do not think they approved of my girls, but that was long ago, and I had always been very quiet, even then. They were working people, kind, sensible, tolerant. Good people, my neighbours: all except the man and woman who kept the restaurant on the ground floor. They were a bad couple; the man a flashy, smarmy-haired little pompous rat; the woman a short-legged, hard-faced shrew of about forty. I went there at first because I thought it would save trouble, and they gave me an omelette with a cockroach in it. They drank heavily, quarrelled and screamed until dawn sometimes. Their place was frequented by their friends and by foreigners on the spree, and they bawled and sang and shrieked above the blaring radio until four or five in the morning. The man was odiously ingratiating: the woman too: she had a high screaming laugh, more truly metallic than I have ever heard from a human throat. She could let it rip at will, and she did whenever anybody else laughed. It was quite false: she had never really laughed in her life except at a puppy drowning.

They had a waitress whom they did not pay: she made her living from tips and by whoring with the customers. All the sporting men of the place went there after her and you could hear them out-manning one another in deep voices and whooping cachinnation. She was a big wench, fairly pretty, crammed with high spirits. I would have had nothing against her at all, if she had not sung: but she did sing, every morning until lunchtime, while she cleaned the restaurant. She sang very loudly, very affectedly – she was being the quaint pretty girl scrubbing floors and not minding it, I believe – and on one note only. It was a false note, and the damned songs she sang penetrated windows, shutters, floors, everything.

There they were, a pretty crew; and the man had one trick that irritated me more than all the rest. He had an ugly little signboard hanging on the wall, pointing to his restaurant, and every time he passed it he would set it straight. The gesture, indicating ownership, importance, the right to touch, was so automatic that he would do it without even looking to see whether the sign were straight or not. Sometimes he would go out, touch it without looking, and come back. I could have borne anything but that.

To return to this kind of dream of which I have spoken. They were making more noise last night than usual. I wondered whether my neighbours in front would get angry enough to throw a bottle: they did sometimes when the din had been intolerable for many hours past midnight. I felt angry for them: they and all the people around were working families who got up early. Many and many a time have I seen them come out, cross and bleary, robbed of their sleep and robbed of their full day's power by the screaming hooligans below. As time went on I grew angrier on my own account.

Then I was thinking in my chair for a long while. In separated waves the noise pierced through, but when I got up to find my bomb I was no longer angry. I was far within myself, but I recalled my anger, for myself and for those other people, and I examined it: it was very red, emotional and raw: roughly triangular.

My bomb was one of the small kind that we used to call a *citron*. I do not know its technical description, but it was a hand grenade, shaped like a lemon. I had kept one, because I liked

THE LEMON

its form. I found it in my box of different shapes, kicked off my
slippers and went quietly downstairs. As I went down the shrieks
and laughter increased. In the lobby inside the front door (it is
always open except in the winter) there are the fuse-boxes for
the whole house. I drew the white porcelain bridge that controlled the restaurant's electricity, and as their lights went out I
heard the huge, anticipated shriek and the waitress's unbridled
scream as one of the men grabbed her in the dark.

The electricity is always breaking down in this street, and
everyone has candles ready. I waited a moment until I saw the
dim glow reflected, and then I went into the street. In the darkness outside the open restaurant door I stood and looked in: the
girl was out of the room; the rest were gabbling about a second
candle. They were all drunk. The woman let out a burst of her
cackle and I drew the pin. It was, I remembered, a seven-second
fuse, so I counted five before lobbing it in. It was remarkable
that the people looked at the bomb as it landed, and not towards
the place it came from, as I had expected.

It went off with a great orange flower of light that blossomed
momentarily in the whole street. I pushed back the electric fuse
and went silently upstairs, pursued by the familiar smell of dust.

There was no possibility of detection. All the neighbours would
be at their windows, not looking down the stairs.

Now the thing that worries me about all this was the moral
aspect. The withdrawal of the fuse was an act of lunatic cunning
that would never have occurred to me as myself. I do not think
that I even knew which was the right box. But the fact that I
did withdraw it is terribly significant: at some time in my journey
downstairs my play, my pretence of being a man – and hence my
control – must have merged into a sense of reality and uncontrol.

This train of thought must have started in the morning before
I sat down with my book, it must have started unconsciously
when I looked down into the street and saw a mess of plate glass
still heaped in the gutter and the people staring: and it must
have been that that wrecked my reading, a deep, well-founded
distrust of that single element in the dream – dream or physical
reality, it does not matter which.

The essence of the matter is that the action of withdrawing the fuse was the action of a psychopath. And the consequences are bad. I do not mean the bodily consequences: detection is impossible. No; the consequences of an action that one recognizes as undoubtedly psychotic are that one must take measures against the possibility of a repetition: if once the lapse is established, to go on living would be criminal in an honest man.

And it is so soon established: one question is enough. 'Did you draw that porcelain bridge that holds the wire, and did you leave it so that you could push it back in the dark?' If the answer is yes, you must then say 'You did not know where the fuse box was: you know almost nothing about electricity. But your unconscious mind had noted the place and the function of the bridge; long ago, perhaps. It formed an intention, against the time when it could take over control. The intent was criminal. The thing that formed it must be cut off. The only moral issue now before you is the recognition of this fact.'

The Last Pool

'THIS IS the last pool,' he said again, as he stood by the side of it with the water running over the toes of his waders. He had said the same thing at each of the five pools below it, and he had meant that if he did not catch a trout he would go home. Each pool in turn had yielded nothing, not even a rise to save the face of his resolution. Each time he meant it more, and now he meant it entirely: beyond this pool was a long flat stretch of river, difficult to fish and notoriously barren; to circumvent both it and the small private lake beyond meant a tedious hot walk in waders already too warm for comfort.

The last pool was certainly the best pool for size and looks; it stood high above a series of chaotic rapids, and an almost unbroken rim of rock enclosed it. At the top end the river came clear over a wall of black basalt four or five feet high, curving over in green water before it broke into two main cascades that came down in foam to the pool. Even now, after weeks of drought, the top quarter of the pool was white, and the water had a menacing roar to it. The outlet was one single column of racing water, a broad mortal jet that came through a black gate of rock in the pool's lower rim; it was from this that it had its name of Goileadair, or, as some said, the Kettle. The sides of Goileadair were sheer-to, and down the middle of it was a shingle bed, piled there by the two competing falls above. The highest part of the shingle was out of the water now, and quite dry.

There was a sombre air about this last pool – little colour, for the valley just here narrowed to a gorge with a great deal of naked rock to its sides. The Scots pines that had taken footing in the crag to the left showed darkly above, and the flash of the falling water accentuated the black polish of the half-sunken rocks. In Conan's time they drowned lepers here.

The gorge was beautiful, this man, this James Aislabie, observed to himself; but it was a harsh, grim kind of beauty, God forbid. He sat down on one of the smooth rocks that marked the end of the pool, the edge of the cleft that let the water out; the river slid fast and silently between these rounded edges, its surface curved and tense. It ran over his dangling feet with an insistent pressure and a grateful coolness; and in ten minutes the all-pervading roar that filled the gorge no longer reached the threshold of his hearing.

At the top end a yellow wagtail perched on a flat stone and stood bowing there and bobbing, and as James Aislabie watched the bird – a fine bird in the glory of his feathers – a fish leapt out of the foam a little to the one side of it. It was a small white fish, a sea-trout of perhaps half a pound or less, but it was a sight pleasant enough to a man who had fished long hours in the heat of the day without the sight of a fish at all.

All day long the weary length of the river, with its difficult, reed-grown banks lower down, and the beat of the sun on his back: the disastrous lowness of the water, with its shining surface and his cast lying awkwardly curled upon it, and his hot boots and the grinding strap on his shoulder. The bad, short, laboured casts as his arms grew more and more tired, the glare on the water as his eye followed the place where his fly ought to be, and the swirling water. When he lay in bed thinking about fishing he did not recall these things, nor the flies cracked off, pulled off, dropped, lost high up in trees.

He considered the best way to fish this pool, and he thought about changing his fly. He had no confidence in the fly he was using and none in the only other fly he had left, which was far too big. However, he cut off the one and tied on the other: it was more a gesture of piety than anything else. The name of the fly escaped him; somebody's Fancy, or possibly Indispensable, he thought, as he pulled the knot tight round the black, shining eye. It seemed but decent to do the thing correctly, although his belief in his motions had almost wholly gone.

His faith in the day's fishing had gone in three stages. At first, on the flat, easy stretches of the lower river, he had been keenly expectant, had made each cast with extreme care: he knew that some fair sea-trout, two- and three-pounders, had been caught within the week, and he hoped with each new cast that he should see the white flash of a turning fish and hear the scream of his reel. Then as the hours passed he had begun to hope rather desperately for just one fish, one, to save him from the wretchedness of having nothing at all. He pictured to himself the beauty of the fish, its gleaming sides, its black spots, the square tail and the fine, strong head, the heft of a good one dead in his hand. The vision grew clearer and more desirable still as he became more and more certain that he was going to catch nothing. It seemed, towards the end of the day, so very unlikely that any fish should want to take an artificial fly tied to a piece of gut; it was so improbable that there were any fish in that river, that if it had not been for some nagging persistence in the back of his mind he would have gone home about tea-time.

The feathers were smoothed, the cast was tried; he stood up and worked out a good line, facing the falls at the top of the Goileadair. His arm was rested, and he cast well; the line shot handsomely through his fingers, and the new fly dropped into the eddy at the outer side of the right-hand fall. It settled for a moment while the current carried down the slack; Aislabie's hand, as though it had an eye, took the line and drew it in, while he stared after the racing spot on the surface that should cover his fly. He was just about to lift his line off the water when some tiny variation stopped him. Was the cast moving a trifle across the current? It was, and the movement increased. With a quiet, smooth firmness it glided across and then upstream: there was a swirl under it that checked his quick strike. Aislabie stood there with the coiled line in his fingers.

'Wait. Oh wait,' he whispered, and he let a coil slip out through the rings.

Then came the pull; a firm pull, rather than the jerk of a little fish. Aislabie struck, with a straight, tight line; he struck too hard from over-anxiety. He had not finished the lashing upward stroke before his rod sprang to violent life. The rod top whipped down to the water, and two coils of line shot from his detaining fingers, and the reel gave a flying screech. In the middle of a pool a huge fish flashed three-quarters of its length into the air: it shook its head, poised there for an instant and fell sideways. In that instant Aislabie had seen every spot on it – the impression burnt itself in as a flash of lightning does. A silver, fresh-run cock-salmon, the heaviest he had ever seen alive. He had even seen the gleam of his cast between the strong beaked jaws.

Before the splash had settled it leapt again, clear of the water this time, and stood on its tail, worrying its head from side to side. Aislabie dropped his rod top: his hands were trembling so much that he could hardly find the knob of the reel, and his heart hammered in the back of his throat. His mind was devoid of coherent, conscious ideas: there was only a sort of cold exultation.

Then came a period of short, frenzied rushes across and across the pool, while Aislabie did nothing but endeavour to keep a tight line. This was not too difficult, as the fish went to and fro across the middle water, keeping roughly the same distance from him. His sense returned, and with it the depressing certainty that he was going to lose his cast for sure and probably most of his line as well. His reason conscientiously told him that only a silly man would hope to land a thirty-pound salmon with a short trout rod and fifty yards of line, a 3X cast and a little fly that a salmon should never have touched.

A salmon had no right to be there: only three, and small fish they were, had been taken in the river in the past twenty years. The top of his desire had been a two- or three-pound sea-trout, weighed by a friendly scale.

His body and the rest of his mind fought the salmon with every particle of skill and resource he had. A wild hope began to glow there in his heart; he put a stronger check on the fish, and the salmon responded with a strength that made the running line bite into his fingers.

So far the salmon had made no attempt to run up or down stream, and at present the only danger lay in the long, dividing finger of the bank of shingle between the incoming falls: if the run took the cast across one of its stones and then the fish were to turn, the cast would surely break. He became aware of this at the same moment that he saw the salmon turn just below the surface at the right-band side of the pool and rush directly at the spit of shingle. Its shoulders were barely covered and he could see the wake it made, curving away right-handed to cross the tip of the spit. Plainly the salmon meant to go up into the deep hole at the foot of the left-hand fall. This would do two things: first, the curving rush would carry the line, if not the cast, over the bare rocks; and second, it would in all probability run the line clean off his reel, in which case it would tauten, stretch to the breaking-point in an infinitesimal fragment of time, break at the weakest point – he had a fleeting vision of the knot joining cast and line – and leave him with a still, lifeless rod.

As the wake neared the point, he leaned his rod out to the left horizontally and checked the racing line with all the force it could bear. The rod bent and quivered to the butt and the salmon's curve flattened perceptibly; it cleared the point several feet below the bare stones, but still the fish bore up right-handed. Aislabie could check no more. Suddenly he let go altogether, and his reel ran out free and screaming. He felt the knot between line and backing pass up through the rings, knocking as it went, and a bitter wave of disappointment welled up around his heart. There was very little backing – he had been careless – and that little was frayed and stiff. He could not gain any distance by wading into the pool; it was neck-deep a foot from where he stood.

The salmon took no notice of the slackened pressure; it sped on into the boil of the fall, to the topmost limit of the pool, and dived into the deep, slack water on the further side of the fall, the inward side under the falling water. There it lay, with its side and belly fins spread and its gills working violently: from time to time it worried, nuzzled against the water-worn rock, trying to dislodge the fly; but the hook was well home.

Aislabie stood there with a couple of yards of backing still on his reel, and for the first time he felt a reasonable hope. He had little enough ground for it, since the line was angled about a rock, and the salmon, should it wish to stay where it was, could not be moved. Still, ambition swelled up and took entire possession of him, so that he could hardly breathe. He saw the fish dead on the shore and wiped the loose scales from his hand – he would have to tail the salmon, for he had neither gaff nor net: he settled in his mind how to attach it to his bicycle.

The salmon, angered and disturbed by the thrumming that the taut line made in the fall, moved across the current and then quite slowly down into the quieter water. Aislabie left it alone until it was farther down than the shingle bed and then he bore gently on the line. The salmon, fiery as ever, hurled itself into the air twice, skittering along on its tail, and rushed straight across to the right-hand pool and back. It paused a moment, and then started a savage, exhausting series of short runs up and down the left-hand half of the pool. Had it not kept to the far side, right under the steep bank, the line would have crossed the middle bar every time, and it would certainly have parted. As it was, Aislabie, standing as high as ever he could, was just able to keep a straight line and a continual slight check on the salmon. Then, when the fish came over again to the hither side, he could bear more strongly against the pull, and now he felt that the salmon's first splendid flush of strength had gone.

His greatest fear was that if he should manage to tire the fish to a dangerous point, it would go downstream, through the pouring lip of the pool, down the strong column of water, and there, among the precipitous black rocks, he could not hope to hold it for a moment.

Time rushed by, marked only by the passage of crises; twice he had slipped on a mossy piece of stone, once the salmon had bored into the only small patch of weed in the pool, and many times his line had dragged perilously over the bare rocks. Long ago he had noticed, with a hurried glance at his top ring, that the sun had left the trees. By now he felt that he knew the fish intimately well, could foretell its reactions, could think in front of it. It was a stupid, angry fish, he thought, with little of the sharp wit of a trout; a clever fish would have been off in less than five minutes. His own reactions, the working of the rod, the instant reeling-in, the varied check, were quite automatic by now;

he did not think of them at all. As the fish began to tire in good earnest, to make shorter rushes, he pressed it harder and harder, allowing no moment of rest. Often as it turned he saw the white of its belly.

'It will go down any minute now,' he said, and with half an eye he marked three loose stones. He shuffled one between his feet, and when the salmon turned heavily down the current he had it there to throw with his free hand. It was his one chance, a remote chance, but his luck was with him. The salmon was near the surface, just above the very strong rush of current, and the stone splashed six inches from its nose. It turned and ran upstream.

Quite soon after this the salmon began to tire so much that it was rolling in the water, and he could draw it towards him ten and twenty yards before it would run. At last he brought it into the side, curved with exhaustion and seeming half-dead. He towed it gently up the bank to the one place where the rock ran down to within a couple of feet of the surface. With slow, blundering haste he changed his rod to the other hand, knelt down, muttering 'Calmly, calmly . . .' and made a foolish, impetuous grasp at the salmon. His fingers slipped incapably on the scales, and the salmon shot away with enormous power. The rest and the touch of his hand had renewed its courage and strength. He had known it, he said, and a lowering premonition of failure had been upon him as he knelt.

It was a weary battle now; his strength seemed to have gone into the fish. The consciousness of his own ineptitude tired him more than anything else. He realized now that his arms were as heavy as they could well be, that his reeling hand was about to be seized with a cramp, that he was going to make some last fatal error.

With a headstrong wilfulness, he bore on the salmon, disregarding his frail, frayed cast. The fish sank in the depths, and he pumped it out with the force he would have used with tackle fit for a salmon. His foolishness answered; the salmon made a last flagging run, tried three leaps, each weaker than the last, and lay drifting on the surface.

Now that he could see victory, Aislabie's desperate courage left him; he wasted vital time gaping, tied in an agony of indecision. His body and mind were so tired that he could hardly think.

The salmon came drifting down on the current on the near side of the pool. It was not going fast, for it was not in the main stream, but to one side of it. The fish passed him, and he stood impotently staring: it was downstream of him now, drifting towards the out-pouring fall, drifting faster. A queer eddy took the inert body, swirled it out of the current into the slack water of an overhung bay just to the one side of the fall's top.

With an awakening gasp he came out of his trance and ran heavily down the bank to the rock over the bay. He dared not draw the salmon along the bank now, so near the strong current, for he had left it so long that its strength might well be reviving, and one stroke of its tail would carry it into the run, over the edge and away. He knew that he must tail the fish there as it lay or lose it.

The rock on which he stood overhung the water by four or five feet; three feet down, below the usual high-water mark, a narrow sloping ledge jutted out. The fish was on the top of the water, filling this little cut-off basin, a demi-lune made by a backward swirl from the fierce stream that ran at right-angles to its mouth. He put his left foot down to the water-polished ledge – there was not an honest sharp edge of rock anywhere – put his right leg out behind and knelt on the smooth rock, facing up the pool. His right hand, holding his rod, stretched as far as it could over the flat top on which he had been standing.

He was oppressed by a sense of strong, present danger, and when he was in position he paused to collect himself. Peering down, he saw the fish from its dorsal fin to its tail; its head was under the rock and out of sight. It had sunk lower, and now lay in some two feet of water. Just above the tail fin he saw a faint band of lighter scales, the place where his hand had grasped before.

Now he let his arm down to the water, and as he touched the surface he felt his left knee move. There was a patch of dark wet moss under it, and the rubber of his waders was slipping gently on it, downwards. The movement was very gradual, but the slightest motion of his body increased it. He brought his hand back to steady himself, but all his weight was on his left knee, and his hand found no resting place to thrust upon. He put his rod down, quite gently, for any abrupt movement would be fatal, and sought with terrible eagerness for a hand-hold; there was none anywhere in the compass of his reach. His right elbow stayed him for a moment, and by a huge muscular contraction he seemed almost to recover his poise. But his elbow could not grip on the mossy rock; the tuft of moss and grass on which it relied slid from under it, and he felt his weight swaying over on to his unsupported left side. He knew he was falling then. It was quite impossible to get his balance again, and even the smallest movement made him slide a minute, sickening, irrecoverable distance. His right hand, as though working by itself, still searched every inch of the smooth rock for a hold. There was none. He slid further. His whole body was tense to the extremity of its power, and the tension was unbearable. It was a relief when he fell at last – he no longer had to do anything now; it was decided for him now. He observed that his reason was working perfectly well although he was terrified and sweating with the fear of death.

'Right,' he said aloud, and let himself go. His hand, already under water and within a foot of the salmon's tail, dropped right on to the lighter patch of scales: he gripped with a kind of furious reaction just as his face hit the water and his mouth and nose filled chokingly.

The salmon gave a vast, galvanic lunge which momentarily checked his downward fall so that his body was asprawl when it hit the dark racing water. His face was set in a horrible grimace, but his fragmentary thought 'Oh God, the speed . . .' had no horror in it.

It was like coming out of an anaesthetic. He was quite happy, and he was aware that he was conscious before he opened his eyes. As he had supposed, there were people around him, and they were talking, although at a great distance still. He looked placidly at the grey shingle alongside his cheek and somewhat out of focus because of its nearness, he saw the battered head of the salmon.

They were wrangling softly about where the priest was to be found, and Dr Niel said again, 'I tell you he will certainly be at Tobin's – we sent for him – my own patient, for all love. Hurry now, Jack, will you? You can take the poor man's bicycle from by the bridge . . . Surely to God it must be the biggest fish that ever ran up this river.'

Aislabie smiled secretly: a voice said, 'He has come to,' and another, so anxious and kind, 'Can we ease you, Mister, as you lie?' The doctor was speaking too in a professional voice; but Aislabie could not bring himself away from his deep innermost glow; he smiled again, and drew in the smell of the fresh-run fish.

The Handmaiden

'SO IT IS SETTLED, THEN?'

'Yes. It is settled,' she said; and since she was a woman who liked to cope with difficulties at once she stood up and walked straight to the door.

'You're not going *now*, are you?' cried Edward, in an unbelieving tone.

She turned in the opening and smiled. 'Never mind, Edward my dear,' she said, to smooth away the unhappiness she thought he was concealing. 'It really won't be anything at all. I don't mind it.'

'Oh,' he said, and there was a pause. She stood looking back, for the oh still hung up in the air, inconclusive; but all he said was, 'I was just wondering, in that case, whether you would mind coming back by the village. I am right out of tobacco. Since you will be in that direction . . .' The untimeliness of his request seemed to become more apparent as he uttered it and his voice trailed away, ending in something between a cough and a laugh, with the word 'anticlimax' thrown in.

'Of course,' she cried, keeping the surprise and disappointment out of her voice and nodding too vigorously. 'A box of Henry Clays and a yellow tin of panatellas.'

What an extraordinarily crass thing to produce, she thought, walking rapidly up the path: but perhaps he had meant to say something quite different. Perhaps this something else had turned out to be in the wrong key altogether while it was actually on its way – emotional or dramatic – and he had hurriedly substituted this awkward piece about cigars. That must certainly be the case, for no one could call Edward blockish. How stupid not to have thought of it at the time. But that had been altogether

233

typical of the discussion: polite, oh so considerate, ham-handed. At the very moment when they most needed to be even closer than usual they had somehow flown miles apart and had found themselves obliged to make blundering, muddled signals across the painful gulf with no common language any more.

How had it begun? And who had started it? She could not tell; but she felt the cold of loneliness and she walked faster up the hill. She had been married for more than ten years now, and she was no longer equipped for individuality: everything in what she thought of as her only genuine life had been doubled and made real by sharing, and this solitude was desolation itself. 'Mrs Grattan,' she murmured, emphasizing the Mrs: and a little later, 'I am in a silly, silly flap.'

At the top of the path she stopped, turned round and sat on a hummock. Their house lay below her, and she gazed studiously down upon it, calming herself with an enumeration of its charms: there were plenty of them, in all conscience; and once the water was piped from La Higuela there would be even more. Lawns . . .

La Higuela. She raised her eyes to look in the direction of the hidden village, and because they had been staring down for so long she saw the whole landscape with a sudden freshness – the colours all tuned sharper, the perspectives subtly changed, everything much more important. No longer blunted by familiarity, the view acquired a mysterious significance: a false significance, perhaps, but for the moment this was a portentous landscape, one that might be waiting for some huge event, the Second Coming or the Antichrist, a chariot of fire, the Annunciation.

The feeling of imminence passed almost as soon as she had formulated it; but the freshness stayed. This was how they had first seen the country: rounded bosomy little hills in the foreground, all neatly planted with almonds, precise little trees on a pink ground, like embroidery; beyond them, filling the middle distance, an ocean of olives; and then the sierra, sharp against the sky. She let her eyes run from the far left, run steadily along the deserted scene, strangely empty and uninhabited apart from the innumerable host of the olive-trees, along the crests beyond, some snowy and remote, some craggy and quite near; from left to right, taking in the ruined castle, the half-seen abandoned monastery (it had a lovely baroque court, grass-grown and silent, invisible from here), the crumbling triumphal arch among its cypresses, until she reached the hermitage. Here she paused for a moment, gazing affectionately at its little rounded apse, and then swung her head full right for the dramatic contrast, the spectacular set-piece that never failed to come off – the dazzling sweep of sea, the whole pure curve of the bay with the mountains running down to the Mediterranean at the far end, the long coastal plain, bright green with sugar-cane and checkered with different-coloured fields (they were already cutting in some places), the villages flashing white, the round walled town on its mole-hill, the Moorish fortress on the island, and all along the shore the white hem that meant there had been a storm in Africa.

This was how they had first seen it. There was the same even all-embracing light from the sun behind her, gently warm in the soft unclouded midwinter sky, ripening the bananas and the custard-apples and reflecting colour so brilliantly that she could see that the cloth hanging from a window three miles away was blue. Even the flecks of sail on the luminous sea might have been the same, unmoved.

One change there was, but it lay below her, not in the general scene: they had found the house dead and now it was alive. That made a great deal of difference, she thought, looking down on it as objectively as she could. In all this vast expanse of country there were only about seven houses visible, and two of them were ruined. A landscape had to have living houses in it (the remote toy villages of the plain did not count), and this was a living house, beautiful, reasonably-sized, deep in its own land for privacy, built round a patio and surrounded by gardens; and although from this plunging angle she could see little but its pale tiles – nearly all their pink drained out by the sun – she could place the arches of the covered walk exactly and each wrought-iron screen, each well-proportioned opening on to the outside world. The two courts lay open to her view; but so, she noticed

with distress, did her little walled garden. Or at least parts of it:
all the lily-bed and most of the tamarisks. They had overdone
the trimming of the trees, which was a bore, because the walled
garden was where she sun-bathed; and much as she liked the
local peasants she had no wish to play Susannah to any yokel's
elder, however picturesque. They would have a pool there, she
reflected, when the water came from La Higuela, or a fountain
at the very least; and what was now a tawny patch would be
real grass, and Irish green.

She was above the house but no great way from it through the
air, quite near enough to hear the singing. It was Conchita, of
course. After a moment she attended to the song, a flattened
version of a record the radio had been plugging these last months,
and shrugged with a slight impatience. Conchita could sing fla-
menco so beautifully . . . but it was no use going on and on. She
must be singing in the drawing-room. How odd. Conchita had
a strong sense of the proprieties, stronger than Paula Grattan's,
and she had never been heard to utter except in the kitchen or
the court outside it. She *was* in the drawing-room: Paula saw the
window open and a mop come out. What of it? she said, faintly
disgusted at having stared so long to prove her tiny point. What
did it matter? Yet it added a little to her returning sense of – not
exactly of displeasure, which sounded pompous, but of *not being
pleased*. And although she went on in a more equable state than
she had started out, this feeling came back to her more than once
in the course of her walk.

It was a damned thing, this going to La Sartén. A damned thing.
But it was no good anticipating the encounter. She knew what
she had to say, had rehearsed it several times: why go through
the whole process twice in the same day?

She walked along the sandy road through the olives, trying to
keep her mind serene and blank; and for a while she thought she
was succeeding. She took an intelligent interest in a hoopoe that
was obviously wintering here, well north of its usual limits, a
charming cinnamon-coloured bird with black and white bars that
walked busily, short-legged, in front of her, rising every now and

then to flit a hundred yards farther on, raising its crest each time it took off or landed; but then she found that her fingers were picking convulsively at her balled-up handkerchief and must have been doing so for the last half mile.

They had talked over their plan so often and for so long now that it had come to seem quite reasonable, even quite ordinary: no longer wildly abnormal, grotesque, impossible to phrase with any decency. Surely, with each encouraging the other, they had distorted their perspective? Now that she was alone, actually walking along the cart-track to La Sartén, with no one to prop up her conviction, the whole thing was beginning to look to her as it must look to the rest of the world. Or was she being stupid again?

Now that it was becoming a practical issue, a matter of immediate action, with such disconcerting speed, the whole thing seemed to her profoundly distasteful. An ugly business. Was it so in fact? Was she not merely trying to shirk the interview ahead? How much was plain jealousy?

The house came in sight. She found herself dawdling, looking with an exaggerated interest at the olives, their ancient trunks split, rent in three, sawed and mutilated over the centuries, standing images of torture, confined in round walls like well-heads, imprisoned; but each with its boughs inhabited by a luminous aerial being that lived on the wind.

This would never do. Half-consciously she checked her hair, face, clothes; and achieving a real silence of mind for the first time that day, she walked straight on through the trees.

Mrs Grattan sat on a straight-backed black chair that had been set for her where the beaten earth met the hearthstone: on her right an immense pot hung darkly over a glow in the cavernous fireplace; to her left the twilight held two or three women dressed in black: aunts. Only in front, sitting on a broken chair and two boxes was there a clearly visible group – Conchita's mother, a female cousin, and another aunt. They were all dressed in black cotton, with black shawls, black stockings, and black rope-soled shoes; they all had eyes screwed up and watering, red-rimmed from their work in the shifting glare of the olive-leaves; they were all of the same indeterminate age, between forty and eighty; and she could not certainly tell one from the other. Her chair-leg was slowly sinking where an undetected spill of soup had softened the ground, and a good deal of her attention was taken up with keeping her balance and at the same time concealing the fact; but enough was free to have received a number of impressions – the oilcloth on the round table smelt just like the oilcloth in the kitchen at Killeen: the hens that walked in and out seemed to be house-trained: the ornaments were of a fair-ground tawdriness past belief: the everyday pots were fit for a museum: they did their washing-up in what must surely be an alabaster sarcophagus. The anecdote about the health of an unknown child at a great distance was drawing to a close, and with it the period of necessarily-wasted time.

Very well, she thought, so this is it. At least I have a better lead-in than I could have expected. In an unemphatic voice she said, 'As you know, ladies, there are no children in my house. My husband and I had always hoped for a child, but now the doctors say we shall never have one. It is I who am barren, not my husband. We had thought of adoption, but you cannot tell whose child it might be; and it rarely succeeds. What we hope is to find a young woman of good character and a very respectable family whose parents will allow her to bear my husband a baby. We know that this might injure the young woman's chances of marrying, but we should provide her with a handsome dowry. We have often discussed it . . .'

Yes: very often. It was her suggestion in the first place: she had never forgotten Edward's delight at her supposed pregnancy long ago, nor the way he had sung about the house, laughing and saying, 'Now we shall not all die.' And apart from that there were so many, many reasons: everything in favour of it.

And now this had seemed the perfect – not *opportunity*, that odious, exploiting word, all wrong – but rather combination of circumstances. This family was healthy, desperately poor, and manless, having been on the losing side in the civil war; they were anti-clerical and therefore not subject to the priest; the girl

herself was clean, beautifully built, and now that she had been
fed properly, outstandingly attractive. How brutish and ugly it
all sounded: but those were the raw facts, and they were un-
changeable.

Ugly. Yet in their own private language it had all become so
quickly stylized, dulcified, attenuated; they had been facetious
about the patter of little feet, the happy event, bawds, interesting
condition, the onlie begetter.

Then again they had had one of their enthusiasms about
Conchita and her family; had been silly, attributing all sorts of
earthy virtues to them. Why were they both still so silly, after
years and years of adult life? She did not even like these people
at all, she reflected, looking at them. Those who were in the light
might just as well have been in the dark: there was nothing
to be told from those closed, lined, concerned faces. Dim, dim
creatures, almost extinguished by the burden of their life. No
human contact. She could not tell what they thought of the pro-
posal nor what they thought of her.

Having said what she had to say right to the very end, she sat
there, physically relaxed now that the chair had stopped sinking,
but exhausted and empty. The sun, coming in at a wider angle,
lit the side of her small head, still held up quite straight: with
her ash-blonde hair and her grey eyes, and with a composed,
even remote expression on her face, she looked incredibly distinguished; and, in that dark, huddled room, incredibly foreign. She
also seemed indifferent to the outcome of her speech.

The aunt who spoke the heaviest dialect was still going on and
on about some place of pilgrimage far away to the north, in
the Pyrenees, where childless people went on foot, climbing the
mountain to couple with their heads in a holy saucepan: at least
that was what it sounded like. She could only be sure of understanding Conchita's mother, who spoke something like standard
Spanish.

What did they think? Many and many a time had she
inveighed against the Spaniards' stupid affectation of being high
and proud, of never smiling, of concealing their emotions in this
silly, theatrical way; often had she wished to bang their heads

together and make them behave naturally; but never so much as now. 'They caught it from the Moors,' she repeated, and all at once she became aware that for some minutes past she had been driving her wedding-ring into the knuckle of the opposing finger with painful force. Her hands were clasped on her lap: she looked at them. They clasped, loosened, moved over one another, and clasped again. Dear me, she thought, I am *wringing my hands*: so people really do: I am *amazed*.

The hoopoe was still there, drinking at a pool left from the autumn rain: it lowered its long curved beak, raised it vertically, closed its eyes and swallowed glug-glug-glug, like a hen. 'Lord,' she said, 'what wouldn't I give for a drink! A stiff one.' For a while she hesitated between the cold, roborative kick of a martini and the immediate lift of whiskey: gin was the right thing for a bawd, however, and she would have it the moment she reached home. She could see the misted glass with the olive looming faintly through and a sliver of lemon from their own untreated tree: a bowl of pine-kernels too, and some salted almonds. Conchita was very good with drinks. Edward had taught her the whole ceremony.

How astonishing that she should have come from La Sartén, thought Paula: practically a cave-dwelling. In her maid's uniform – long black dress, frilly apron, cap and streamers – she looked like a drawing from an old bound volume of *Punch*. To be sure, the clothes were natural enough in Spain, where so many things looked as though they had escaped from the nineties; but Conchita also behaved like a maid in one of those archaic pictures. You would have said she was the product of generations of good service, trained by the housekeeper of some big place in the country: she looked so much the part that it was absurd to hear Spanish coming from her mouth rather than a gentle brogue. Modest, good, and oh so pretty. It made one smile to look at her.

It *was* astonishing. But at one time she had thought it even more so: in those days she had thought Conchita quite the prettiest, brightest girl she had ever seen, and had meant to teach her to read – to bring out her innumerable latent virtues, intelligence, taste and all the rest of it. How grossly unfair, and at this point how horribly suspect, to blame the child for not being what she had never claimed to be: Conchita might be rather stupid, resistant to learning, a besotted and firmly illiterate watcher of the television, but she still remained pretty, diligent, honest, industrious, reliable . . . And she could sew beautifully, insisted Paula Grattan, topping the hill above their house, and as for washing – 'Oh my God,' she whispered, stock-still on the hidden path.

Clear below her in the small walled garden stood a figure wearing a familiar housecoat, poised there in the sun. Another squeal pierced up through the still air, and as she uttered it Conchita darted into the tamarisks. The soft branches waved; from beneath their feathery covering came another cry, the excited whoop of amorous pursuit and ritual flight. For a moment the girl reappeared at the edge of the tamarisks, struggling, the blue coat held by unseen hands in the bush, pulled open and showing her long white legs, her belly, her high young bosom. Then she toppled beneath the heavy foliage: shrill protests, diminishing; a slap. Silence.

Her first reaction was incandescent anger. She stood rigid there with her fists and her teeth clenched and all the foul words she had ever heard rushed through her mind. 'In *my* garden,' she said hoarsely. 'In *my* garden – in *my* housecoat – under my very eyes, the bitch.'

Her knees were trembling and she sat down, turning her head away from the garden. She scrabbled blindly in her bag for a cigarette: her face was set and very pale.

She could not light the cigarette and she threw it impatiently away. Her whole being was seething with fury and malignance: a torrent of disconnected ejaculations raced through her injured spirit: 'Couldn't wait for it – the putrid little whore – the odious, lecherous bastard – bald and fat – I always thought she was a tart – sly, sly as a cat – a cat on heat – in my own garden, the swine – turning the house into a brothel.' But all this only served to relieve her immediate rage; beneath it a monstrous suspicion was taking form, thrusting up through the anger.

How long had this been going on? Had they been making a fool of her since the beginning? Did they do it every time she went out? She remembered Conchita's singing 'the moment they had the house to themselves'. But with a far deeper stab she returned to the knowledge that Edward had asked her to go round by La Higuela: under the stress of her interview she had entirely forgotten about his cigars and she was back long before they could have expected her. Had he really done that? Had he really sent her out of the way? She could almost swear she had seen a handful of cigars in the box last night when she was tidying round his chair. In that case it *was* just a pretext; his painfully awkward words were . . . oh surely not? The mounting cold put out her anger: her intelligence swept the declamatory nonsense to one side and began to probe the real question. She searched back and back into her memory: who had started the idea in the first place? Who had renewed it when Conchita arrived? She thought *she* had. Most probably, though she could not remember the occasion. But had it been planted in her mind? She wanted the truth, nothing else at all; but it was terribly elusive. Even in this last discussion, which had brought things to the plane of action and which had ended so clumsily, who had been the real initiator? Where had this dreadful lack of sympathy come from? At one time she had thought it was from her own suppressed jealousy; was it really from his awareness?

Suppose he had already got the girl with child, wouldn't he then send her off for this ghastly interview so as to have it all legalized after the event? This was a new theory that came forcing itself in, together with a bitter resentment of the heartless insensitivity that *could* ask her to walk another couple of miles after such a party, that *could* agree to her offer to make all the arrangements singlehanded, that *could* send her to say, 'My husband wishes to use your daughter for breeding purposes. What will you take for her virginity?' without a scrap of moral support. Though indeed he spoke almost no Spanish, cried another of her voices; and it was true that he – it was not fair to . . .

She brushed all that aside and with passionate concentration she burrowed through the history of words, gestures, moods, tones of voice, to find the truth; but she could not ever be sure that she had it; she could not ever be sure that she was not successfully lying to herself, either believing what she wanted to believe or insisting upon martyrdom.

She turned her head from side to side: she could not keep her mind needle-sharp and cold. She was too tired, dispirited, and sad, sad. The renewed desolation of loneliness struck her with infinitely greater force and she bowed her face into her hands: tears ran between her fingers to the dusty ground.

In time she returned to the ordinary, demanding world. She was disgusted with the scene she had made and with the poisonous, dirtying, ugly things she had said; she was disgusted with the whole thing and she was weary through and through. But while she was repairing the worst of the havoc done to her face ('My God,' she said to the little mirror, 'what a wreck') she found that her judgment had fixed rock-hard upon a decision. She would go down to the house and find out whether there were cigars left in that box or not. If there were not, if it was empty in fact, then he might just have yielded to a sudden burst of goatishness: *that* she could cope with – that would be a recognizable Edward. But if there *were* . . . why then she would have been a complacent fool for all this while. She would have been genuinely deceived and she would have to make a fundamental reassessment, since the Edward who could send her (she prayed she was not blaspheming him) on such an errand, and for such a purpose, would be a stranger to her, a man she had never really known; perhaps even an enemy. Everything she had ever heard about cold duplicity in marriage came back to her: tales of unsuspected change, malevolence, concealed bitterness.

But she had to know. She had to know one way or the other. And suppressing a little habitual whimper to Edward (her invariable recourse in unhappiness till then), she walked down the path.

Before coming to the door itself she made a noise; she was

ashamed of doing so, but she had to – it would not be bearable to catch them, to stumble right on to the beast with two backs and meet its hatred. So shoving the iron garden-gate to and fro she advertised her presence: a harsh metallic clangour.

She did not know quite what she had expected, but it was certainly not the front-door half open and Conchita's face peering through the gap. Sickened by the noise she had made – the grating of the iron had pierced through and through her aching head – and perhaps encouraged by the scared little face, she walked straight forward, brushing her hands.

The girl stood back, retreating into the hall. She was still buttoning her black dress and at the same time trying to confine stray wisps of hair. She was ivory pale, and Paula Grattan could hardly make out what she was saying.

Paula's senses were unnaturally acute: she was aware that there was something here she had not expected at all, a tension in the house that did not match with her own. The hypotheses raced through her head and she was already more than half way to the answer when, glancing over her shoulder, she saw a slim youth glide away by the garden wall.

Conchita followed her eyes: stifled a despairing cry but not a flaming blush. Paula caught some distracted words about 'a cousin, who happened to be passing by', and turned away to gaze at the maiolica on the hall table while she mastered her own feelings and let Conchita do the same. Without turning round she asked where Edward was. He had gone to the village for tobacco – he had none left – had started a little after the señora – he meant to surprise her on the road.

Listening attentively to this, Paula chose her most beloved vase, the roundest, as an offering. She closed her eyes and let it drop: the pot exploded like a bomb. 'When you have swept up the pieces, my dear,' she said, 'be very kind and bring me a martini in the drawing-room. And Conchita, you must take great care with men; it is terrible what they can do to a woman.' She walked along the hall towards the door, called, 'Never mind about the drink,' and hurried out of the house on Edward's track.

On the Wolfsberg

WHEN SHE CAME out of the mindless, ruminating state that walking often induced she found that the moon had risen: a gibbous moon behind hazy cloud, but enough to flood the world with diffuse light. She also found that she had no notion where the road was going to, nor why she was walking along it so eagerly, nor indeed who or where she was.

As far as she could tell she had never seen these vast rolling mountains, with their moonwards sides gleaming a soft grey and their deep coombs as black as velvet and the white ribbon of a road that ran on and on, vanishing behind spurs and shoulders but always reappearing higher up on the next flank beyond until at last it was lost in the general merging of cloud and sky and moonlight.

'This is the damnedest thing,' she said, amused, 'I have absolutely no notion of . . .' She looked attentively at the road: it was a metalled road, but clearly few people ever used it – plants stood knee-high in the middle, and brambles reached from either side, flat on the surface. The even slope ran upwards, with no hint of its destination ahead, no high perched village, no lights anywhere, high or low: all around the vast field of view, nothing but these soft hills for ever, limitless peace and silence; and on her right a dark mass with jagged peaks against the sky.

'I must have been lying in the grass,' she said uncertainly, picking dry wisps and fern from her clothes. 'But where? When? How come?' There was no answer at all; a vagueness like that of the grey mountains; but a placid vagueness – she was not particularly concerned or upset even when a concentrated effort brought no response.

'The great thing in these cases is not to press,' she said. 'It is like trying to force a tune – if you leave it alone, five minutes later or perhaps the next day you will find the whole orchestra booming away in your head, apropos of nothing. I have only to let a few synapses clear and I shall be able to call myself by name. I shall be able to fill out an hotel card – surname, Christian name, maiden name, date and place of birth, profession, nationality.' She walked on, whistling Death and the Maiden in an undertone, and presently she was floating along at her former steady pace.

'Amnesia, amnesio,' she sang, after a while. 'What a caper. How much is there left? A great deal, I find: speech centres unaffected, technical memory unimpaired.' She repeated the alphabet, the cranial nerves of the dogfish, the list of elements. 'I am a woman, of course; I never had any doubt of that. Youngish: sound in wind and limb.' She glanced at her hand. 'No ring: but that's not evidence. And I am *myself*, that's sure. What I am looking for is the label.' Her mind flitted away in a long digression – how much was label a component of identity? How much epoch, nationality, with all their values and associations? Take the social context away from a parcel of reflexes conditioned by that context and what remains? Something, nevertheless: the size of a dried pea or even smaller, but irreducible and enough for the statement *I am me* to carry some conviction.

'However,' she said at last, 'my sex is certain, and the time is the present, whatever that may mean: the question is, what is myself doing in these mountains?'

Here the road led her round to the westward side, still warm from the sun, and wafts of aromatic air surrounded her. 'I can't put a name to these smells,' she said, 'nor can I attach them to any sort of association: I don't know them at any level. So I must be abroad.' This reasoning was confirmed when she found a milestone by the road. 1.3 km, clear in the moonlight. 'Kilometres. So this is certainly Abroad, as I said.'

Far away, carrying a great way, there came the call of a midwife toad, repeated at solemn intervals: 'Ayltes obstetricans,' she murmured; and reflecting upon the immense silence in which the sound was produced – a silence that seemed part of the moonlight and the huge expanse of shadowed mountain – she concluded that she must herself be an urban creature, used to a continual background of noise. 'Some time ago, a mile back perhaps,' she observed, 'I heard running water on the far side of the valley; and that amazed me too.'

For an indeterminate time, still walking steadily, she contemplated the peaceful infinity of rounded hills below her, the slope falling sharply from the road, and the mountains above and beyond her: it was not in any way a hostile landscape nor, though bare of trees, a savage one; but rather detached, almost irrelevant – a landscape for vague wandering rather than incisive thought. 'You would say the farther side was as clear as day,' she said, 'but when you look close everything is uncertain. The folds merge together; there is no telling where one begins and the other ends – as soft as clouds from an aeroplane. These mountains . . .' All at once she cried, 'Mountains! In my very last letter – such a pompous letter – I wrote "leaving geology and everything else aside, from a strictly anthropocentric point of view, mountains are there as an analgesic." It was my very last letter to –.' And looking at them the name was almost there, hovering half-formed in her throat; but it faded, no longer to be grasped, before she could bring it to the level of perception. 'Never mind,' she said. 'I shall catch it unawares, in time.'

Yet time had lost its usual flow, and indeed almost all its meaning: that is to say, in so far as time differed from mere succession. A raucous voice from the sky startled her, breaking her train of thought – a voice that wound about, trumpeting overhead. 'Heavens!' she cried, peering up. 'What can it be? No owl ever carried on like that.' A farther trumpeting to the north, and the voice drew off to join it. Her wits returned and she said, 'Why, nycticorax nycticorax, of course. But it might have been an ostrich, judging by the row . . . Amnesia: it is an obvious refuge from distress, from an intolerable situation: everyone knows that. But I feel no particular distress; no heartbreak, no depression. Only a pleasing melancholy, engendered by this prodigious wild romantic prospect. And perhaps a sort of bruised feeling . . . I suppose,' she cried, laying her hand upon her bosom, 'I suppose I have not been knocked on the head and raped, with all that grass on my back?

'No, of course I have not: everything is perfectly intact. And I do so despise women who are perpetually being raped, or almost raped, or in situations where they might have been raped – trains, cabins, lifts, lonely woods – the lot.'

The road was turning slowly out of the light of the moon: for another hundred yards she still had her faint shadow for company, and then it was gone. In the soft darkness only the white track could be seen, and with nothing, not even moths, to distract her mind, she thought more about this feeling of a bruise. It was in her heart, and as she probed its nature it was so very like a physical pain that she could almost define it anatomically.

None of this helped her in her search for a label, but it did take away from her amusement. By the time she walked out of the darkness nothing sharp or clear had flashed into her mind, yet enough of an atmosphere in some way connected with this bruise had drifted near enough to the threshold of apprehension for her to say, 'If it is as bad as all that, I do not want to find it. Just let me walk along like this.' Another waft of scent drifted across. 'I love this road.'

The scents were extraordinarily varied; there was one as sweet as orange-blossom but far more piercing, another like pot-pourri, and one that must surely have been rosemary; and she thought she had been entirely taken up with her attempt at classifying them when she saw a piece of paper on the road.

Her automatic cry, 'Let it be nothing symbolic, for God's sake. No more of those square old symbols,' showed her that in fact some part of her mind had been running in quite another direction. 'No more symbols,' she went on nevertheless, 'and nothing *directed*: I have had digs enough to last me the rest of my life. If it says anything in the line of *expense of spirit in a waste of shame* I shall blaspheme.'

It was not of that nature at all. Tilting it to the best light she made out a set of diagrams, possibly directions for solving a Chinese puzzle, an interlocking wooden ball.

She opened her fingers, let it plane gently to the ground, and walked on. But the realization that some busy autonomous process had been burrowing in that direction took away the very last of her amusement: she felt an anxious, dreary expression settle on her face and she found that the elasticity had gone from her stride.

Her whistling was a failure too. 'It occurs to me,' she said, after a long course in the darkness, two miles at least, 'that the reason why I do not really care where this road is going is that I do not care where I am going either: not a damn, alas.'

Moonlight again, even brighter now; and with the change of light there was some subtle alteration in the atmosphere, the landscape and the sky – a certain air of menace. She noticed it at once, but she said, 'Nothing can threaten me: nothing can threaten me now.'

She must have reached some kind of pass, for now the road no longer climbed. After a quarter of a mile of flat it began to slope down, still in this noiseless silvery everlasting universe, the easiest road in the world to follow. And although at present the silence had something frozen and indeed inimical about it, she sank deep into its cold heart.

Down and down, so detached from her body that she could have left it to float on ahead, and so removed from any ordinary consideration that the wolf did not cause her any extreme surprise.

He was a big wolf, lean, long-legged and gaunt, and he was drifting along on the mountainside above her and somewhat behind, moving silently on a track parallel with her own. He reached the inky shadow of a rock, and she saw his eyes gleam green.

It did not surprise her very much; and although at first her heart beat hard and quick and she felt weakness in her knees, this died away and she and her pursuer moved on steadily, the wolf paying no overt attention to her and she watching him out of the corner of her eye as he loped through the clumps of thyme. Presently she heard a soft dump as he leapt down on to the road, crossed, and took up his position on her left, still a long stone's throw away, neither gaining nor losing ground.

He was easier to see now, and although the moonlight never gave a really sharp view of him at any one time, the countless glimpses built up a perfect image: he was enormously strong.

'It would be a laugh if he turned out to be no more than a prodigious great dog,' she said, and she was surprised to find tears running down her face. 'But it is more likely he is just some damned symbol, longing for a romp.'

She wiped away her tears and sniffed, and at the sound the wolf's ears pricked up. They walked on. Half a mile later she called out 'Hey!' and the wolf froze, so that she could see him perfectly: a huge brute, quite six feet long with his mangy tail; and in spite of his silver flanks he looked indescribably mean. After some repetitions of this he sprang up on to the road and followed immediately behind, his shadow clear on the whiteness; and sometimes he snuffled on her track. But she was growing bored with the wolf, bored with watching, bored with tension.

At last anger flared up: she turned and cried, 'What kind of a goddam symbol are you, anyhow?' At this point the wolf was sniffing about a milestone: he kept his eye on her and deliberately cocked his leg. 'A symbol cocking its leg, for God's sake,' she exclaimed. 'I never knew wolves did that. Unless indeed it is symbol upon symbol.' She picked up a stone and walked back along the road: the wolf crouched, rigid, glaring. She called out, 'Here's for you, canis lupus,' and as her arm whipped up she knew who she was and that Hugh Lupus was an empty selfish man, hollow and false: false through and through. The knowledge came faster than the flying stone.